# COUNTERS

To Nick

Tony Taylor

October 2011

# COUNTERS

## A NOVEL

## TONY TAYLOR

iUniverse, Inc.
New York  Lincoln  Shanghai

# COUNTERS

iUniverse books may be ordered through booksellers or by contacting:

iUniverse
2021 Pine Lake Road, Suite 100
Lincoln, NE 68512
www.iuniverse.com
1-800-Authors (1-800-288-4677)

Because of the dynamic nature of the Internet, any Web addresses or links contained in this book may have changed since publication and may no longer be valid.

This is a work of fiction. All of the characters, names, incidents, organizations, and dialogue in this novel are either the products of the author's imagination or are used fictitiously.

ISBN: 978-0-595-46427-2 (pbk)
ISBN: 978-0-595-70229-9 (cloth)
ISBN: 978-0-595-90721-2 (ebk)

Printed in the United States of America

*For Jan, who counts for me in every sense of the word.*

# *Thanks to:*

My daughter, Chelsea, who coined the word "warmones" at age 12 and graciously allowed me to use it in the story.

My mother, the poet and the *first* Elizabeth Taylor.

My writer's group: Pat Gifford, Paige Shenker, Liz Haims, Stanley Hart, Jon Streeter, Cookie Townsley, and Greg Fitze, for moral and literary support.

Especially Pat Gifford and Paige Shenker for wonderful critiques and advice beyond the call of duty.

My friend, Jim Fussner, for the cover and interior artwork, encouragement, and valued advice.

My wife, Jan, for advice, reality checks, moral support, and keeping me on the straight and narrow.

Meridith Brucker, for inspirational teaching and valuable critiques.

To Philip Gernhard for writing the lyrics of "Snoopy vs The Red Baron," and Charles L. Green, DBA Tashko Music, for permission to use them. Also to The Royal Guardsmen, for the thumping bass beat and roaring engines of the same song booming from the jukebox during many lazy, hazy evenings in the DOOM club bar.

Larry Peterson, for providing real-life inspiration for the episodes of flying without an airplane, especially the first mission shootdown.

All my classmates in the University of Hard Knocks at Danang: those who made it back, those who took a detour for a vacation at the Hanoi Hilton, and those who did not return.

# Prologue

Engines thunder. Vibration grabs and shakes you by the seat and rattles the instruments in their cages. Air-conditioned wind fills your nostrils with the odor of metal and quick-dries the sweat soaking your flight suit. Bright sunlight glitters from specks in the concrete runway, floods the instruments, burns sharp detail into the retinas. Stand on the brakes. The plane creeps a few feet down the centerline anyway, straining to get loose.

Brakes off, throttles up! Afterburners explode, and a blunt inertial hand pushes you back against the seat as the plane lurches down the runway. Everything happens at once, but your mind spaces it out. After many trips down the concrete, the things that happened *bang-bang-bang* on the first takeoff now come at slow count, and there's time to watch it happen, to understand and not surrender to the sheer screaming pace.

Strangle the stick with your right gloved hand, middle finger holding down the nose wheel steering button. Guard both throttles with your left hand while you do an instrument scan: Exhaust Gas Temperature, green; RPM, 100 percent and steady; hydraulic pressure good. A few little kicks on the left rudder pedal stop the nose from drifting and turn it back toward the centerline until the airspeed comes off the peg at eighty knots and it's time to release the nose wheel button. Another quick scan: airspeed, a hundred, one-twenty, ease back on the stick. The two-thousand-foot marker flashes by on the right. Another scan: RPM, good; EGT good. The nose starts up—a little more, a little more. Hold!

The wheels lift off, the wings wobble, and *thunk!*—the gear handle comes up solidly in your left hand, and the flaps start up while you click the trim button atop the stick with your right thumb. Check the landing gear: three blinkers left-nose-right change to safe-safe-safe, and the vent blows air-conditioned fog until you turn down the control. Pull the throttles out of burner, then nestle them right back behind the detent, 98 percent RPM to give your wingman a couple to catch up on.

The nose points high into the blue, white fluffball clouds race by, airspeed's on the mark, call the turnout of traffic. "Demon Flight, right turnout." Look back for the wingman. There he is below, small and distant inside the turn, catching up steadily. Glance down at the wild beauty of the countryside surrounding Danang.

# 1

A long time ago, a hawk soared through a cathedral blue sky. It wheeled in a gliding turn, beat its wings once against the air, and drew quick rapacious eyes across mountains to brown parched earth and cactus.

A long time ago, a boy rode naked through an early morning desert. Hot sun and cold wind—fire and ice—competed against his skin. He spun his motorcycle across the ground, kicking rooster tails of sand against dry brush and cactus. There was no fear of sandpaper earth, no sense of danger from a bare-skinned spill, for the boy was a child—a six-foot, one-inch growing child who knew nothing of accident, injury, dismemberment, death—who would study those lessons tomorrow, thank you, but not today. Today, it would be sufficient to be wild and free.

His eyes turned up to the hawk. Its white underside was almost lost against the brightness of the sky. He veered to stay beneath the bird. He whistled up a parched arroyo, shimmied across loose gravel at the top, nearly lost it, nearly laid the machine on its side, but powered the rear wheel around and came back upright. He wound his way up a mineral path past ocotillo, creosote bush, jumping cholla, paloverde, past giant sentinels of saguaro cactus, to the top of the hill.

He slid broadside to a stop. He surveyed the living desert, the great Sonoran Desert of Arizona. Saguaro-stubbled mountains diamond-etched their profiles across his retinas, beautiful brown against an enormous overturned bowl of crystal blue sky. He could not understand; he was awed that such a plain color as brown could be so varied, so beautiful, so inspired. The pungent odor of a creosote bush wafted through his nostrils. The hawk soared above.

Today was the end of freedom. High school had fallen behind; college loomed ahead. Tomorrow he traded freedom and Arizona for Colorado and discipline.

The hawk folded its wings and dived, stooping to a hapless desert rabbit. The boy envied the bird its everlasting wildness, wished he, too, could soar forever through canyons of saguaro. The hawk struck and rose heavily into the air beating the white feathers of underwings against the wind, carrying a struggling furry package impaled on razor talons.

The boy gunned the cycle down the other slope of the hill, going airborne over a small hump. The wind played cool fingers through his short brown hair and pinched his nipples. He loved the power between his legs, the feel of leather and metal, the dominance over a machine—and was oblivious to the machine's reciprocal power.

He'd lived in the desert all his life, and he loved it. He was its child. It was his home.

•          •          •

Seven years later, he walked across a black asphalt sea, older and a bit taller, a gangling young man. He was a fledgling hawk now, shaped by the art and discipline of military flying, but a boy still lurked inside.

White block letters over the entrance to the air terminal shouted at his eyes:

PHI CANG SAIGON TANSONNHUT

He puzzled at the meaning and smiled inwardly. The sign probably said, "Welcome and Affectionate Salutations to All Who Enter the Glorious Tan Son Nhut Air Base, Home of Seventh Air Force, Only Minutes from Beautiful Saigon." Or maybe not; he couldn't know. Maybe it read, "Welcome to the Dung Heap of Despair—Abandon Cheer, All Ye Who Enter."

First Lieutenant Steve Mylder paused on the tarmac, lifted the front of his blue serge flight cap above a widow's peak of close-cropped brown hair, and wiped a film of moisture from his forehead. Deep-set English blue eyes glanced down past a slightly oversize nose and surveyed the front of a tall, gangly body. He smoothed his khaki shirt at the belt line of his khaki trousers and checked that the fly, buckle, and buttons made a proper military line.

The air smelt rainy and felt muggy. A solid overcast hid the mid-afternoon sky. Steve tacked around oily puddles dotting the shining wet tarmac. Asphalt ripples and patches rode across the surface like waves and froth, washing against a terminal building, which sank slowly into the blacktop sea.

*Desolate*, he thought. *The whole country is sinking.*

He found his bags embedded in a pile of suitcases, trunks, duffels, and garment bags dumped onto the dusty concrete floor in the middle of a large room in the terminal. Dishwater light filtering from the bottom of the gray overcast through grimy windows provided the only illumination. He wondered that someone had found the optimism to bring a tennis racquet; it was sloppily tied with heavy brown twine to the handle of an overflowing duckbill flight bag. Another optimist had brought a golf bag.

*They're not going where I'm going,* he realized. *Somewhere the sun shines and the grass grows, but it ain't Danang.*

Steve saw no need to change his opinion or mild depression on the ride to the Visiting Officer's Quarters. On his way into the office, however, he was pleased to find a familiar face. Vaguely familiar, that is, because the last time he'd seen it, it had been smoothly shaven; now it was prolifically mustachioed.

"Don," he called to the flight-suited man who brushed by him on the way out. "Don Casper."

Don turned abruptly. "First Lieutenant Steven W. Mylder!" he mocked pleasantly. "My, my, look what the cat dragged in. I haven't seen you since the Academy."

"Couldn't let you guys have all the fun." He did not feel the gusto that he projected.

"How long you been here? What're you flying?"

"Just got here. Going up to Danang in F-4s," Steve said. "How 'bout you?"

"Oh, I've been around a couple of months." There was an unmistakable swagger in Don's attitude. "I'm in Thuds. Out of Korat."

Steve suffered a pang of envy. "Thud" was the endearing name given to the F-105, a high-performance fighter otherwise known as the Thunderchief. It was a hot plane, sleek and clean, although not as hot as the F-4C Phantom II that Steve flew. The critical difference was that the Thud had but a single seat, while the Phantom was a two-pilot plane with an aircraft commander in the front seat to do most of the flying and a pilot in the backseat to do almost everything *except* pilot. Steve was in the back.

"Meet me at the O-club tonight," Don said. "We can drink and yak about the Blue Zoo. We could troll for girls, too, but there's not many you'd look at twice unless you're snockered."

Steve found his quarters: an austere but comfortable single room and bath. There was a bed covered by an army blanket, a small closet, a chest of drawers with a mirror, a desk and chair, and a brown-painted steam radiator that had probably never seen use. He flung his cap onto the dresser, unfolded his long frame onto the bed, yawned, and stretched his arms overhead, intending to rest for just a few minutes.

# 2

The Teletype had made a mistake. At least that was the story. Steve wondered if it were a minor cover-up—the simplest, easiest way to cut a man a little slack, to acknowledge the social, human side that could never be accommodated officially. Or maybe it had really happened that way. Maybe the simplest explanation really was the best.

The names had come down by Teletype from the gods that be at the Pentagon, or the Seventh Air Force, or wherever the decision had been made and the authority had been sufficient to make it. By Teletype, sixty-eight names had arrived in England in the middle of November 1966 at Wing Headquarters at RAF Bentwaters/Woodbridge. Sixty-eight pilots' names had been drawn from a hat, or who-knows-what roulette wheel of random selection. They were to report to SEA. Southeast Asia. ASAP. As Soon As Possible.

It had wiped out the equivalent of a squadron, although it was spread fairly evenly over all three squadrons in Steve's wing. Sixty-eight lucky pilots (many considered themselves fortunate to fight in the only available war) would get their affairs in order immediately and await further instructions, which were expected within ten days.

Steve's name was not on the list. He was greatly relieved. But a few days later came word that there was an unreadable name on the list. The Teletype, clattering ill-formed gray letters onto pulp-yellow paper fed from a roll, had stumbled and badly mangled name number twenty-three, as Teletypes were sometimes wont to do.

...

| | |
|---|---|
| 17. 1LT DEEVERSON, SF | 18. CPT TANNER, HC |
| 19. CPT STEVENS, KL | 20. 1LT TAYLOR, AH |
| 21. 1LT MEYERS, JJ | 22. MAJ STALVERT, AP |
| 23. 1##++O++@+I++^,)/R *%^^ | 24. 2LT ALBERTS, RA |
| 25. CPT MALOVSKY, PB | 26. 1LT STYLES, WI |

...

A First Lieutenant, probably. Had *O* and *I* and ended in *R*. Maybe. A query was sent. Two days later, and no answer. Another query brought back the reply: *Garbled in transmission*. Seventh Air Force requested a repeat. The query was sent a third time. Six days after the initial message, a name returned intact.

Meanwhile, First Lieutenant Hoskins, James R., had irresponsibly gotten married and now expected to go on a honeymoon. He'd already made the plans.

"Would anyone like to volunteer to take Hoskins's place?"

No one stepped forward.

Steve was Hoskins's friend. He'd gone to the wedding. After a few days of agitated cerebration, he was astounded to hear himself say, "Yes," when what he really wanted to say was "NO, NO, NO!" He was not a volunteer type of guy. He wasn't a warlike type of guy, either, even though he was a fighter pilot and proud of it. It had just never occurred to him quite as viscerally as then that the central occupation of fighter pilots was fighting. Until then, the central activity had been tooling a hot machine through wide open spaces.

*Why am I doing this?* he wondered.

> Well, Hoskins was his friend. Sure, but they weren't *that* close, and …
> They'd get him anyway. In a few months or a year or so, another list would come down. But maybe it wouldn't …
> After beginning poorly in England (his squadron commander was unimpressed, Steve was behind the eight ball), this could be a fresh start. But jumping into a war is a fresh start? …
> He owed it to his country …
> It was the right thing to do …
> It would further his career …
> Everybody else was doing it …

There was something to each of these reasons, but not one of them was by itself compelling. Not one. Even in total, all the reasons he could think of didn't add up to going to Vietnam. There are some decisions in life that have no rationale. This was one of them.

Or maybe there was something else. Something at the gut level. Maybe there was still just a little bit of a naked boy on a motorcycle in Steve. Maybe there was just a little bit of a wilder side in Lieutenant Mylder.

A few days later, he got his orders. After four years of tax-paid education at the Air Force Academy, another expensive year in pilot training, a month of survival school in Nevada, a leisurely winter and spring at F-4 upgrade school (the pilots fondly referred to it as six weeks of training jam-packed into six months), and countless hours of in-house schooling and training missions in England, it was time to do something real.

Payback time.

Six months after Steve received his orders and packed off to fight his war, James Hoskins belatedly received orders to Southeast Asia. Hoskins would never return home.

# 3

Steve woke in a sweat, trapped in the cockpit of a plane that would not respond, that swam slowly, oh so slowly, through a sky of blue gelatin. He thrashed from side to side to dodge blobs of bullets whizzing by. Someone on the ground was shooting at him; someone was trying to kill him. Before the dream dissolved, he noted with curiosity that he was not over Vietnam; it was the Air Force Academy that sprawled in rectangular forms below him, and the natives who fired their guns were not Viet Cong but cadets.

Steve showered, dressed in slacks and a sports shirt, and walked three blocks to the Tan Son Nhut Officer's Club. A solid overcast still roofed the world, but it had risen to several thousand feet. The last of the day's light trickled to the ground, and already dull colors faded into shades of gray.

Social animals and large flying mammals packed the Tan Son Nhut O-club. Steve ambled into a bar. Voices buzzed. Bottles and glasses plied cheerfully from hand to mouth. There was bragging and swaggering and a modicum of staggering. It was similar to most officer's clubs that Steve had frequented, only more so—*about an order of magnitude more*, he estimated. His mood lifted. This was a familiar world.

He wandered from the first bar through a hallway lined on both sides with slot machines and players, and entered a second bar just as unruly as the first. Vietnamese waitresses traversed well-worn routes between tables, zigging petite bottoms around outstretched grasping hands, zagging around upturned puckered lips. They were efficient but disconnected, Steve thought. Offended? Bored? This was not their world. What thoughts flickered behind the vacuous smiles painted on those faces? Contempt? Indifference? How many worked for the enemy? He briefly considered his chances for scoring, but he decided not to try. Don Casper was right: there weren't any he'd look at twice.

He savored the activity—the hubbub, the camaraderie, the high-flying tipsy decadence of the club. *This is really it*, he thought. *I'm in a war. If you have to die in the morning, you might as well enjoy the night before.* This was the team, the action, where it was at. Soon he, too, would play in that game in the sky, in the sport known as air combat, and after a hard day's war, come home to roost and strut in an O-club bar.

A shrill inner voice asked, *How the hell do you fit in here?* It was not the masterful voice of a fighter pilot. It was an unsure boy's voice, a journalist's voice—the kind that questions and wheedles and cajoles but never provides means or answers. Even deeper than this nagging, beyond this insecurity, at his roots, Steve suffered a deep and abiding personal problem: fear of dying.

Gone was the cocky self-confidence of the naked boy; gone was time to defer the lessons of accident, injury, dismemberment, death. A fall to the sandpaper earth had become a high-probability event. Tomorrow was here, and in *this* tomorrow it was insufficient to be wild and free.

"Jesus, Don, this place is unbelievable. Is it always like this?" Steve had found his friend meditatively sipping a beer in a third bar.

Don smiled, lifting his mug in a mock toast. "Continual party, Babe, all hours of the day and night, sorta like Vegas. What else is there to do in Vietnam?" The smile came through knowing eyes empowered by two months of combat experience. That small span put an enormous gulf between them.

Don raised the mug to his lips, and when it came down to the table, foam glistened from a darkly luxurious mustache. His face was ruggedly handsome, primal. It spoke Warrior, Virile Man of the World, Slayer of Dragons, Prince and Master of Single-seat Fighters. It spoke of things Steve might become.

If he survived.

Unspoiled innocence shone from Steve's face. Light blue eyes smiled out from an unremarkable visage, a face of crowds, a face whose only mild oddity was that it was designed with a nose slightly larger than he would have measured and cut himself.

It was a minor flaw. He was only aware of it when he was near a girl he wanted to meet, and in those cases, the more desperately he wanted to meet her, the larger the nose loomed in his consciousness and the more it assumed iceberg dimensions, enormous gawky hidden roots of nose spreading massively to the depths of his soul, lurking to shipwreck a potentially meaningful relationship and a toss in bed, only the innocent tip jutting above the flesh, offering a blurred profile to the periphery of pulchritude-filled vision. Actually, it was comic; he had even brought himself to laugh about it once.

"What're you up to, Don? What're you doing in Saigon?"

"Went to Okinawa for a couple days' R & R." Don's speech was slow but not slurred as he tossed back the dregs of another beer. "Back to Korat tomorrow." He looked at his watch. "Gotta hop on a C-123 at zero four hundred this morning."

"Does that mean you're turning in early?"

"Naw." Don smiled broadly, laughing. "What gives you that notion, man? Life is too short to waste on sleep, I'll catch up on the plane. How 'bout you? When you going up to Danang?"

"I'm due Saturday. How hard is it to get a hop out of here?"

"Piece 'a cake. Go down to Base Ops, and you'll get something in a couple hours." Don smirked. "Hell, they don't discriminate. They even give rides to FNGs."

"FNG. Yeah, that's one I know." Steve smiled. Fucking New Guy.

They had dinner—two T-bones, Don's rare and Steve's medium—and returned to drinking.

They bantered and reminisced. The Air Force Academy was their last common experience, and they returned to it. Colorado sun punched holes through the dreary overcast of Vietnam as they relived pranks and mischief, basic cadet summer, Saturday morning inspections and parades, the misery of Hell Week, Thunderbirds thundering in tight formations of Super Sabre jets over the enormous grassy parade field during the halcyon days of late spring, freshly mowed smells of graduation wafting through their nostrils and memories.

They flew to separate pilot training bases, one in T-33 T-birds, the other in T-38 Talons, and a year later, after the winning of wings and the kissing good-bye of girlfriends, split to their post-graduate training bases to fly their Phantoms and their Thuds after learning to survive in the mountains of Nevada and gamble in the casinos of Reno.

Steve went to England, and Don went to North Carolina. Then Don came to Vietnam.

"How many missions you flown?" Steve pumped for information.

Don spoke of flak puffballs by day and hose streams of red hot tracers by night, of blossoming bombs and sizzling napalm and firecracker-popping CBUs spattering over darkly verdant countryside. Don talked and enjoyed talking because he was a player in the heat of the game, a veteran of hunters, a steely-eyed Prince of Predators.

Don talked and Steve listened. War stories had always bored him, but now he listened intently. It concentrated his attention wonderfully to know that tomorrow he would face those same bullets, drop those same bombs, consort and achieve first-name basis and drinking privileges with General Death. A hawk soared, and a boy wondered what he had gotten himself into.

Don's mustache glistened with foam, and Steve put his finger surreptitiously to the skin between his own upper lip and ship-wrecking nose. The skin was smooth—not even slightly fuzzy.

He made a decision. He vowed he had shaved above his upper lip for the last time until his war was done. He would join the ranks of Hairy Young Dragon Slayers. A white scarf fluttered in a mental wind. A Sopwith Camel barrel-rolled around a Fokker, and a personal battle to the death was joined between two mustachioed grinning Captains of the Air.

Finally, Steve had enough. At one o'clock in the morning, he faded, ready to return to his room. "You really goin' to stick it out the rest'a the night?" he asked, fog banks colliding in his brain.

"You betcha." Don's speech was only mildly slurred despite the ocean of beer he'd put away. "Life's short. I'm gonna hang around, maybe chase one'a those waitresses. They're not half bad lookin', you know, come right down to it."

"'Member what the training films said. Don't catch somethin' that'll rot your dong off."

They said good-bye. It was the last time that they would ever see each other.

Steve felt almost in control—almost not tipsy—as he left. An inner copilot navigated as if through an obstacle course: *Okay, up from the chair smoothly, around the table, don't bump it. There. You're doing well; you almost didn't stumble when you made that turn.*

He stopped in his tracks as he left the club, gazing upward in wonder.

The sky! In the middle of the night, a strange illumination stretched shadows across the ground.

Flares! Three of them floated high above, flickering, trailing bright smoke as they drifted slowly downward, lighting the landscape almost as well as stadium lights illuminate a night football game. Steve watched, hypnotized, then heard a distant *whump-whump,* He guessed the sound came from mortar rounds fired from the base into the jungle, not the other way around. Incoming rounds would probably generate pandemonium.

The overcast and a haze in the air caught light from the flares and returned it, making it seem as if he were beneath a giant inverted bowl, as if his whole world were under that bowl and nothing else existed. He was closed off, hermetically sealed from the outside.

# 4

*Clayton Daily Star*

## Lt. Mylder sends first dispatch from Vietnam

Lt. Steven W. Mylder, the Clayton Star's unofficial war correspondent, has arrived in Vietnam and sent his first dispatch, which will be published tomorrow.

The Air Force officer, a 24-year-old graduate of Clayton High School, is the son of Dr. and Mrs. Harold G. Mylder, 921 Beaufort Drive. He will fly copilot on an F-4C fighter-bomber, which he describes as "incredibly ugly, but powerful, fast and two times better than anything else ever built."

Lt. Mylder graduated from the United States Air Force Academy in 1964 (the first and only Clayton graduate of the Academy) and attended pilot training for one year in Alabama. After pilot training, he attended Air Force Survival School and F-4C Training School before joining an operational squadron in England. He requested duty in Vietnam and left Clayton in early January for jungle survival training in the Philippines after a short visit with his parents.

Lt. Mylder volunteered to write about his Vietnam flying experiences and will report in a series of dispatches which will be cleared by the Air Force. In tomorrow's column, he will write about his arrival in Vietnam.

# 5

Demon Flight, two F-4Cs, took off north, then began a right turn, angling across a corner of Danang Bay and out over the Gulf of Tonkin. Cloud shadows mottled the morning sunlit water into the distance as far as Steve could see.

Steve was in Demon Lead. He watched Demon Two come in on a constant angle, a classic indicator of a collision course: first a tiny model airplane in the distance, then a bigger model, and finally a very big and very real plane, indeed. Two round-headed bugs sat fore and aft in the other cockpits, dark sun visors pulled down, big compound bug eyes staring right at him. The plane parked off their right wing just a few feet away, nearly thirty tons of metal, fuel, meat, and bones. Thirty tons of ugly elegance bobbed up and down ever so slightly, a rhinoceros ballerina quivering in arabesque.

Virgil Demopoulis flew the other plane from the backseat. Frank Bender sat casually in the front, arms up along the canopy rails. Virgil raised his left gloved hand into sight from the throttles and wobbled it ever so slightly, a whimsical wave, at Steve.

Demon Two moved out a couple of wing widths to relax—flying in precise fingertip formation is hard work—and the plane reduced to a manageable perspective. The canopy bulged out like the eye of a Cyclops near the front of a squat, beefy body, as fighters go. The plane had uptilted wingtips, downtilted tail slabs, a drooping, warty black nose, and a bad skin condition of olive-brown camouflage. Six "snake eye" five-hundred-pound bombs hung from the ejection racks beneath the wings, and a big gun—a long gray cylinder, a vile instrument of evil—clung with metal lug teeth to the belly of the beast, cold steel barrels protruding forward. Demon Two was a repulsive, dangerous-looking animal.

*Beautiful,* Steve thought. *Power, grace, charm!* A motorcycle spun across a mental desert.

The two planes continued a shallow right turn, making a big circle as they climbed out over the Gulf of Tonkin. Steve looked down at gray-green water washing into foam on a golden sandy beach. After almost 360 degrees of turn, Demon Flight rolled out, pointing northwest. Still climbing, it passed almost directly over Danang airfield. Steve saw a motley queue of airplanes—all sizes, shapes, purposes—on the taxiways waiting for takeoff. He watched a C-130 cargo plane begin a lumbering roll down the runway.

"You've got it," Captain Patrick Truhaft breathed over the intercom, and Steve took the stick and rattled it ever so slightly. "I've got it." He relished having control again, the dominance over a powerful, fast machine. He checked the airspeed and altitude, walked the throttles back a quarter inch with his left hand. A trickle of sweat departed his left armpit and rolled down his side. "Could you turn the temperature down a little, sir?"

For such a big plane, the cockpit space of the Phantom was almost criminally minuscule. Steve's long frame was shoehorned into the rear cockpit. Instrument consoles hemmed him in on the left and right, the canopy arched inches over his helmet, the stick rose close between his thighs, and narrow foot wells beneath the front instrument panel enclosed his legs forward of the knees. There had been more room in the much smaller planes Steve had flown in pilot training. This was not a job for the claustrophobic.

He squirmed, trying to find comfort. Already, only five minutes into the flight, the hard padding of the seat dug into his rear. Already there was a faint but building pressure in his bladder. Five minutes gone and ninety more to go, give or take a little.

Air roared at four hundred knots past the smooth plastic of the canopy just inches from Steve's head, but he didn't notice it; the foam rubber of the headset inside the helmet encased his ears, and through the headphones came the raspy, semiregular sound of breathing—his own and Truhaft's, an unintended duet. There was mostly silence between them except for the breathing, the silence of two pilots in hermetically sealed worlds. Occasionally, Truhaft pointed out something on the ground—this valley, that ridge of peaks, a road, a village tucked into jungle—professionally and impersonally training a young bird in the hawk-eat-hawk ways of attack and survival flying. But mostly there was the silence of breathing.

And the silence of thoughts. Daydream bullets hit Demon Lead hard. *Whack-whack.* There was an explosion behind them in the left engine, and a suddenly unbalanced turbine began vibrating violently. Steve's teeth rattled, and the plane pitched and rolled out of control.

After a while, Truhaft began humming the Air Force song. Steve wanted to join in, but he hesitated at an uninvited camaraderie.

# 6

*Clayton Daily Star*

## Lt. Mylder arrives in Vietnam

By Lt. Steven W. Mylder

Vietnam is not like Arizona! Everything is too green, there is too much vegetation, very little bare ground, and no cactus at all. Even though it is wintertime, we are close enough to the equator that the days are not much shorter than the nights. It rains most of the time.

I left Clayton just three weeks ago, but it seems like three years! I spent a day in San Francisco, then I left from Travis Air Force Base, traveling with Denny, a buddy I met there. We flew to Clark Air Base in the Philippines for Jungle Survival school.

We camped out in the jungle, thirty pilots, mostly Air Force, but some Marines. They gave us sharp machetes and admonished us not to cut off our fingers and toes. They taught us to hide our parachutes as soon as we hit the ground and then get away fast. They showed us plants to eat and pointed out that bugs are a good source of protein. The plants tasted bad, but the good news was that there were a *lot* of bugs, big ones! No *thanks*! Then, after a few days in base camp, they turned us out in two-man teams to "escape and evade," and after we had an hour's head start, they turned loose the native Negritos who were paid to hunt us.

It was no contest. They tracked us down in 20 minutes! We might as well have left billboards saying "200 yards to the next exit for Denny and Steve." Then they turned us loose again because that was part of the game, and we spent the rest of the day running. That night we slept on the side of a mountain. It was a *terrible* night! I kept sliding down the slope. There were clouds of mosquitoes and *rats*! Three or four of them crawled over us, and they rattled our empty food tins around all night.

The next day helicopters came to pick us up. We had a day to rest, then Denny departed, and I left the day after that. I spent two days at Ton Son Nhut Air Base near Saigon and then got a hop on a C-130 cargo plane to Danang.

•        •        •

Steve listed across the tarmac, bobbing like a crane with a short leg as he lugged a heavy green flight bag on one side, a garment bag and briefcase on the other. A film of moisture clung to his skin. He stopped halfway to the operations building to renew his grip on the baggage. The ever-present overcast loomed above.

Two F-4s in tight formation drove out of the gloom into the traffic pattern, screaming in hoarse-throated harmony, trailing twin streams of dirty black smoke. Steve craned his neck to follow. The lead plane broke formation almost directly overhead, pitching out crisply into the turn to downwind. Steve had counted to four when the wingman slapped into 60 degrees of bank and pulled two gs to follow the leader. The whine of turbines cascaded down in pitch as the planes angled away.

A long, green awning stretched from the operations building to the tarmac. Someone waited beneath the awning. He peered intently at the name tag sewn over the left breast of Steve's flight suit. "Steve?" the someone asked.

"Yes."

"I'm Avery." The first lieutenant held out a hand. "Avery Aughton." Steve put down his bags and shook the hand. The lieutenant's grip was firm and self-confident.

Steve smiled. "I didn't expect anyone."

"Oh, don't feel special; we do this for all the new pilots. You're in my squadron."

"Great," Steve answered lamely.

Avery was not small except in comparison to Steve's six foot two; he stood four inches shorter. When he moved, it was with a well-oiled fluidity which conjured a symphony of muscles just beneath the skin, and when he stopped, it was to strike a jauntily akimbo pose that shouted "fighter pilot." Blond, nearly white hair crept from under the edges of his flight cap, contrasting sharply with green eyes flashing from a square-jawed, smooth-shaven face.

Steve touched his own upper lip almost unconsciously. It was smooth, too.

Avery wore a standard cotton flight suit like Steve's, but Avery's was neat and new while Steve's had seen over a year's worth of sweat and washings. Counterpointing the white bars sewn onto Steve's shoulders, Avery's insignia were black cloth on green patches attached to the shoulders by Velcro so that they could be ripped off if it came time to "escape and evade." The name tag was similarly attached above the zipper over the left breast. And the boots were different;

Steve's were standard heavy black leather, but Avery's had panels of canvas along the sides and looked lighter and more comfortable.

The differences were both functional and vain. Steve felt vaguely unfashionable.

"How was the trip?"

"Cattle car," Steve replied. "One of the worst flights I ever had. We must have landed at every runway between here and Saigon. And that reminds me; I'm looking for the first latrine available." He glanced at the sky. "I've seen more weather in the last week than in a year back home. Do you ... do *we* fly in this junk?"

"Naw, not much." Avery's face was pleasantly Nordic, cheerful. "This is the rainy season. We go to early morning briefings and CNX—that's 'cancel'—for weather, then screw around all day, drink at the bar, or catch Zs so we're happy and relaxed and we can kill more Commies." Avery's faint grin widened slightly, but Steve wasn't sure he was joking.

"Com'on, I've got the crew truck out back." Avery led the way into Base Ops while Steve staggered behind with his baggage. He dumped the bags on the floor beside the door, visited the latrine, and then the two young men resumed their way through the air-conditioned, military green-and-cream interior of the building. When they exited on the street side, a new clammy layer of moisture condensed on Steve's freshly cooled skin.

Five white delta-winged airplanes, each a foot long, flew in painted echelon across the side of a large blue-paneled van. Large block letters proclaimed "THE MiG KILLERS."

"Wow," Steve exclaimed, meaning to project 50 percent gentle sarcasm but achieving closer to 100 percent true awe. "An ace squadron!" He looked askance toward Avery. "Any of 'em yours?"

Avery looked uncomfortable. "Well, no. I've only flown three missions ..." He continued quickly, "... but they were damn good ones. Twenty Charlies KBA on the last one."

"KBA?"

"Killed By Air. The FAC—that's Forward Air Controller ..."

"I know, I know," Steve protested.

"The FAC takes a WAG after you drop ..."

"WAG?"

Avery grinned. "You *are* wet behind the ears. Wild-Assed-Guess. They take a WAG at the body count and pass it over the radio. It doesn't count for anything—just a warm, fuzzy feeling. Makes you feel like you've 'done your duty,' and it gives Seventh Air Force a hard-on; they like big KBAs. Anyhow, we burned their asses with napalm and spattered 'em with the gun."

Avery backed out of the parking space and turned north onto a road paralleling the runway on the east side. A soft drizzle began peppering the windshield, and Avery worked the wipers sporadically.

The base was even more depressing than Tan Son Nhut. The unmarked narrow asphalt road was lined on both sides by dirt pathways dotted with puddles of water, and the empty fields they passed were choked with weeds. Telephone and power lines ran starkly along the road atop ugly form-cast concrete towers. Buildings were one- or two-story affairs, many of them built with dingy white plaster walls topped by low-pitched corrugated metal roofs. They broadcast an air of dilapidation and decay. The only uplifting sight Steve found was the rise of mountains out of the ground and into the clouds a few miles ahead.

Steve grinned at Avery. "Three missions, huh?"

"Right." Avery frowned. "And now you're the FNG—that's Fucking New Guy. I'm sure as hell glad I'm not at the bottom of the totem pole any more." He grinned wryly at Steve. "We get new people every few days, but you're the first GIB in a couple of weeks. There're two more coming in tomorrow. Another wad of cannon fodder, oh boy!"

GIB. Guy In Back. Pilot but not pilot. The guy in the backseat ran the radar, navigated, set the comm channels, read the maps, and did housekeeping chores while the guy in front, the aircraft commander, did most of the flying and got most of the fun. The GIB got a little stick time each flight, usually. Every other flight, he got to make a landing to maintain proficiency.

"Have you been shot at? What's it like? Are you scheduled every day?" The questions tumbled out against his will.

"Youth wants to know," Avery commented sarcastically. "Yeah, sure, I've been shot at. Triple A, automatic weapons, the usual stuff. The Triple A makes those nice puffy clouds, but you usually can't see the AW during the daytime. Sometimes the only way you know is the FAC tells you they're shooting at you. Or you bring home a few holes."

Avery cycled the windshield wipers.

"We're flying days now, along with Blue Squadron. Red is on nights. Oh, yeah, we're Green Squadron, by the way. Welcome aboard." Avery extended his hand again.

Steve shook it again. "Thanks."

"We fly—or at least we're scheduled—every day, mostly once a day, some-times twice. Saturdays and Sundays, too. The only way you can tell it's Sunday around here is there's comics in the newspaper."

Avery slowed and turned right off the main road through a gate flanked by barbed wire fences. An air policeman saluted as they passed through. Steve noticed a sandbag bunker at the side of the gate.

"This is the Air Force compound. Our wing is housed here, along with some other flying units, support groups, and the usual paper pushers. I'll take you over to Wing Headquarters so you can process in. That'll take an hour or two; you can leave your bags in the van if you want; nobody'll run off with them. You can call me when you're done, and we'll go over to Operations to meet the colonels and majors and good ole boys." He looked askance at Steve. "Then we can get together at the DOOM club and wet our whiskers. You do drink, don't you?"

"DOOM club?"

Avery pointed forward through the windshield. There was a wide, one-story building just ahead where the road turned hard right. A red sign hung beneath the peak of the roof above the entrance. White embellished lettering announced:

DANANG OFFICERS OPEN MESS

"It ain't much, but it's ours, by gawd."

# 7

At Wing Headquarters, Steve saw four different clerks and filled out fifteen forms, each requiring name, rank, service number, date of birth, and combinations of twenty other items of personal information which should have been well known to every bureaucrat in the Air Force by now. He had writer's cramp as he walked out the door through the drizzle to the waiting van.

He had made a successful transition. He was a new piece of property belonging to a new Air Force organization, and somewhere, no doubt, his essence was captured in a single line on a form in backward inventory order: *Mylder, S.W., 1Lt, Pilot, Fighter, Air Force, Standard, One each.*

Avery Aughton had come back to pick him up. "We lost a crew last week and just cleared out their stuff, so the pilot's bunk is open for you in one of the hootches," Avery said. "We'll go by there and dump your bags, and then I'll take you over to Squadron."

*Great. I hope they cleared out his ghost, too,* Steve thought. Out loud, he said, "How long before I start flying?"

"Oh, four, five days. There's a little in-house training course to go through first."

Steve walked into an alcove of his new hootch, then crept softly to avoid waking one of his new roomies, who was sleeping in the bottom of one of the two double-decker beds. He heaved his bags up to the empty bunk above the roommate, who grunted and rolled from one side to the other without waking, dragging an army regulation blanket around with him.

They left the compound and continued north along the road traveled earlier. The drizzle had stopped. After a half mile, the road turned left toward the runway. They entered another guard gate, drove a hundred feet, and parked in front of a trim clapboard building painted a refreshing mint green, not the regulation olive that colored everything else.

"Home," Avery announced as they got out of the van. Corrugated metal covered the roof. A small antenna sprouted from the peak. Five MiGs ran diagonally across the front door, similar to those on the van except that these were bright red. A sandbag bunker squatted along the west side of the building, its doorless entrance gaping like a toothless mouth. Steve imagined it swallowing pilots whole. Beside the squadron building door, a wooden sign carved with an eagle's head in bas-relief announced "Green Squadron."

Across the road was a low, white clapboard building enclosed inside a barbed wire fence. Stacks of sandbags rose high beside the walls, up to the tops of the windows.

"The Wing Command Post," Avery explained. "It doubles as the Intelligence building."

A sign at the pinnacle of the roof proclaimed: 666 TFW PHIGHTING PHAN-TOMS.

A hundred feet west, the road ran into a broad expanse of concrete whose function was as a parking lot to a mighty fleet of aircraft and substrate for flotillas of hangars and other buildings. Steve saw a bewildering array of airplanes, mostly Air Force, but also Marine, Navy, and even a few Army planes. There were transports and fighters and utilities and choppers and a few small bombers, and even a few trainers, some of them in neat rows, some parked in nearly random clusters—fighters here, cargos there, more fighters there and there. He saw two Thuds, a C-130 Hercules, an F-100 Super Sabre, a scattering of Navy A-6s and A-4s, a C-47 Gooney Bird, a Navy F-4, some tiny O-1 Bird Dogs nearly lost among their big brother fighters, an F-102 Delta Dagger, and more that he couldn't name.

"Most of those are transients," Avery said. "They'll bug out when the weather clears." He pointed northwest over the concrete toward rows of squat gray metal barriers that covered acres and acres of concrete.

"Ours are over there."

The barriers formed revetments. Thick steel walls full of sand provided three walls for each roofless room, open in front. In each revetment crouched a camouflaged F-4C Phantom II, an ugly misshapen aerospace troll hunched forward to pounce on innocent children or unwary Sunday strollers.

They crossed the road to the Wing Command Post. "This is where El Hombre spends most of his time," Avery said. "He likes to meet new pilots fresh off the hay wagon, so we'll do that first." They walked through a barbed wire gate into the building, and were ushered into a large office by a sergeant. Avery introduced Steve to the wing commander.

"Colonel Sanger, sir, this is our new guy, Steve Mylder, fresh out of jungle survival school."

Steve tensed and saluted the colonel in Air Force tans behind the desk. Colonel William D. Sanger rolled his chair back slightly, propped his elbows on armrests, and, with slow deliberation, made a steeple with his fingertips. He nodded a salute back to Steve and smiled.

It was not pleasant. It was the frozen smile of a voracious, hard-eyed predatory animal, except that it was asymmetric, flowing up one side of his face but not the other. It was a knowing, Machiavellian, probably evil smile. Long moments dragged by, and the colonel did not speak. The fingers tapped lazily together just in front of his nose. His eyes bored right through Steve's, through the brain and out the back of his skull.

The colonel was a big man, as tall as Steve but heavier and more muscular. A short lock of black hair draped carelessly down the side of his forehead in a vaguely Hitleresque style. There was no mustache, but there tried to be—blackness lurked just beneath the surface of the skin, pushing to get out. Indeed, it appeared that hair grew, or wanted to grow, from every surface of his body. Tufts sprang from his ears. A black jungle began at the crease of his neck and flowed down in a dark mat to disappear beneath the "V" of a short-sleeve uniform shirt. It grew out again through the arm holes to march down both arms, a dense growth of black vegetation thinning finally to clumps along the backs of his hands and the first joints of his fingers. The man was a walking hair ball. Steve thought that a significant fraction of the colonel's energy must be consumed by the process of pushing hair out of pores.

"Sir, I was stationed in England. Sir." He had to say something, anything. The ball was in his court; he had to justify himself. Guilty! He was guilty already. What did he do?

The colonel nodded. "I know, lad." The voice was deceptively mild, soft-spoken, casual.

"F-4s." Stupid. Really stupid.

"Yes."

"I just arrived this afternoon. Sir."

"So you came over here to help us shoot down some MiGs and win the war, did you?" He was smiling.

"Ahhh.... Yes sir, that's why I'm here."

After no more than five minutes in the colonel's office, Steve was sweating and extremely uncomfortable. He'd rather be shot down in combat than traffic with this man.

A little later they crossed the road to Green Squadron Ops. Avery introduced Steve to the squadron commander, Lieutenant Colonel Parsons, a pleasant man who peered through wire-rimmed glasses. He was the opposite of Sanger; he actually tried to put Steve at ease.

Next he met the squadron operations officer.

"Major Scott, this is Steve Mylder just off the plane from Saigon. He's come over to help us rip some new Commie assholes."

Avery's introduction was so outrageous that Steve knew the major must have a sense of humor, although all he could see was a wiry, slight man with a facial expression of perpetual worry.

"Stay on his good side," Avery advised later. "He makes the life-or-death decisions around here." Steve looked puzzled. "He schedules. I mean, do you fly hairy missions or easy ones."

Avery introduced Steve to several other people: a hodgepodge of captains, majors, and lieutenants whose faces and names he instantly forgot. There was one, however, who stood radically apart from the rest.

"Sub-Lieutenant Sam, this is Steve Mylder. He's an asshole pilot from England, and you'd better be good to him because he's the only one you out-rank."

Sam had a long, narrow face and was even woollier than Colonel Sanger, but this was not surprising since Sam was a collie. He pranced excitedly around Steve as if this were the most important meeting of his young doggy life. White spots in all the right places accented a magnificent coat of shiny brown fur, and Steve's inevitable first thought was, "Lassie! What's a beautiful pup like you doing in a hole like this?" Steve wasn't a dog person, but it was immediately apparent that this handsome animal was one of the nicest people he'd ever met. Sam liked him, and he liked Sam back, and whatever the reason for the instant chemistry, Steve had made a friend.

"His full name and rank is Sub-Lieutenant Sam the Collie, but you can call him Sam. He showed up a couple of weeks ago, just after I arrived," Avery explained. "We knew right away he was a good boy, so we made him a member of the squadron."

They'd finished the rounds. Avery grinned. "Let's go to the DOOM club and drink."

•    •    •

They had been drinking beer for about an hour and felt no pain when Colonel Sanger walked in from a cold drizzle, a lock of black hair pasted wetly to his forehead.

It was said of Colonel William D. Sanger that he kept a pen of bunny rabbits behind his trailer—four or five nice, white, cuddly little things with long silky ears and cute, twitchy little noses. It was said that the pen needed periodic replenishment since the colonel liked to kill a bunny each Sunday; he derived considerable pleasure from twisting their heads off (a hands-on, back-to-nature experience, so to speak). He skinned them himself and gave them to his Vietnamese housekeeper to cook for Sunday dinner. It was said that he loved rabbit stew, the kind made from tender young bunnies. It was said that he especially liked the eyeballs—he popped them out with his thumbs and ate them raw.

The DOOM club bar went silent for a heartbeat, then picked up again, for the colonel was apparently in a good mood—he was scowling. A path cleared as he strode to the bar.

"Good evenin', sir; how ya doin'?" First Lieutenant Lux Luxington the Third ventured and received a barely perceptible nod of the head in reply. The colonel ordered a gin martini, "dry, up," and turned to lean back against the bar while he watched a clutch of first lieutenants, all of them Guys In Back, loitering at the dart board. It was Steve's turn to throw, and he put the first two darts smack on target.

"Whoa, hot shit!" the colonel exclaimed, regarding Steve with fresh eyes. "I'm gonna put you in the front seat and send you up to Package 1," he joked.

Steve smiled nervously.

The colonel ambled over to the dart board and put his palm over the center, hairy stubby fingers splayed out.

"Com'on, put it right there between the fingers."

Steve's jaw fell open. His co-GIBs urged him on, laughing, teetering on their feet. "Do it, do it!" they chanted.

"Com'on, do it," the colonel taunted, looking around the group. "I thought you lads were hot pilots." He zeroed in on Steve. "Front-seaters can nail it between the fingers every time."

A hubbub of drunk laughter and a buzzing of voices whirled in Steve's head. He hesitated. He balked. He shook his head from side to side.

"Ahhh, yer a goddamn washer woman," the colonel snorted and walked away.

•           •           •

*Clayton Daily Star*

## Pilots live in "hootches" at Danang

By Lt. Steven W. Mylder

Danang is a disaster area. Not much was expected, but those minimal expectations proved optimistic. The place is like a broken-down village no one bothered to put back together. The Air Force section consists of stark, ill-put-together buildings and tents on an irregular network of sometimes paved roads. The sidewalks are mud when it's raining and dust when it's not.

The sun hasn't shone while I've been here. It drizzled for about half the day yesterday and a little today until everything was sloshy, but as soon as the rain stopped, the dust began rising. Except for the dust, things never dry out. Bed sheets always feel damp and gritty. Clothes left in lockers acquire a slow growth of vegetation after a few months.

We live in barrack-type buildings called hootches. The interiors are partitioned into several smaller living areas consisting of two double-decker beds, four lockers, and an opening (not a door) into the hall. The bunks are enclosed in mosquito netting so that the bugs can't get to us. The floor is concrete, the walls are screen wire and the ceiling is open right to the roof. It sounds bad, but our hootch is surprisingly comfortable. It has a strange charm, perhaps that of being lived in, and may not be too hard to grow fond of.

Have the grim realities of war taken away our sense of humor? Not at all! Note the cheery name of our officer's club: the "DOOM" club—for "Danang Officer's Open Mess."

Despite grievous deprivations, the pilots are fairly comfortable and happy here. We didn't expect a palace and, by God, we didn't get one!

My first mission was scheduled for today but canceled because of weather. I'm scheduled again tomorrow. An easy one.

• • •

Lt. Col. R. W. Gannis
666 TFW Public Information Office

Sir:

I made the changes you wanted and took your suggestion about toning down negative comments. I hope this meets your approval.

Lt. S. W. Mylder

# 8

Demon Flight. An easy mission. For beginners.

Steve and Virgil Demopoulis, another new GIB, walked fifty yards along the dirt path from the hootch to the asphalt road, then fifty yards more along the road to the DOOM club for breakfast. The sun slanted almost cheerily through a high, thin cloud cover. A small flock of sparrows scrabbled angrily among themselves—a moving rumpus fluttering from field to road to scraggly grass patches along the dusty path—fighting their own version of an air war for reasons known only to birds. Every minute or so, a formation of fighters roared off the runway a half-mile away.

The two GIBs picked their way around two large stacks of fresh lumber that workmen had dumped across the sidewalk leading to the entrance of the club. On the left side of the building, the foundation for a substantial addition was in mid excavation. Abandoned shovels stood like sentinels in mounds of earth. The smell of freshly turned dirt and new lumber blended pleasantly in Steve's nostrils.

They came into a large, breezy room fronted by an entire wall of wire screening that joined it to the outside. Twenty or thirty plain wooden tables accompanied by plain plastic chairs littered the concrete floor. There were no cloths on the tables, no curtains for the windows, and no decorations on the walls. A cafeteria counter ran along one wall, at the end of which stood a table holding condiments and utensils.

They slid their trays along the counter. Steve heaped his plate with scrambled eggs and bacon. Virgil got a sweet roll. They both took black coffee. They sat at a table by the screened wall near the entrance, watching planes take off. Cool, damp air moved slowly across their faces. After a while, Virgil went back for a coffee refill.

"You'll need to piss that away in a few hours," Steve clucked, "and you won't have the opportunity." The F-4, unlike some other fighters, had no "relief" tube.

"Yes, Mother Mylder." Virgil smiled and reached down into the helmet bag beside his chair. He held up a baby bottle that he'd bought at the BX. It was filled with water. "If that happens, first I just drink this bottle—and then I fill it up again."

Steve returned an indulgent smile. "Yeah, I know the trick. And if it happens again, you just drink it and fill it again, right?"

Virgil laughed and triumphantly held up a second baby bottle. "Two of 'em. See?"

Despite a mildly feisty exterior and a gently sarcastic humor, Virgil Demopoulis exuded an agreeable, carefree presence. Large, dark brown innocent eyes dominated a pleasant face beneath a short mop of black hair. Almost everything about Virgil said, "Ehhh! Don't sweat it," but his physical motion sang a different tune. His every movement was smooth, as if his joints were lined with satin. Even simple physical motions—the lifting of a fork, the lacing of a boot—were as graceful as ballet and conveyed a dynamic charm. His walk was cat-like, even tiger-like, as if to say, "You may think this critter is fuzzy and cuddly, but use caution—there are some really sharp claws under the fur." It gave him an air of competence, gave him a compact, self-sufficient core. Steve figured that Virgil, like a cat, could land on his feet if dropped upside down from any height.

Virgil had arrived a day later than Steve with two other GIBs. The four of them had taken the miniature in-house training course on ground and air procedures, rules of combat, squadron and wing policies, local flying hazards, and local area diseases associated with local area women (as well as a host of other admonitions, cautions, caveats, and warnings).

They had spent an afternoon cutting and taping maps, dividing Vietnam into bite-size military pieces. The region just above the DMZ, or Demilitarized Zone, was named Tallyho for completely obscure reasons. Steve drew the boundaries with his black felt pen and plastic straight-edge, wrote "Tallyho" in the center, and *zip-zip-zip* marched off north with his marker along the narrow ribbon of North Vietnam trapped between Laos and the Gulf of Tonkin. He marked "Package 1" above "Tallyho," "Package 2" above "Package 1," and so forth, up into the heart of enemy land where the country bulged into a bulb containing Hanoi in the center of its nether region. There he marked "Package 5" on the large half of the bulb west of Hanoi, and "Package 6" on the eastern half containing Hanoi near its leftmost edge.

"Package?" Steve had asked. He had received a shrug in reply.

"Don't ask; it's just the military's way of naming things."

*Snip-snip-snip* went Steve's scissors, splitting whole districts, counties, peoples, cities, regions, and cultures into convenient packets for flight suit pockets and knee clipboards. The local area went into Steve's left thigh pocket, and a parcel of countryside extending from twenty miles south to fifty miles north of the

DMZ—the map of the day—was trapped beneath the checklist on the clipboard on the table beside his plate.

They'd received a supply of fat anti-malaria pills that they washed down with difficulty, but religiously, each day, for the mosquitoes were fierce. They'd accumulated new dog tags, Geneva Convention ID cards, new flight suits ("Coverall, Flying, Man's, Very Light K-2B"), jungle boots with green canvas siding, and army blankets for their bunks. They collected green netted survival vests containing an emergency radio ("XMTR/RCVR, Guard, RT-10"), flares, a signal mirror, a medical kit, and an emergency food ration "with Pemmican Bar and Nutritious Fruit Cake Portion." They picked up standard military issue .38 caliber revolvers and bullets for the vests. They were issued helmets with plastic pulldown visors, anti-g suit leggings, face-fitting oxygen masks, orange-handled parachute knives for the specially made pouches near the groins of the flight suits, and strongly webbed parachute harnesses to hook into the parachutes that were built into the ejection seats.

They were trained, supplied, and fortified. They were ready to fly and fight.

The squadron van swung by the club to pick them up at 0830. Airman First Class McNish, the squadron orderly, drove. "Hi, Sub-Lieutenant Sam the Collie," Steve said cheerfully as the young dog met them inside the door of Squadron Ops, tail wagging enthusiastically, nails clicking on the linoleum tile floor. Steve gave him a friendly rub.

"Say, what happened to you, boy?" The edge of Sam's left ear was bleeding, and Steve found a deep nick.

McNish came in the door behind them. "Well, sir, I took him along for a ride over to Red Squadron barracks yesterday, and he tangled with Charley." He took the collie's head between his hands and playfully shook it.

"Charley? Who the hell's Charley?"

McNish gave a crooked grin. "He's Red Squadron's cur. A real ugly black and white dog and a real scrappy son of a bitch, literally. He and Sam don't get along at all. I nearly lost a finger getting them apart." McNish held up his left hand. The forefinger was bandaged.

Demon Flight gathered in one of the squadron's small briefing rooms. The four pilots, two for each plane, sat in government issue gray metal chairs around two gray metal tables pushed together in the center of the room. A blackboard covered most of one wall. An overhead fluorescent light buzzed and flickered just below the threshold of aggravation. The tables didn't quite match in height, so there was a small ledge in the center. Steve rested his elbows on one of the tables. It wobbled.

Patrick Truhaft was Steve's front-seater in Demon Lead; Major Frank Bender would fly Demon Two from the front, with Virgil in back.

Truhaft was a lean man with a crew cut topping a tight, controlled face. He was confident, intense, serious—deadly serious. He had flown forty-five missions and was still alive. Steve had flown none and could very well be dead on the first one, he thought.

Captain Patrick A. Truhaft had been a member of the first Air Force Academy graduating class, Academy '59. Steve was impressed. Truhaft was one of the gods the upperclassmen had talked about in Steve's first year, the year after the class of 1959 had departed.

Those gods, those anointed ones, those members of the Golden Class, had endured their first years under surrogate upperclassmen from the Air Force officer corps, most of them West Pointers, who rode them, broke them down to the fundamentals, then gathered the pieces together, put the chips into molds, stoked the fires and melted them down. The pieces had run together, becoming entirely new living beings. Those gods had cooled and cured, hardening pupas inside rigid cocoons of discipline, until the molds came apart and metal shone through.

They'd entered as pimply faced teenage civilians—self-absorbed, weak, undisciplined, concerned about hair and looks and girlfriends and cars and their positions in the pecking order of the wishy-washy civilian world. They'd exited as military men, rugged and dependable and self-disciplined, ready to fight and sacrifice their lives out of a fierce love of country and military tradition.

At least that's what happened to Patrick Truhaft, Steve surmised. He had come in a boy and exited a man, an intense man with a mission and a will and a passion to serve his God and his country.

It had not happened to Steve. The Academy tore him down in that first brutal year. He and his classmates were stripped of personal dignity and honor, intimidated by hazing, assaulted by a thousand psychological ploys designed to break them apart, to purge all remnants of childhood, and the system ultimately reduced them to fragments. But the regathering process of the upper-class years—the putting together of the pieces, the forging, the molding—went somehow awry for Steve.

The Academy had taken him apart, all the fine parts of a watch dismantled—gears, springs, pivots, and hands in a small disorganized pile on a gray metal table top—but it hadn't quite gotten him together again. The parts were rearranged, some were missing, some were extra, and the watch tick-tocked, but it didn't seem to chime with self-confident love of country and military tradition.

It tinkled; it rattled with doubts, fears, and misgivings. Yet it still told time to fair accuracy and ran adequately to all appearances. Or so Steve felt.

Sam wandered in and listened to the briefing, tail thumping against the wall. A few minutes later, Crew Chief Thornton came to the door of the small room, a tall fatigue-clad professional wearing a face habitually troubled by the vagaries of keeping a sophisticated fighting machine in good working order. "You've got four high-drag Mark 82 Snake-eyes apiece, sir," he announced, speaking of five-hundred-pound bombs, "and centerline guns as well."

There was also an experimental camera mounted under Demon Lead's right wing. Thornton's crew had to rewire the arming circuits to accommodate it. The arming circuit for the gun now ran through the rear cockpit, through a switch called the "consent switch" tucked away on Steve's right instrument console. Steve wrote "Gun-Con Sw" on his clipboard.

Truhaft resumed the briefing. "We're targeted for a defoliating escort just below the DMZ." The flight would stay high and watch while C-119 Flying Boxcar transports skimmed over the jungle top, spraying orange vegetable death. "If they pick up any fire, we go down and zap 'em with the Snake-eyes or the guns," he explained. Next, he patiently went through the formation briefing checklist item by item. This was clearly an easy mission—a milk run—yet the others listened intently to a routine they'd heard to the point of yawning indifference on training flights in their previous units.

The briefing ended. Steve smiled nervously at Frank Bender and Virgil. Major Frank Bender had only two combat missions under his belt so far. Virgil was his back-seater, and like Steve, he had none.

Frank Bender was a quiet, pleasant man of medium height, slightly on the high side of average weight. There was nothing much to distinguish him from others; he might have been a small town businessman—a banker or accountant—who just happened to wear a flight suit to work. There was no obvious burning passion in the man, nor any other trait of extraordinary comment, either good or bad. Yet in a few hours, his name would echo across every Air Force base in Southeast Asia.

The four pilots walked across the tarmac toward the revetments, dangling buckles and straps from parachute harnesses. They carried their helmets by the chin straps—like buckets, with clipboards and checklists stuffed in where the brains usually go—in their left hands.

Sam followed them, tail wagging, a big collie grin on his face. "Woof!" *I'm a fighter pilot, too!*

"Stay, Sam, stay." They motioned him away with big sweeping motions of their right arms. "Damn dog's gonna get blown away by somebody's engines."

"Woof," Sam replied and followed them until they reached the revetments, then turned back on his own.

They split into two pairs at the second row of revetments and went in separate directions. Steve's plane was in the third stall of the second row, tail number "536" painted in large letters against the dull camouflage. The plane's great bulbous black nose jutted forward, drooping slightly like a Jimmy Durante schnoz, the infrared sensor growing like a wart from the bottom. Except the F-4C was not a Jimmy Durante type of airplane; it had no sense of humor at all. It was sophisticated but brutish—impolite, ugly, and brusque. It was more like a Cyrano de Bergerac of fighter airplanes, and lesser mortal fighters would do well not to cross it or tweak its nose. *The son of a bitch can beat anything in the sky*, Steve thought with unambiguous pride. A hawk soared above a deep canyon of his imagination.

Steve climbed the metal ladder that hung against the plane from the lip of the front cockpit, stepped along the top of the engine intake ramp to the rear cockpit, checked first that the red-flagged safety pins were in his ejection seat, and then stretched over the seat to turn on the power for the inertial navigation system. A yellow APU, or auxiliary power unit, cart behind the airplane chugged loudly and merrily, umbilical air and electric lines crawling from it to rise into the belly button of the airplane. Truhaft began the pre-flight walk-around.

Two rows of revetments away, Frank Bender and Virgil Demopoulis began their pre-flight procedures. Virgil lowered himself gingerly into the rear Martin-Baker ejection seat, snapped his harness into the built-in parachute, collected the shoulder straps and inserted their loops over the tongue of the seat belt, along with the "gold key" at the end of a lanyard that would provide automatic opening of the chute if he had to eject. He connected the oxygen and intercom lines, plugged his g-suit hose into the socket in the console along his left armrest, strapped his clipboard around his left thigh, and wrapped the long Velcro straps of his checklist around his right thigh.

Continuing his strapping-in synchrony with Virgil two rows away, Steve, in Demon Lead, leaned forward to attach leg restraints around his calves, the restraints that would jerk his legs and knees back from the rudder pedals in the automatic ejection sequence so that he would not leave bloody stumped legs behind with the plane—so that he would not depart two feet shorter than he'd entered. There was something final about this act; it was a commitment of sorts, he thought. It was an irreversible wiring-in of the pilot to the aircraft.

Flak came up in his mind and hit the airplane, *thump*, and there was an explosion and a sickening yaw and roll, and Steve was out of the plane, tumbling through cold air, the sting of cockpit debris on his face and in his eyes. *I'm going to make it. Don't let up, don't lapse. Gonna make it.*

Truhaft called over the intercom, "Ready for the engines?"

"Yes sir," Steve answered.

Two rows over, in Demon Two, Virgil took gloves from the chest pocket of his flight suit and pulled them on—right hand, left hand—wiggled his fingers whimsically, and sat back to wait. After a minute, Frank called.

"Engines?"

"Right."

The two planes taxied and rendezvoused in the last check area. They parked in echelon formation, engines whining and canopies open. Four pairs of pilot's arms rested in view along the canopy sills so that the ground crew could see that it was safe to go beneath the planes. The ground crew removed the last of the "WARNING, REMOVE BEFORE FLIGHT" red flags from the bombs and guns, checked for leaks, and then waved the formation on with a salute. The canopies came down, and there was a slight popping in Steve's ears as the pressurization kicked in.

They taxied again, and Truhaft called the control tower. "Demon Flight of two, number one for runway three-five right."

They were ready to fly.

# 9

*Clayton Daily Star*

## Lt. Mylder Flies First Mission. Disaster!

By Lt. Steven W. Mylder

Counter number one. I will explain that in a moment.

We were Demon Flight, two F-4Cs. It was an escort mission just south of the DMZ. We took off and angled across Vietnam, heading northwest, Pat and I in Demon Lead, and Frank and Virgil in Demon Two. Everybody except Pat was new. He had 45 missions, Frank had two, and this was the first one for Virgil and me.

The land rose into foothills and became full-blown green-covered mountains. We contacted the FAC (Forward Air Controller) on the radio. He was flying a small airplane somewhere below us. We never even saw him. He gave us the location of the aircraft we were to provide cover for. We soon found it and orbited 10,000 feet overhead while it worked the jungle way down below, skimming just above the tree tops, spraying defoliant to strip the top cover off so the enemy would have one less place to hide.

•          •          •

The mission was dull. Captain Truhaft flew the plane in large, lazy circles while Steve watched a Flying Boxcar skim the treetops far below, a toy airplane spraying water over a toothpick and tassel forest mounted on papier-mâché mountains.

Truhaft had hummed the Air Force song three times since takeoff. Then he cycled through the rest of the service songs.

*Hm hm hmmm hmmm hmmm-hmmm-hmmmm-mm-hm ...*
*To the shores of Tripoli ...*

Steve fiddled with the radar. He pointed the antenna—located inside the plane's bulbous nose—downward and watched it paint the coast onto the screen in front of him. He found the funny scalloped section that flanked the DMZ. Out on the water were a few bright orange blips surrounded by dark. *Navy ships,* he reckoned.

*Anchors aweigh, my boys,*
*hmmmm-hm hm-hmmmm …*

So far, so good. Nothing had happened.

*Flying is ninety-nine percent boredom,* Steve reminded himself, twiddling the radar, practicing lockups on clumps of ground clutter.

*How many roads must a man walk down,*
*Before you call him a man?*

*Huh?* Steve thought. *Dylan?*

•          •          •

After a while, the defoliating aircraft finished spraying and left. We queried the forward air controller, who informed us he had nothing else for us to do. We requested permission to go on an armed reconnaissance mission into the region just north of the DMZ.

•          •          •

"Want to get a counter?" Truhaft asked.

The question was rhetorical. Truhaft wanted a counter; he didn't care what Steve wanted.

"Sure," Steve answered easily, but he thought, *No, no, no! I don't want a counter. Tomorrow!*

Today it was sufficient to be mild and free.

"Let's do it, sir!"

•          •          •

Crossing the DMZ, the mission became a "counter" because we were going into the north. The standard tour of duty for pilots stationed here is 100 combat missions over North Vietnam. After that, you get to go home. South Vietnam doesn't count, no matter how many times you fly there, or how shot up you get.

We arrived over the coastal plains, about ten miles inland from the Gulf of Tonkin.

The most striking thing in the area just north of the DMZ is the incredible number of bomb craters. They're everywhere! The land is like the moon—full of holes, with nothing living in sight. There is no sign of human activity in the day-time. Most of the action happens at night or during bad weather when the enemy repairs bridges and sends trucks and sampans with supplies and muni-tions toward the border.

We followed Highway 1 north, presently spotted a bridge, and went down to take it out. It was an overnight construction—an earth-fill across a stream. We made one run and dropped our full load of bombs, getting a direct hit. Frank and Virgil in the other plane stayed high and watched.

Climbing to altitude again, we searched for another target. After cruising several miles further north, we found a transport boat coasting lazily down a river.

●          ●          ●

"There's one of them down there." Truhaft's breath came fast through the intercom. "See the sucker?"

He dipped the left wing, and Steve saw it, too. A boat drifted down the river, a small boat pointed at both ends.

Truhaft called over the radio. "Demon Flight, there's a sampan down there on the river about a klick north of the bend. See it?"

There was silence, punctuated by heavy breathing, for about ten seconds. Tru-haft swept the plane in an erratic left turn, rolling out every few seconds before turning in again to spoil any ground gunner's lead. Jinking, it was called. Steve saw Demon Two inside their turn a thousand feet away, banked up steeply onto its left side, searching.

"Got it." Frank's voice was squeezed by g-forces.

"Arm up, Demon," Truhaft called. "Lead goes in first with guns, then you drop your load behind us, Two."

*Click-click* went the radio—a universal, voiceless acknowledgment.

*Are we really doing this?* Steve wondered. *What if it's civilian? We don't know for sure.* He was an intruder, a burglar in an unfamiliar house, creeping in to rape the wife and kill the children, expecting the husband to open up with a shotgun.

He read the short arming checklist for the gun out loud, and Truhaft acknowledged each step. They continued the jerky turn, descending slightly until they were a few miles north of the sampan, then rolled into a steep bank. Truhaft hauled back on the stick, pressing both pilots into their seats with three gs of force. Steve's g-suit bladder inflated, pressuring the blood in his legs and gut to keep it in his head to help him stay conscious. He tightened his abdomen and grunted quietly to keep blackness away.

The Phantom rolled out on course, descending as if on a steep, hot, final approach for landing. Truhaft jinked hard left, then right, then settled on a straight course with the small white dot of his gunsight wallowing slowly around the sampan. Steve glanced at the airspeed indicator, saw five hundred knots, and then watched outside as the forest canopy rose alarmingly, coming up to smack them.

"Damn!" Truhaft grunted as the plane jerked right—four gs—then left until they were in a steeply climbing turn, throttles up to full power. "Our gun didn't work, Two. Why don't you make a pass while we figure out what went wrong."

*Click-click.*

"Check all the circuit breakers back there," Truhaft snapped.

Steve pushed up with his left arm against the canopy bow and bent over to look along the right wall of the cockpit where rows of black buttons hid.

"They're all okay," he reported.

"I'm de-arming. Now let's go through the checklist once more to make sure we got it right."

They leveled at ten thousand feet and watched Two make its pass far below, a hawk plummeting toward its prey. Two pulled off left, and a few seconds later, the bombs went off but missed.

"Crap, crap, crap!" Truhaft was intensely frustrated. "You were long by fifty yards, Two. We'll go through one more time. You follow with the gun, then we have to get outta here."

"Rog, Lead."

"Okay, let's try it again."

Steve thought about the wing policy of one pass per target. The exposure went up, and the odds for survival went down drastically. He'd been briefed on it just two days before. He decided not to raise the issue.

Again the treetops rushed by. Again the gun refused to fire.

Truhaft's voice was cold this time. "Did you check the consent switch? Remember, they wired the gun through it."

"Oh, shit! That's it. I'm sorry, I didn't even think about it. Okay, it's on now."

Truhaft was resigned, almost patient. "Too late, we don't have enough gas." His voice became tinny over the radio: "Demon Lead is off, Bingo, heading south."

A few seconds later, Frank called. "We got him, Lead. We hosed him good."

●         ●         ●

We circled overhead briefly and then went down for a strafing pass. Our gun wouldn't fire, so our wingman came in behind. He missed. We made another unsuccessful pass and then pulled off, heading south for home. Frank and Virgil, behind us, called a direct hit on the boat.

Then, disaster.

●         ●         ●

"We got a little problem, Lead. We took a hit."

Frank Bender's voice came over the radio calmly, like a banker talking to his customer: *We found a little problem on your loan application, sir.*

●         ●         ●

Our wingman was hit!

We pulled up left and looked back. Demon Two was a half-mile behind, streaming smoke from the right engine. The plane was losing hydraulic pressure rapidly and would soon have no flight controls.

We called for Frank to head for the sea, and just about the same time, the plane went unstable. It started rolling, and the nose began to come up. We were five miles inland.

●         ●         ●

"GET OUT, GET OUT!" Truhaft shouted over the radio. "GET OUTTA THERE!"

Steve keyed the mike button on his throttles and added to the chorus, "PUNCH OUT, PUNCH OUT."

"It's not too bad." Frank's voice came back calmly, as if he were out for a Sunday drive. "We're going to stick with it just a little longer."

"Not too bad?" Truhaft said to Steve. "Look at them!"

The plane stood on its tail at the apex of a climb, then fell backward and wallowed—inverted—as it began to roll the left wing toward the ground.

Thus began a minor spectacle of the Vietnam air war, and an exploit that would become an anecdotal pearl among fighter pilots that would illuminate an arcane but occasionally useful quirk of the Phantom and that would earn a modicum of celebrity for the flying skill and sangfroid of Frank Bender.

•          •          •

Demon Two began a loop but completed only a quarter of it and ended pointing straight up at 12,000 feet, out of airspeed. At this point we expected Frank and Virgil to spin and bail out. Ejection here meant almost certain capture. We wanted to get out over the water, but there didn't seem to be that choice.

They stayed with the plane as it flipped and went into the first stage of a spin—roll and left yaw onto the plane's back. But then it started to recover, nose almost straight down. We switched to the emergency frequency and called for rescue. Meanwhile, Two went through an incredible series of gyrations. It began a shaky pull-up through level and up again into another vertical stall. Again, it gyrated at the top, barely escaped a spin, and came out in a steep dive, heading roughly in the direction of the gulf. The nose started up again. By now, we saw fire trailing from the right engine.

•          •          •

"That right engine's starting to burn pretty bad, Two. Shut it down, shut down the goddamn right ..." Truhaft's voice was cool, but not that cool. "... oh, shit. Pull it up, PULL IT UP!"

Steve was helpless. He was a passenger. Truhaft flew the plane and made the decisions. The only thing Steve felt competent to do was change the radio channels. He watched the Phantom roll and climb and dive, and he caught a distant glimpse of Virgil and Frank, two small dots in a cockpit, as they came by on the way up to the top of another giant loop, and he knew that they were passengers, too, because without hydraulic pressure the Phantom was totally uncontrollable. They were on a wild-assed roller coaster ride, inverted and every which way but right side up, death at the end of the last chute. They were about to lose it, to lay a giant powerful motorcycle hard on its side against the sandpaper earth.

Steve shivered and not because he was cold. Sweat gushed from every pore of his body.

*... ninety-nine percent boredom ... and one percent stark terror.*

•      •      •

It happened again and again! The plane continued through several more stalls, changing direction, attitude, and altitude violently, sometimes pulling out left, sometimes right, but somehow maintaining a slight, average motion toward the water. It was like taking three steps forward and two steps back on the way to the gulf.

After a long, long time, the plane passed over the beach. The gyrations had gradually damped out and now they were in a descending, nose-high, slight left bank over the ocean.

At five miles out to sea, 5,000 feet altitude and still descending, we saw the first chute: Virgil's. Beautiful sight! Ten subjective years later (but probably no more than twenty seconds), Frank's chute blossomed. The plane continued a left spiraling turn and exploded into the water, forming the northern apex of a triangle with the chutes marking the lower two corners. Black smoke boiled into the sky.

The chutes continued down for at least two more minutes while we heard their emergency beepers over Guard channel. Virgil hit the water first, about six miles off the coast, and Frank landed about a mile farther out.

We circled low and saw both men in their rafts beside the chutes. After a few more minutes, we saw a helicopter coming in from the southwest and vectored him toward the chutes.

Virgil lit his smoke flare, and we saw the marker dye in the water around his raft. We had to leave for home just as the helicopter was hovering over him because we were dangerously low on fuel.

•      •      •

"What the hell happened?" Sanger demanded, climbing the ladder to the cockpit before Truhaft or Steve had unstrapped.

*Guilty.* A gavel thundered down in Steve's head. *Guilty.* His forgetfulness had cost an airplane and nearly cost the lives of his comrades. But he didn't mention the consent switch, and no one asked about it.

•          •          •

Frank and Virgil were returned to base that evening unharmed. We went to the DOOM Club to celebrate and get the answer to our big question: how did Frank fly the airplane without controls?

The answer was simple but reflected extreme flying skill: the F-4C has a tiny amount of "slosh" in the rudder system, even without hydraulic pressure, so that either pilot can, with considerable effort, move the rudder a little in either direction. That was all the control Frank had—the ailerons were neutral, the "slab" was up, but there was that tiny amount of movement of the rudder that he used to control the roll and to keep them out of spins. When the plane was going up, he plugged in the burner on his left engine. When it was coming down, he pulled back the throttle. Basically he had a tiger by the tail, guiding it by tweaking the tail all the way out to the sea.

On the way to the DOOM Club, Virgil made this off-handed comment that I'll never forget: "Well, that's one down, only 99 to go."

•          •          •

Lt. Col. R. W. Gannis
666 TFW Public Information Office

Sir:

You are completely right. I should not have speculated about the sampan, and should have emphasized that it was an enemy transport boat so that no one could come to the mistaken conclusion that it might have been civilian. I changed that and also took out the part about getting drunk at the O-club.

I hope you approve of the current version. Thank you very much for the interest in my writing.

Lt. S. W. Mylder

# 10

Three pilots in flight suits gaggled at the counter of the DOOM club barroom. Earlier they had wolfed down cafeteria meals and then loped into the bar. A few hours later, they were still there: Steve, Avery Aughton, and a new guy named Mike Ross.

The bar grew like a tumor out of the side of the main building. It was a pitiful, temporary thing with harsh lighting, a dusty linoleum floor, and rickety tables. A makeshift wooden counter stood at the far end of the small room.

On the positive side, the barkeep, an ambitious moonlighting airman, was cheerful and competent, and there was a lot to drink. What else was there for antsy pilots to do? There were no women—camaraderie and drinking were about it.

The small room jostled with pilots and energy—standing room only. Smoke from cigarettes and cigars layered the air. A jukebox in the corner thumped deep bass as The Royal Guardsmen belted out the noisy, everlasting duel of "Snoopy vs The Red Baron."

*Ten, twenty, thirty, forty, fifty or more,*
*The bloody Red Baron was runnin' up a score.*
*Eighty men died tryin' to end that spree,*
*Of the bloody Red Baron of Germany.*

The sound of revving airplane engines—Fokker versus Camel—growled from the speakers and reverberated off of bare plasterboard walls into the air.

Steve watched a group play Liar's Dice. *Rattle, rattle* went the cup, then *bang* down on the table. The roller tilted the cup between his hands to shade it from the prying eyes of his cohorts and peeked beneath the cup. Then he lifted it with a flourish. There was boisterous laughter.

At another table, Heck Sluder presided over his regular poker game, a noisy intermingling of pilots from Red and Green Squadrons. At the counter, a pack of fliers flew through a conversation. A major's hands went around and around in the air, fighting a dogfight in the dusky skies over the counter as captains and lieutenants absorbed the action from nearby clouds of smoke.

*The den of the hunters.* Steve put a finger to his upper lip. It was smooth.

43

As was inevitable in these kinds of gatherings, the conversation of the three pilots started at the home base of flying.

"How do you get upgraded to the front seat around here?" Mike Ross, the newest GIB in the squadron, pushed perfectly coifed black hair to the side with the palm of his hand, smoothing an invisible muss. His mouth curled beneath a hawk nose into a disarmingly friendly smile. Steve hated him.

Mike exuded the faint but unmistakable odor of money and aristocracy. He was aloof and superior until he turned on that charming smile. He had probably grown up in a well-connected family and had everything he'd ever wanted. He stood six feet tall and had a lean athletic build, neatly combed black hair, and dark brown eyes. On top of that, he was extraordinarily handsome. *With those Hollywood good looks*, Steve thought, *Mike Ross must do exceptionally well with the ladies.*

Steve did not do that well with the ladies. He was always conscious of his somewhat gawky presence and big-nosed frontage. His was an ever-present, crushing shyness that turned his tongue and brain to mush in the company of the opposite sex and that put the ladies on an unassailable pedestal—pure, beautiful, perfect, and all too often beyond reach.

"Ha!" Avery laughed. "You don't get promoted to the front seat. You die and get resurrected as a front-seater." He smiled indulgently. "How do you think? You volunteer to be a hero for another hundred missions and come back on a second tour."

"How about Luxington?" Mike asked. "He's in the front seat, and this is his first tour."

"First Lieutenant Lewis Luxington the Third." Avery's smile turned crooked, and his voice dripped with scorn. "That asswipe. I don't know how the hell he did it. He was in the pilot training class ahead of me at Willie, but he wasn't anything special. He got on somebody's good side, or maybe his daddy bought it for him. If I ever get the chance, I'm gonna punch him out."

"Wow," Steve responded sarcastically.

Avery shadowboxed, throwing punches at a hapless invisible opponent. "Bap, bap!" he grunted with two left jabs, then crossed with a lightning right. *Good*, Steve thought. Fast and efficient, even after four beers. Avery could probably handle himself.

"I was boxing champ in college."

Steve believed it. He knew boxing. For some reason, maybe because of his height and long arms, the squadron sports team leaders had chosen him for intramural boxing his first year at the Academy. After a few exhausting and nose-bloodied fights in which he demonstrated a total lack of aptitude and motivation for the sport, he was taken off and put on a football team. This was a little better—he was agile and a good runner—but not much. After a few weeks, he tried out for the varsity tennis team. He made it and was allowed to quit intramurals. Tennis he loved.

Eventually their talk veered toward women, as was inevitable in any gathering of pilots. First flying. Then sex. It was a subject with which Steve had never attained comfort.

Avery was more than comfortable. He entertained them with stories of exploits, for it turned out that he was not only a fierce air warrior (to listen to him, at least), but also a grand soldier of feminine hearts.

There was Tricia Walcot, whom he'd nailed in the Dean's office at the University of Minnesota. Not all that extraordinary, but Dean Walcot would certainly have been surprised if he'd walked in to discover his daughter flat on her back on his desk. And Alice Stansfield, the blue-nosed rich bitch who was cold stone to lesser mortals, but warm putty in Avery's hands.

High school had been an especially fertile rutting ground, and he recounted with relish Betty, Jill, Kate, Mary (one through three), Sandra, Barbara, Jane, Sue (one and two), Ida, the Stevens sisters (twins), Patty, Phyllis (sweet Phyllis), Janine, … and on and on, for there were scores of them, scores of scores. He'd lost count.

And especially there had been Virginia Graham, the unknown beauty who came out of nowhere to play a dazzling classical piano piece for a school assembly and capture the attention and hormones of all the pubescent males at Richmond High. She was innocent, subtle, intelligent, high class, so good as to be unapproachable, and exotically, voluptuously erotic in the backseat of Avery's car.

He couldn't help it. The conquistador proclivity expressed itself through his jeans and ran through his blood. And the girls couldn't help it, either. They and Avery drew together irresistibly, bees and flowers, to a trysting ground of youth. They needed him as much as he needed them to relieve their burden of virginity, to scratch a hormonal itch. What better man than a warrior to flutter their maiden hearts and flush their cheeks, to warm their breasts and bottoms, to ultimately fill them with screams, sighs, and satisfaction.

The affairs were temporary, but there was nothing malicious—purposes were served on both sides. Avery was as much usee as user. His was a square, solid Norse face, not that good looking, but the girls sought him out nevertheless. It wasn't that he was artificial. He wasn't. It wasn't that he was a glib talker. He wasn't, although he was certainly intelligent and articulate. There was some combination of boyish charm and wickedness that the ladies found devastatingly attractive. He was deadly in the arena of combat seduction.

Until then, few challenges had gone unmet, and few fortresses had been unsuccessfully assailed. Soon, however, Avery was to meet an impregnable woman.

# 11

The next week flew by. Steve found himself on the schedule every morning for an "in-country"—a sortie in South Vietnam. A *non*-counter. However, the dark overcast and rain had returned, and most of his flights were canceled for weather.

There was an exception: a flight with Major Scott, the operations officer. They flew under the weather thirty miles southwest, flying Two in a two-ship formation. They hooked up with an FAC putt-putting at low altitude in an O-1 Bird Dog. The sun beamed through the clouds, dappling the land, painting spots of blazing green. Steve saw reflections of clouds and sun in hundreds of smooth puddles and sheets of rainwater, and when they racked up into a steep turn, he looked straight down and—yes—his own plane scudded across the water mirror, trailing a line of black smoke.

The FAC sent them down on a patch of jungle surrounded by clear farmland. "Suspected Viet Cong encampment," he told them. "Hit my smoke," he said, punching a Willie Pete (white phosphorous marking rocket) into the tangled vegetation.

They followed Lead around a large oval pattern, watched from above as the tiny airplane made its shallow run-in, and saw the yet tinier napalm tanks separate and gyrate, blinking sunlight into dark jungle, crumbling, bursting, spewing fierce clouds of bright flame below the leafy surface, illuminating the jungle with strange orange light from within. Then they were down on their own run, and the plane lurched slightly as the tanks separated, and they were off in a steep climbing left turn, looking over their shoulders for their drop.

One pass apiece and done! The FAC gave them five KBAs.

Scott laughed. "He's blowing it out his ass. He can't see a damn thing under that jungle canopy."

On the way back, they flew into rain, droplets streaking the plastic canopy over Steve's head, and split off from Lead for a radar approach.

"You want the landing?" Scott asked.

"Sure."

"You've got the airplane." The stick rattled in Steve's hand.

He flew a good approach, asking Scott to lower the gear and flaps. There was no flap lever and only an emergency gear handle in the rear cockpit—a major source of irritation for the GIBs. He craned to see around the front seat, which blocked most of the view of the runway.

Landings from the back were flown by keeping equal amounts of runway edge on both sides of the front seat, setting up a collision course with an unseen aim point. It required faith that the concrete really existed and that an invisible airplane did not wait beneath them for takeoff—faith that all the things that should, would, and the things that shouldn't, wouldn't. It was like driving a car with a black windshield by watching the curb out the side window. Steve was almost comforted by the slight pressure of Scott's hand on the stick in the other cockpit. Almost. And he resented it. He could fly the damn airplane better than anybody.

He spiked the Phantom onto the runway in the approved semi-carrier-landing manner. The long shock absorbers compressed to smooth the transition to concrete flying as if the wheels had gently kissed the earth. The F-4 had started out as a Navy plane and was designed for violent landings. After almost two years of flying this plane, Steve still marveled at the ability of the beefy landing gear to turn controlled crashes into delicate touchdowns.

They climbed down from the plane and walked side by side from the revetments to the maintenance shack. Steve liked these post-flight moments because there was an easy camaraderie between pilots, a bonding that arose from shared danger. They talked and joked, and it was not rank versus rank or front versus back, but two sweaty people who had put their lives on the line in a monster machine in a monster war and survived. It was relief. It was almost friendship.

They debriefed for maintenance and intelligence and then returned to Squadron Ops where Steve made an entry into the Hero Book.

The front entrance of the Green Squadron building opened into Major Scott's operations area. A waist-high wooden counter surrounded a Plexiglas scheduling board where the major grease-penciled pilots' names, airplane tail numbers, and takeoff times. Other rooms branched out from the operations area, including two briefing rooms, two small offices, and the ready room. One of the two small offices belonged to Lieutenant Colonel Parsons, the squadron commander. The second office, stuffed with two desks, three chairs, and two waste cans, belonged to the orderly, Airman McNish, and anyone else who needed to sit at a desk to type a form or compose a memo. Steve had sat there already to type dispatches to the *Clayton Daily Star*. As he stood at the counter scribbling in the Hero Book, he glanced through the open door of the office and saw McNish tap-tapping haltingly with two fingers at the typewriter. About five words per minute, Steve guessed.

The squadron Hero Book was a large accountant's record book, cloth-bound in black with red-trimmed corners and spine. Full of lined blank pages when new, now the Hero Book was half-filled with the pen-and-penciled scrawl of weary but elated pilots back from a hard day's war. The Hero Book provided the story line for the citations for medals. Lots of Air Medals, occasional Distinguished Flying Crosses, and much rarer Silver Stars had sprung from its pages.

It was the GIB's duty to make an entry after each mission. This was not taken very seriously, and the book encompassed a great deal of whimsical bravado. It fell to the hapless awards and decorations officer to winnow the wheat from the chaff, because a hundred wars had been won during the great and brave flights chronicled in the Hero Book, but there were only enough medals for one war.

Finally, the weight of the paperwork equaled the weight of the airplane, which was the requisite for finishing a mission. Steve understood implicitly that the major had evaluated him and was satisfied with his performance. The evaluation had been informal but the result was tangible. The reward—was it worth the effort?—was graduation from the limbo of training status into the ranks of the fully combat-ready.

Steve was qualified to fight.

The rest of the day was his to do as he pleased, and Steve was about to leave, but a commotion caught his attention and prompted him to stick his head through the doorway into the ready room. He focused on two pilots. He had met them both. They stood toe to toe: Captain Heck Sluder and Major Karl Jasper.

"You fucking pussy," the captain said.

Sluder was a big, rawboned redneck from Alabama, who was loud and obnoxious, complete with a large nose dominating a rough pockmarked red face. Jasper was much smaller than Sluder, almost runty, with pinched features and a trace of a mustache that gave him the face of a rodent. The major had seemed aloof and alone when Steve first met him.

Sluder leaned into the already thin space separating the two pilots and stuck his face into the major's. His voice twanged through his nose.

"You fuck face asshole, don't ever go on a sortie with me when we have guns. There might be an accident."

Steve wondered if he'd heard what he thought he'd heard.

The major didn't answer, but neither did he wither from what seemed a vicious onslaught.

Sluder abruptly straight-armed the major, catching his shoulder, spinning him around, and in the same movement stalked away.

"Goddamn son of a bitch," he announced loudly to the world as he passed through the same doorway Steve had lurked in. Their eyes locked momentarily. Steve sensed a pickup truck barreling over a hill.

The major's flight cap had come off, and he retrieved it from the floor as Steve came into the room.

"Are you all right, sir?"

Jasper turned big, dark eyes on Steve. They were the eyes of a buck caught in the headlights of a fast approaching pickup with a rifle rack over the rear window. He grinned a joyless grin, turned, and walked out the door.

"What the hell was that about?" Steve asked the only other occupant of the room, Harry Taint, who had sat calmly reading a *Playboy* magazine while the confrontation had proceeded. "How does a captain get away with screwing around with a major like that?"

Harry smiled over the top of his magazine, shifted his beanpole frame in the chair and shrugged. "They were just havin' a little love fest. If the maj-ja hadn't been a maj-ja, he would'a got some more love pats." His words lilted in a soft Southern-fried accent that was as pleasing to Steve as Sluder's speech had been obnoxious. *There's more than one kind of Southern accent*, he realized for the first time, *or maybe there's more than one kind of Southerner.*

"That's a strange kind of love." Steve laughed, then he suddenly had a flash. "Is the major, uhh … is Jasper, uhh, …" He almost couldn't say it, but he finally said the word in a lowered voice: "Is he … gay?"

Harry Taint was amused. "Well now, that might be one of his problems, too. I don't know, but the main thang is—"

Steve felt something wet touch his hand from behind and reflexively jerked away.

"Sam!"

Sub-Lieutenant Sam had clicked into the room over the rust-red linoleum tiles, tail wagging, and had come straight to Steve.

"Sam, you handsome dog you!"

Sam graciously nodded his noble brown and white head, and looked up with big brown, collie eyes. Steve gave him a friendly rumple and checked the ear that had been hurt in the fight with Charley. It was nearly healed, but there would be a permanent ragged edge.

Harry commented, "Dawg likes to fight. Gonna get himself killed." He put his magazine away in a rack stuffed with an eclectic mixture of flying manuals, magazines, and paperback novels.

"We're all gonna get killed, but y'all have a good day, anyway," Harry said. "See you at the club." He departed.

Steve idly browsed the ready room with Sam snuffing around beside him.

The ready room, the biggest room in the building, was the social center of choice when pilots were required to hang around operations. Rows of overhead fluorescent lamps shone down on stacks of nested formfitting white plastic chairs, which littered the floor along the walls—there were enough to seat all seventy pilots. A coffee bar of oak-stained plywood, obviously built by amateur carpenters, occupied a corner. Maps, photos, blackboards, and flying notices cluttered their allocated wall spaces, along with two special areas bordered by red and black stripes titled "FLYING SAFETY" and "EXPLOSIVES SAFETY." On the wall behind the coffee bar was a wooden plaque with the squadron logo carved in bas-relief: an eagle's head speeding ferociously behind a thin, green flying delta, grim eagle's jaw firmly set in determination. Below this resolute avian head (the Chicken Hawk, they fondly called it) was carved and painted in bold letters, "Green Squadron."

Sam and Steve found the "ANUS AWARD"—a white plastic toilet seat hanging vertically against the wall. Smiling, Steve lifted the lid. Within, framed by the laurels of the seat, was the title "Goof of the Week" above a memo from Wing headquarters signed by the wing commander himself, Colonel William D. Sanger.

To: All Wing Pilots

Subject: Taxi Procedures

1.  For the third time this month, damage was incurred in a revetment due to use of excessive power pulling out of the chocks. This time a rolling tool chest was blown over the wall and destroyed.

2.  This will cease. Pilots will use MINIMUM power coming out of the revetments.

3.  I will personally debrief the next pilot guilty of disregarding this instruction.

Handwritten in red ink in the space below the body of the memo: "Attaboy, Lux, you got a tool chest. You can probably get an APU if you run it up to 90 percent."

Steve assumed "Lux" was the Luxington he had heard about, the first lieutenant front-seater. He pictured a clown in a flying suit, red hair flowing out around the helmet, but this was unfair—it was a delicate balancing act to use those enormous twin engines to get fifty-nine thousand pounds rolling without wreaking havoc behind the F-4.

Steve had a fervid desire to not meet Sanger again. He'd heard other pilots talk about the colonel, and it was always in hushed voices intermixed with covert glances, as if an omniscient and omnipotent Sanger might fry them with lightning.

Sam trotted dutifully beside Steve as he came back into the operations room to poke through nooks and crannies and paraphernalia that he hadn't detailed before.

There was a grease board showing pilot statistics. It was divided into two parts, the left side for the aircraft commanders (ACs) and the right side for the GIBs. On the left, Steve read that "The Average AC" was thirty-two years old and had 3,166 flying hours. There was a cartoon of a rickety old geezer receiving a blood transfusion. On the right, "The Average Pilot" was twenty-four and had flown for 532 hours. A cartoon showed a virile young stud receiving the hungry embrace of a voluptuous woman.

Screwed into the wall near the ops area was a large display where Major Scott tallied missions flown by all the pilots. The display was a major watering hole for their attention: the counter board.

The simple title at the top of the counter board was "Missions Flown." There was a grid of lines set in a black wooden frame behind a plastic sheet. Down the left column were the pilots' names, all seventy of them. Then thirty-one narrow columns marched across the center, one for each day of the month. The tallies were kept there in the rows along each name—a red *1* for a counter, a black *1* for a non-counter. The *1*s marched across, red and black, without regard to weekends, but there were gaps for weather or R & R or sick leave or other sundry reasons. Of the rightmost three columns, the first totaled the "in-country" missions in black numerals, the second, the counters in red, and the third, the sum of the two in black. Steve's eyes ran down the rows and stopped at a familiar name.

"Scott, Walter". *Really*, Steve flashed. It was "Sir" to him.

Sir Walter Scott had eighty-three counters. He'd be finishing soon except that he was among key people in the wing who had signed up to a fixed-length tour of eighteen months to provide continuity. Counters didn't count for Scott. It was possible that he would still be here when Steve was gone.

*Oops, what's this?* On the bottom of the counter board were taped two notes that hadn't been there an hour earlier, the fruit of McNish's earlier tickety-tapping. There were two lists of pilot's names in one-to-one correspondence to the two four-ship formations scheduled for the following morning.

The second list jumped off the board and hit Steve in the face. One name in particular flew into his eyeballs through suddenly dilated pupils, traveled up optic nerves, and jumped violently into his brain's image processing center, magnifying itself grotesquely out of all proportion. An extra load of adrenaline dumped into his system.

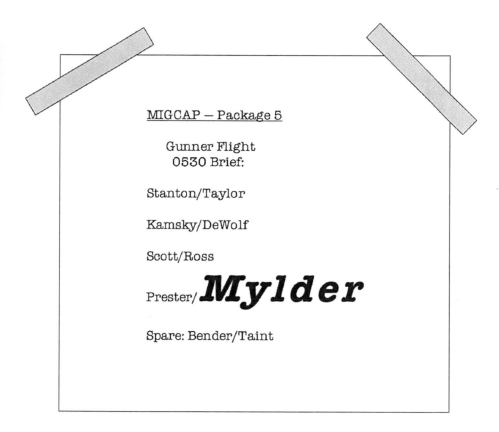

MIGCAP — Package 5

Gunner Flight
0530 Brief:

Stanton/Taylor

Kamsky/DeWolf

Scott/Ross

Prester/**Mylder**

Spare: Bender/Taint

MIGCAP! They would troll for MiGs.

This was it. Here's the opportunity. The fighter pilot's first dream and most ardent desire was to shoot down a MiG. *Then how come my stomach is lurching,* Steve thought.

He glanced back at the counter board to find his front-seater.

"Prester, John." Twenty-three counters. The name sounded peculiarly familiar, but Steve couldn't recall ever seeing him.

He found his own name near the bottom of the board. Beside "Mylder, Steve," a red *1* and a black *1* were tallied, separated by a few empty columns. Total: two missions, one counter. Still only ninety-nine to go.

# 12

Avery Aughton had a vision. It was quick, unexpected, and vivid. It would invade his dreams.

He and Patrick Truhaft were newly paired together as a permanent team, like a marriage, aircraft commander and pilot. They flew their first mission together as a "road recce" into Route Package 1, one of the southernmost partitions of convenience of North Vietnam by the U.S. military. A road recce was a pilot's dream, an armed reconnaissance into a free-fire zone to look for targets of opportunity.

They had six five-hundred-pound bombs, three below the inboard pylon of each wing, and a large Vulcan 20 millimeter cannon pod mounted on the centerline. A three-hundred-seventy-gallon fuel tank occupied the outboard pylon of each wing.

They made a left turn out of traffic from runway one-seven left and climbed north, out over the Gulf of Tonkin, "feet wet," leveling at twelve thousand feet and turning northwest to parallel the coast. After fifteen minutes, they'd traveled almost a hundred and twenty nautical miles, and were north of the DMZ, nearly over the apparently desolate city of Dong Hoi. They turned west and angled across the coast, "feet dry."

The land was a moonscape—empty and deserted. No cars plied Highway 1 below, wending its scenic hole-filled way along the coast all the way from Saigon to Hanoi. No trains carrying loads of gawking tourists chuff-hummed along the rails just west of a highway dissected by bombs into disconnected, dashed line segments. No teeming crowds of happy shoppers massed the nonexistent malls of the lonely city of Dong Hoi. The land was vacant and devoid of content. The lights were out—"Nobody home."

So it seemed. But before they'd gone a mile inland, little black puff-balls—"Triple A," for anti-aircraft artillery—began to blossom around them, hinting that the world below was not totally uninhabited after all. Truhaft began jinking, flying a series of random turns to keep the gunners off their aim.

"I saw it, I saw it!" Avery yelled over the intercom, excitement ringing in his voice. (This was not the vision.)

"What? Where?"

"The Triple A. I saw the muzzle flashes on the ground. Look, look! It's four o'clock, about to go under the wing."

Truhaft rolled the plane onto the right wing.

"I don't …"

"See the crook of the river, where it comes close to Highway 1?"

"Yeah?"

"It's about halfway between … Look! You see it?" Two pinpoints of light danced on the ground.

Truhaft's answer was gleeful. "Got it." He hauled in two gs, the nose came up, and the turn tightened until the target came through two o'clock. Then he rolled more, past 90 degrees of bank, and pulled inverted, keeping the gs on. The nose came around and down to the target. Truhaft rolled upright in a steep dive.

"Eleven thousand, ten thousand, nine thousand, …" Avery called from the backseat. He saw tracers streak by the airplane on both sides from dead ahead. "… seven thousand, six thousand, five thousand, four thousand, …" He began to wonder if Truhaft was getting target fixation—an unfortunate condition in which a pilot hypnotizes himself and flies into the ground—and tightened his grip on the stick just as the gs snapped in for the pullout.

"Right down the barrel," Truhaft grunted.

They feinted left, then pulled off hard right, climbing to look over their shoulders.

"Hot damn," Avery yelled. (This was not the vision either.) A beautiful gray-black flower—a lovely blossom of smoke—grew from the precise place where Avery had first seen the guns. That was one gun that would be out of commission for a while. As he watched, though, there were more pin-pricks of light from a low hill to the south. This time they were AW (automatic weapons), small cousins of Triple A. "Do you see …?"

"Got 'em," Truhaft answered. "I only dropped two bombs. We'll give their friends the rest."

There were three AW sites that they could see and probably more that they couldn't. They popped back up to eleven thousand feet and repeated the first bomb run, but this time on the easternmost site. They pressed down to four thousand feet again, pickled two more bombs, and the first gun was gone. They repeated the sequence with their last two bombs, and the second gun was gone. The pilots were ecstatic.

After the pull-off, they leveled at three thousand feet and jinked out over the Gulf, then made a sweeping turn to the left, over the land again, until they were headed south toward the guns. Truhaft armed the centerline gun pod. He continued to jink, then started the run-in with a shallow dive, steadying the nose. Again, tracers streamed by the canopy on both sides and above. It was a head-to-head duel, a high noon gun battle, and the bad guy had drawn first.

*B-R-R-R-R-R-R-P*

*A cosmic fart!* Avery thought. *A four-thousand-round-per-minute cosmic fart.* The whole plane shook and decelerated slightly as Truhaft triggered a two-second burst of 20 millimeter projectiles toward the target. The gun was a miniature rocket engine, spewing a momentum stream of heavy slugs and hot death.

*B-R-R-R-R-R-R-R-R-R-R-R-P*

The second burst was longer, and Avery felt the plane pitch and yaw as Truhaft worked the stick and rudder to hose the target.

*B-R-R-R-R-R-R-R-R-R-R-R-R-R-R-R-R-R-R-R-R-P*

Another long, ripping cosmic fart sounded while the nose stayed down, tree tops whizzing by at impossible speeds on both sides of the canopy. They were pressing this one hard, and for the second time, Avery's hand began tightening around the stick as Truhaft finally bounced the airplane slightly, a micro pull-up. They leveled just above the tree tops.

"Bingo," Truhaft called over the intercom. "Bingo" meant they were down to the minimum safe fuel level. "Time to go home."

"Was that a pissing contest, or was it a pissing contest? How'd it look up there?" Avery was joyful.

"Good, good! I could see their muzzle flashes right up to the last burst until I dragged dead-nuts right across the gun, and then it stopped, and I saw a little red mist. Scratch another gunner."

They stayed just above the surface at four hundred knots as treetops and rice paddies and bomb-cratered brown earth flashed beneath them. This was the safest possible altitude—no gunner, no weapon on the ground had a chance. They were gone before anyone could even whip out a revolver for a lucky shot. *This is the safest altitude*, Avery thought, *unless the pilot sneezes*, and he rested his hand lightly on the stick grip.

They blazed across a beautiful lonely beach at an altitude of fifty feet, white sand glistening in the sunlight, surf rolling in long tubes toward the shore. Avery took it in with a glance, and in a blink-of-an-eye moment, his consciousness registered an image so strange, so incongruous to expectation that he would remember it as long as he lived. (*This* was the vision.)

Down on the beach below, on the white sand looking up at them, was a single person on the entire wide expanse of sand ...

A girl in a red bikini.

Sun bathing! Less than a hundred feet away, she was lying on her right side on a towel, propped up on an elbow, a hand shading her eyes against the sun. Black hair. Light brown skin. Voluptuous, nubile body bursting in hormonal blossom.

There was a tenth of a second at the most when she was in his field of view. In a tenth of a second, the plane traveled seventy feet across the beach, and his eyes were in precisely the right spot tracking at precisely the right rate or he would have missed it completely and not had his dreams perturbed. But the image burned in, and he got more from the lingering aftereffect than the real-time data. She was beautiful and provocative. She looked right into his eyes. He swore that he could see deep pools of brown in her eyes. And she was gone. Avery was so struck that he didn't even think to tell Truhaft what he'd just seen.

As soon as they were over the water, Truhaft pulled into a steep climb, and they sailed into blue sky. There was silence between them. Avery's hormones and warmones embraced in an exquisitely convoluted dance, an exotic mix of chemical urgency. He sat cocooned in his backseat office, alone with a raging hard-on. He was in love with an unattainable woman—nay, an *impregnable* woman! Then he heard Truhaft humming quietly, "Off we go, into the wild blue yonder ..."

Avery laughed and joined in, and together they hummed at first, then cheerfully sang a heartfelt duet. They lowered their voices reverentially for the chorus, "Here's a toast to the host of those who love the vastness of the sky ...," then raised the volume for the last verse, belting out the final lines, "In echelon we carry on! Nothing'll stop the US Air Force!"

•          •          •

## Hero Book entry

*Truhaft/Aughton.*
*Diamond, single-ship, Package 1 road recce.*

    *We came, we saw, we kicked ass. Scratch a Triple-A and 3 AW's. Laid down 6 Mark 82's in pairs, 2 apiece for the AAA and two AW's, used the gun on the last AW, all about 8 miles west of Dong Hoi.*

    *Everything on target! Another definitive blow for freedom, America, decency, mom, and apple pie. This ought to be worth a Silver Star, or a DFC at least, Mr. Awards man, 'tho to tell the truth, the gunners weren't worth a shit. We pissed faster and farther.*

    *Check out the babe in the red bikini sunbathing on the beach 5 miles north of Dong Hoi!!! Dibs.*

# 13

*Clayton Daily Star*

## Clayton pilot flies mission over Hanoi

By Lt. Steven W. Mylder

Two counters. Only ninety-eight to go.

There is nothing that exercises the respiratory and circulatory systems better than a mission to the Hanoi/Haiphong area of North Vietnam. In that respect it could be considered healthful. The area referred to is the northeast corner of North Vietnam up to the Chinese border, containing several points of military interest. It would not be considered a tourist attraction.

My first mission there was no disappointment. If I was scared previously, death was coming in the door on this one.

There are primarily three things to worry about 1. SAMs. The SAM is a long, telephone pole-shaped creature, a surface-to-air missile, which loves to sneak up on pilots unawares and knock them down. A SAM can usually be avoided if seen, but the unseen ones are dangerous. 2. Flak. Flak comes in various sizes and colors and is recognized by its puffy, cloud-like shape when it explodes. (Think of World War II movies and you've got the picture. Some say it's worse here.) It is easily seen, but, since it covers an area, it's difficult to avoid if one should find oneself in the middle of it. 3. MiGs. MiGs are the cleverest of the lot, and are also, themselves, vulnerable. MiGs like to travel in twos and fours, but can sometimes be seen singly. If one spots a lone MiG, one can usually count on more being behind him. MiGs, when they are in the proper mood, are not easily avoided.

On this mission, we, the F-4C Phantoms, were to fly above several flights of F-105 Thunderchiefs (affectionately known as Thuds), escorting them while they went down to bomb. The atmosphere of the mission was previewed when, as we entered the area, our lead ship saw several tracers from the ground pass in front of our flight.

Flying in this area is a considerable strain—psychologically more than phys-ically. There is the necessity to keep a constant watch for defenses, knowing that if you miss something, that is what will probably get you. Aircraft are spread throughout the area. Most often they're your own, but each time you sight a new one, you think MiG!, instead of the Thud which it probably is.

The problems of navigation are confounded because you have little time to consult your instruments for position. You have to go almost solely on your knowledge of the landscape—the shape of these mountains, the curve of this road. Are we over a SAM site? Are these the heavy flak emplacements? How far are we from the gulf?

The land itself seems innocent and peaceful. Large uncultivated areas, mostly hills and mountains, sprout a uniform layer of dull green, almost blue, vegetation. Here and there, a peculiar geographic formation called a karst juts brusquely into the atmosphere, a proud, rocky individual. It's an out-of-context pastoral scene. Except for a few particulars, I think, "I might as well be flying in the States."

The radio—the everpresent, everchattering radio—brings back my attention, which has not had a chance to wander far.

"Tiger Lead is hit!"

"Rog, we're watching him."

"Say, Two, keep your eyes on our five o'clock. I thought I saw some bogies back there."

"OK, he's on fire. He's spinning."

"There's a chute."

"Check your four. CHECK your FOUR!"

"Tiger Lead is down."

"Say, Spike Lead, I think we've got a SAM coming up at our two o'clock."

And so on. This paraphrased sequence of radio calls is generally typical of the confusion we encountered on this mission. Your ears are bombarded by rapid-fire conversations among numerous people on different planes in different flights (formations), all talking nearly simultaneously on the same radio channel.

Discipline generally requires that every radio transmission identifies the "caller" and the "callee." Since this is sometimes forgotten in the heat of the moment, a message like "CHECK your FOUR!" (meaning check your four o'clock position for something *bad* about to happen to you) means that maybe a couple of dozen heads swivel and look in the general area behind their collective right wings, whether the call is meant for them or not.

Tiger Lead, a Thud in another flight, did indeed go down. We don't know yet if the pilot was captured or rescued.

It was with a measure of relief that we moved out of the area and toward the relative safety of Danang. We'll know in a few hours if we're scheduled here again tomorrow.

Time is beginning to pass rapidly, thank God. Yesterday I was wondering whether it was Wednesday or Thursday until I discovered it was Friday.

•          •          •

Lt. Col. R. W. Gannis
666 TFW Public Information Office

Dear Sir:

Enclosed is the resubmission of my next dispatch. As you requested, I took out the description of the "entertainment" we had in the hootch. I agree, it was probably a little too much. I also took out the reference to Playboy magazine, but really I do not see how people back home would object to such a mild form of prurient interest. Nobody would be surprised that a group of healthy males deprived of women would be thinking about sex all the time. And besides, some people just like to READ it.

Nevertheless, I am glad you decided to let me keep in the incident about Lt. Aughton.

Lt. S. W. Mylder

•          •          •

*Clayton Daily Star*

### Lt. Mylder—Interesting life at Danang

By Lt. Steven W. Mylder

Five down, only 95 to go.

One of our pilots has been bitten by a love bug and fallen for a Vietnamese girl. Unfortunately, if he plans to go out with her, the logistics and family problems are going to be really tough, because he met her at a *North* Vietnamese beach. She was *on* it, he was fifty feet *over* it. Avery was flying low a few days ago and saw a woman on the beach all by herself. He was close enough that he could see her eyes. That's when he was smitten. You may think that's a little strange, but there's more. Consider this: She was sunbathing in the middle of a free-fire zone, wearing a red bikini. Now *that's* peculiar. Avery is sorry he told anyone about it, because now he is getting ragged by everybody.

Today begins my second full month at Danang. May it be ever so much more peaceful than the first. There have been adjustments to make—new sights and sounds (and smells) to catalogue—small irritations to overcome. But nothing is insurmountable. I have put back into the subconscious the roar of planes taking off in the early morning, and the sound of our artillery "pom-poming" into the area south of here. When I'm asleep, I simply incorporate the sounds into dreams and snore on.

There is supposedly a battalion of Viet Cong only five miles south of the base, and we have been expecting a mortar attack at any time. So far, nothing has happened, and we are almost inclined to take the information as rumor; except that instances pop up to make it real—such as the discovery of four bullet holes in an airliner which landed here yesterday.

We will be moving into new quarters within a week. Real rooms, mind you—not open-bay barracks. And, as a stroke of fortune, we'll have real air conditioning. We sympathize with the Marines, the "grunts," who live on the other side of the runway. They continue to put up with hootches and tents and such.

You have to hand it to all the ground troops, in an Ernie Pyle sort of way, for doing the dirty jobs they do while living under rotten conditions. We go off and drop our bombs, shoot our guns, never see the results, and seldom pay the piper. We come back to the relative comforts of civilization, eat regular meals, and go to bed on dry sheets. They get off the ground in the morning, wade through rice paddies, get shot up in fire-fights, and afterwards evacuate their dead and wounded. They live face-to-face with fear and death. And at night, they go back to sleep on the same ground they woke up on. They live a tough life and do a hard job. The muddy, foot-slogging, bone-weary soldier is still king as in the past. He gets our respect.

The DOOM club is rather basic as officers' clubs go. There is a cafeteria and a makeshift bar, and that's about it. There have been slight improvements since I arrived—there are now tablecloths and napkin holders on the tables, and salt and pepper shakers instead of cafeteria packets. New construction is in progress—the wood skeleton for a new section is up—so further improvements are in the wind even as I write.

We have hot water finally. Cold water shaves and showers had been the order of the day until now. The catch (Aha!) is that the water is only on from 6 a.m. to 6 p.m. As a consequence, the toilets don't work at night, and it gets pretty foul back in the latrine.

Free time is rampant. Some, like myself, practice their guitars. There is always letter writing, and when that gets tiresome, one can fall back upon the gadgetry he might have bought at the BX—cameras and tape recorders, etc. Some pass the time working crosswords and putting together jigsaw puzzles. Others spend time at the DOOM club or play poker. Some read—*Life, Time, Newsweek*—some sleep, and some go to the beach. A few of us started a chess tournament. You can burn a lot of hours at a time playing chess. As a last resort, one can go to the movie and watch "Bride of Frankenstein."

# 14

Ron Catarsis set up the projector he'd borrowed from Wing Intelligence. Steve sat in one of the folding chairs in the vestibule of the hootch and covertly checked to see who was there and who wasn't. He wasn't sure whether this was the in-crowd or the out-crowd, the good crowd or the bad.

Mike Ross was there. Bad. Lux Luxington wasn't. Good. Avery was there. Good? Sluder too, with his cavernously nasal and obnoxious voice. Bad-bad.

The movie started, but the sound was displaced from the action, and the words came out after the actors spoke. The projector clattered to a halt, and Catarsis tinkered with it.

Harry Taint sat beside Steve, wrapping his wire-frame body around his guitar in a slurry of angles and straight lines, fingering a few new and strange chords to entertain the troops while Catarsis fumbled with latches and knobs. Harry hummed to himself, and the hums came out in a soft Southern accent.

There was the placid face of Frank Bender and the cherub-innocent, smiling face of Virgil Demopoulis, and the poker-shifting eyes of Jim DeWolf, and the faintly sleazy visage of Jaime Hornslug.

Even Sub-Lieutenant Sam was there, visiting for the day from Squadron Ops, perched primly and excitedly at the back wall beside the door, tail thumping the floor, big collie smile stretched across panting collie jaws, eager to enjoy his very first movie. Woof! Pass the popcorn!

The projector chugged again. This time the words came out first, and then the actor's mouths moved. No matter that it was in Spanish. No one understood it, but it didn't really need a lot of words—the message wasn't enhanced by words.

Pat Truhaft wasn't there, nor was Karl Jasper or Jake Phelps. Phil Stanton was. Art Hoppovich wasn't.

The acting was bad. Didn't matter—the message was powerful. The movie didn't suffer.

The actress was ugly, Steve lamented, and the actor had just crawled out of the sewer. These were minor annoyances, but they didn't spoil the fundamental interest. Catarsis had bought the movie in a hole-in-the-wall shop in Angeles city, just outside the gate on his last trip back to Clark. The production values were low, the actors poorly directed. There was a hole in the wall above the bed, the camera seemed bolted to the floor, and the sound was atrocious, but fortunately the action started almost immediately. There was no namby-pamby shuffling about, no lengthy preamble or fore-longed proto-play. The action started right away, and the pilots were riveted into one of the most stimulating, arousing, moving movies they'd seen in many years. Sub-Lieutenant Sam howled plaintively at a climatic moment, drawing intense laughter, and Steve knew that this fine lad was suffering from the lack of a lady friend, although the articulation of the concept was mostly beyond Sam.

The movie was so powerful that it wrought physiological changes in the pilots, and they rubbed their eyes sheepishly, laughed nervously, didn't look at each other, and were slow to stand when the credits stopped rolling and the lights were up. Steve edged away to his bunk alcove, keeping his front away from the crowd.

That evening there was restlessness throughout the hootch, and Steve lay wide-eyed in his bunk in the dark as his friends sighed into the night, probably longing for home, friends, and old times. He sighed long and deeply himself and soon drifted from waking into sleeping dreams.

# 15

"What've you got against Major Jasper?"

The hour was late in the DOOM club bar. Steve checked his watch. Almost midnight. His 0530 briefing approached stealthily.

An hour earlier the room had overflowed with pilots and energy. The jukebox still thundered with the sound of engines and a heavy bass thump as Snoopy and the Red Baron tangled in the skies over Germany.

> *Up in the sky, a man in a plane,*
> *Baron von Richthofen was his name.*
> *Eighty men tried, and eighty men died,*
> *Now they're buried together on the countryside.*

Engines ripped and roared, but most of the denizens of the bar were no longer there to hear them. They'd departed for hootches and sleep, leaving behind the noisy jukebox, a residue of die hards, and an evaporating haze of smoke.

Heck Sluder's nightly poker party was still there. It rambled apace at a nearby table. Steve recognized Jim DeWolf from his own squadron, and there were Calvin Smythe and Ras Farthington from Red and two others he didn't know. The play was reckless and emotive, filled with relentless chatter. Every few minutes, the group exploded in a frenzied cacophony of damns and oohhhs and raucous laughter. Sluder's irritating "haw haw haw" boomed through the din. Steve's ears perked up when he heard them talking about Sam the Collie and Charley the Mongrel, and he strained to hear, but the jukebox dogfight washed over the critical nuggets of information and left him wondering.

The jukebox thumped heavy bass beats and the roar of engines, Camel versus Fokker, Snoopy versus the Red Baron. Steve felt a wind across his face, ripping through his hair, heard wire braces sing, felt controls stiffen as the speed built in a dive toward the Fokker triplane. The Fokker was down to the right, an easy-way turn for the Camel, as opposed to a hard-way left turn against the gyroscopic resistance of the engine.

"Jasper?" Avery Aughton's lip curled contemptuously around the name, pulling Steve back into the bar from his momentary reverie. "You don't know?"

Steve shook his head indulgently.

"That chicken shit! He doesn't fly north. No Package 5s or 6s."

"Can't?"

"Won't. Refuses. The son of a bitch picks and chooses his missions."

"How does he get away with it? Why don't they court-martial him?"

Avery shrugged again. "Beats the shit out of me. I'd have him shot. But at least he pays a price."

"How's that?"

"He's been here over a year and only has fifty-two counters after all that time. Scott won't give him any more. The son of a bitch is rotting in hell." The thought made Avery happy. He smiled. "Better than that, maybe he'll get killed on a pussy in-country. Maybe he'll catch a golden BB."

There were three of them bellied up to the bar: Steve, Avery, and Mike Ross. Steve wondered if this small grouping was becoming a habit. Momentarily, Will Styles from Red Squadron sauntered over to join them, beer in hand. Styles's thick, dark-brown mustache made Steve acutely aware of the visible lack of his own mustachioed progress, although he had assiduously not shaved above his upper lip each and every day since he'd vowed to join ranks with the hairy Princes of the Air.

"Ah, a representative from the enemy," Steve announced. "What brings you around this time of night? Trying to steal our military secrets?"

"We're night flying," Styles answered pleasantly. "I just got canceled for weather."

"Oh, yeah?" Steve was secretly hopeful. Maybe the same weather would stick around long enough to cancel his MIGCAP.

The conversation turned to upgrading to the front seat, as it usually did in any gathering of GIBs. Their prime griping point was their second-class citizenship—their lowly GIBhood—and they drove the front-seaters crazy with harping and moaning on the subject.

"How desperate are you?" Steve asked Styles. "Would you come back for another tour to get the front seat?"

Styles shrugged noncommittally.

"How about you?" Steve asked Avery. "Would you fly another hundred?"

"Fuckin' A, if I don't make it in this tour. I'm tired of being a goddamned water boy. The Air Force fucked up when they put pilots in the backseat. We're not pilots, we're not even copilots, we're navigators and radar operators and radio jockeys and assistant bombardiers. Sure, I'd come back for another tour. I love the front seat *and* my country. I'm gonna kick ass in 'Nam, and then I'm gonna be chief of staff some day."

Avery came across as incredibly cocky without a trace of humility, yet the brassiness was touched by humor. There was a smile in his manner ... almost tongue-in-cheek, almost self-deprecating. Almost. But Steve thought that Avery really meant what he said.

"You think you could make front seat this tour?"

Avery winked. "Who knows? I flew with Colonel Sanger the other day. He liked it. He's going to ask for me again."

Steve winced. "Geeze. How about you, Mike? What do you want to be when you grow up? A front-seater? Or chief of staff?"

Mike had silently absorbed the conversation most of the evening. He nodded his handsome head for a moment before answering. "I'd like the front seat, but I wouldn't come back for another tour. I have a wife and a three-year-old daughter. I'd settle for a tactical squadron in the states for a few years so I could be with them."

Steve's attitude softened slightly. He'd pictured a playboy life for Mike. This was the first Steve had heard he was married.

"Even if it meant backseat F-4?"

"Even if it meant backseat, but I'll bet I could swing the front."

*I'll bet you could*, thought Steve. *I'll just bet you've got connections.*

"Would you duke it out with Avery for chief of staff?"

Mike smiled. "No, he can have that job. I'll be his boss. I'm going to be a US senator."

Steve cocked an eyebrow and looked at Mike with piqued interest. He turned to Styles.

"How about you, Will. Whadda you wanna be?"

Styles smiled and shrugged. "I'm going to be an astronaut. I'm going to test pilot school, then to NASA. In fifteen or twenty years, I'll be the first man on Mars."

Steve was stumped. He searched for signs that they were putting him on. He saw none from the future chief of staff, the eventual senator, the ultimate man on Mars. They were deadly serious. He licked his lips and was suddenly uncertain, suddenly in retreat from the Master of Ceremonies role he had taken at the behest of one or two beers too many.

"All right, Mister Question Man, how about you?" Avery poked at Steve's chest with an imperative finger. "What're you gonna be when *you* grow up?"

"Well, I, ahh ..."

He was taken aback. He put a finger to his upper lip and pensively rubbed the invisible protomustache. He didn't know. Until now he hadn't considered much beyond tooling a hot machine around in wide open spaces, hadn't considered much beyond the immediate imperative of surviving Danang. Maybe he'd go to a tactical squadron like Mike. Maybe he'd try for test pilot school at Edwards like Styles. But where and what would he be in twenty years?

A general? Probably not. Wing commander? Squadron commander? No. He didn't feel like a leader, at least not *that* kind of leader. He had no vision of twenty years. That was a long time ... beyond the horizon. In twenty years, he'd probably be retired from the military and looking around for something to do. If he were still alive.

•        •        •

He climbed the ladder and stepped along the top of the intake ramp to the cockpit. Coffee sweat soaked the armpits of his flight suit even though it was a cool, cloudy day.

He looked into the cockpit, and there, in the dim light beneath the jungle canopy, he saw a battered seat, saw how it had tumbled out of the air and hit the ground on the right side, saw how it had crumbled in the process of bouncing high, maybe twenty feet, before coming down to stay. And there was the blood—dried, black-red, caked into the leafy debris of the forest floor. He hadn't separated from the seat in the ejection, the belt hadn't opened, the butt snapper hadn't worked, and he had tumbled all the way down from the sky still in the seat, gyrating green earth and blue sky filling his vision alternately, *blink-blink-blink* until, *thump*, the pilot had been crushed, unrecognizable, a green flight suit bag full of ruptured flesh and dried blood.

Steve leaned across the seat and turned the inertial navigation switch from "OFF" to "STBY." He looked down at the concrete below him. Sam smiled up with a big collie grin. His tongue lolled between his teeth.

"Shoo, Sam."

"Woof!" Sam replied happily.

•        •        •

"Speedo Flight, check in."
"Two."
"Three."
"Four."

Like a chant, the four F-4s checked in on ground frequency. The inertial navs were aligned, radars on standby. Eight Phantom engines wailed deep-throated Phantom wails, rising in pitch, falling in pitch, straining, howling to break free and lope through the air like avenging furies at the prey. They taxied out in ponderous single file.

A lone dog taxied behind them.

They assembled in echelon in the last check area. The pilot's arms rested on canopy sills in full sight of a watchful crew chief while crewmen ran under the airplanes checking for leaks and open access panels, pushing against the six-hundred-gallon centerline fuel tank to test its security, and finally pulling the red-flagged "REMOVE BEFORE FLIGHT" pins from the four air-to-air Sparrow missiles recessed into the belly of each plane and from the AIM-9 Sidewinder missiles on the outboard pylons of each wing.

Sam sat grinning from the grass beside the concrete pad, tail wagging.

"Speedo Flight, go button one." The flight taxied single file again.

"Two."

"Three."

"Four."

Steve clicked the radio channel selector from three to one and watched as Sam fell in behind them.

"Speedo Lead."

"Two."

"Three."

"Four."

"Danang Tower, Speedo, flight of four, holding for one-seven left."

"Roger, Speedo Flight, you're cleared onto the runway for takeoff and left turnout of traffic. Call Departure Control after airborne."

Sam followed them out onto the runway, number five in a four-ship formation. Steve watched behind as his plane pivoted into place, waved Sam away frantically and ineffectually through the closed canopy as the engines ran up. He keyed his microphone: "Speedo, use caution. Sam is behind us."

"Sam? Say again?"

"Sam the Collie. Behind us."

*Click-click.* What the hell were they going to do? Stop the flight for a damn dog?

They released brakes and lit the burners one plane at a time, diamond flames stabbing out, *KaShooom, KaShooom*—four times *KaShooom*—and finally Five ran up his engine and chased Four down the runway, trailing badly.

# 16

Steve marked a red *1* in the row beside his name on the counter board. Now the numbers marched along quick time: Nine.

Sub-Lieutenant Sam ran to him joyously as he finished an entry in the Hero Book. There was a deep scratch along the collie's muzzle.

"What happened, Sam? Where'd you put that nose of yours? Someplace it didn't belong, huh?"

"Woof!" replied Sam. He pranced and pawed for Steve.

McNish was sheepish and apologetic. "A couple of Red Squadron pilots came by. Farthington and Smythe. I think they were just looking for trouble. They had Charley with them."

Steve remembered them at Sluder's poker game the night before. Was *that* what the conversation about Sam and Charley had been about? Had they planned this maliciously?

"Good grief, McNish," Steve admonished. "If they come over again, don't let them bring the damn dog in."

"I was busier than a one-armed paperhanger trying to keep them apart."

"If it happens again, take Sam over to Intelligence or lock him up in the store-room or something. Poor kid." He inspected the scratch closely, holding Sam's head while the collie tried to back away. "Think we ought to put some iodine or something on that?"

"Probably just leave it alone." McNish squatted down and put a friendly arm around Sam. "I already washed it. It'll heal fine by itself."

"Probably leave a scar, though."

McNish shrugged. "That's life. Full of scars."

Steve looked at him silently. *You're right*, he thought.

Steve knew scars. He had a few. They were psychological rather than physical, but nonetheless real. A lacework of scar tissue covered all the exposed surfaces of his ego, but there were still deep raw gashes that had yet to heal. Most of them had been rendered seven years ago.

The sign above the entrance to the United States Air Force Academy had said "BRING ME MEN," but instead, the country sent its boys. The Academy's mission was to kill them.

The Academy destroyed boys deliberately, systematically, and spit out new creatures at the end of four years—the original material recycled, usually reconstituted as loyal military fighting men ... sometimes not, but always altered.

Seven years ago, Steve had walked through that entrance, up a wide concrete ramp to an enormous pebble-embedded expanse of paving called "The Terrazzo" and into a hellish year-long nightmare of psychological torture. Upperclassmen waited at the top of that ramp in impeccable white-gloved uniforms, hard eyes peering like small glowing stones beneath the silver rims of black-billed wheel caps. They waited in packs and then swooped upon unsuspecting boys as they straggled onto the Terrazzo two or three at a time.

The technique was to swarm a boy like a pack of hyenas cutting a young calf from the herd. Bring him down hard, go for the throat and rip the metaphorical jugular, spill the blood and tear the limbs before the calf had even stopped twitching.

"Hit it for twenty," was the most common phrase Steve heard that day.

"Dumbsmack, dojazz, hit it for twenty."

"Give me twenty big ones, smackwad."

"You're a pimple on the ass of the military, dumbsquat. You're the sorriest excuse for a basic I've ever seen. Hit it for thirty ..."

"Give me forty ..."

"Let's see fifty ..."

"Yes sir!"

"Count, smackjazz."

"Yes sir! One sir, two sir, three sir, four sir, five sir ..."

"One, one, one. That's one, doosmack. One! Get that back straight. Those aren't push-ups. My grandmother can do better push-ups than that. Start over."

"One sir, two sir, ..."

"One, one, one ..."

Steve probably did between five hundred and a thousand push-ups that first sunny, warm-soaked Colorado June day. There was no way of knowing for sure. He did twenty, thirty, forty at a time until his arms turned to rubber and he collapsed on his face and chest, an upperclassman squatting beside him, face inches away, upper class voice screaming into his ear, "Fifty, dumbsquat, I said give me fifty!" When his arms stopped twitching, when he had minimal control over them again, he resumed.

The upperclassmen were all over them like harpies—furies—three or four at once on each new boy, and what kept them going and kept Steve and his classmates functioning was the realization that they could not go home, they could not return to boyhood, they could not return to families and friends wearing the same faces as when they'd left or they would be tagged forever as losers. And so they lasted out that hellish first day—most of them—not for positive motivational reasons, but from fear of everlasting shame.

They carried big duffel bags stuffed with thirty pounds of gear. The upperclassmen ran them in groups five stories up the stairwell from the bottom to the top of Vandenberg hall, then down to the bottom, then up again, down again … two, three, four more times. Few were acclimated to the seven thousand-foot altitude. They were seriously exhausted by the first trip, completely worn down at the end. Steve became the Tail-end Charley. When they hit the top floor of the dorm the last time, he teetered on the verge of unconsciousness.

The upperclassmen stood the boys at a brace against the walls of the dormitory hallway and chewed them out. Steve's face had apparently drained white, his blood gushing from a metaphorical jugular, because one of God's anointed death angels, one of heaven's hyenas, came close and whispered into his ear.

"Sit down."

Steve slumped along the wall to the floor, wheezing, unable to breathe. The upperclassman squatted on his haunches, white-gloved hands draped casually between his knees, put his mouth close to Steve's ear and whispered again.

"All you have to give is one hundred percent. That's all we ask. We don't want any more than everything you've got."

Steve's eyes were glazed. He was nearly senseless.

"A hundred percent, that's all we want. No more, no less. Can you do that? Rest a moment, don't try to answer, just nod."

Steve nodded.

"Yes sir," the words whistled from his throat between great gasps for air, and abruptly he stood at a brace again. He stood because he wanted to. He stood because he was proud. He stood because this upperclassman whose name he would never know had made him rise and brace. Not by order, by admonition, or confrontation, but by the application of a small kindness. He loved this man, this leader, who knew exactly what Steve needed to hear after hours of agony. Those few whispered words were defining. He never forgot the incident—the one moment that kept him from resigning and leaving for home and shame that first day.

It was to be the last kindness he would receive from any upperclassman for the next several months. There were to be many trials far worse than this one, many times when—physically exhausted, utterly humiliated, abjectly depressed—he would burrow beneath his blanket at night and sob quietly, privately to himself, wondering where he would find the will to last another day.

By the end of that first year, he was still there. He had lost some and gained some. The wounds were deep, but he had survived, and out of survival, he had learned one great truth about himself. He knew rather than felt it. It was not in his nature to feel it, not yet, but intellectually he knew *this*—he knew that over the long haul, the only haul that counted, he was one tough son of a bitch. A finisher … not a quitter.

And lo, by the time Steve graduated, gold bars of a second lieutenant on his proud shoulders, the Academy had not completed its mission—it had failed. It had not killed the boy. Somewhere beneath developing scar tissue lurked a free spirit who *still* rode naked through the desert.

# 17

Major Sir Walter Scott flew a mission with each of the new pilots as they came in so that he could match aircraft commanders and GIBs appropriately. New pilots "floated" for the first ten or so missions, paired with more experienced fliers until they got their feet wet, and then Scott married them to semipermanent partners of convenience.

Survivability was a prime consideration. Weak ACs were paired with strong GIBs, weak GIBs with strong ACs, but the majority were in the middle, and in most instances Scott took temperament into account, sometimes on little more than data gleaned at the DOOM club bar.

The paired traits exhibited an odd but semi-consistent pattern—there were aggressive/aggressives and passive/passives, talker/listeners and listener/talkers, drinker/drinkers and teetotaler/teetotalers (although there weren't many of those, a Mormon/Mormon being one example), and many other orientations, psychological axes, and points of view. In a few instances Scott muffed it, whether out of ignorance or carelessness or the mathematical impossibility of combing the hair on a billiard ball without leaving a cowlick, no one knew. There was Luxington/ Catarsis, a jerk/slob team; Sluder/Jenkins, an asshole Southerner/asshole Yankee; and Jasper/Small, a chicken/hawk.

Major Jasper would not fly near Hanoi. He refused to fly any mission hairier than a ho-hum Package 1, or a combat proof over SAM-less territory. Major Jasper didn't like SAMs or Triple A or AW, or indeed anything that might seriously inconvenience his life. How he escaped the draft for Package 5 and 6 missions and got away with it was the subject of frequent conversations, but Major Scott wasn't talking. Jasper's back-seater, Rich Small, who was patriotic from his epidermis to his steel ball-bearing core, couldn't stand him and his picky, wishywashy ways and took every opportunity to fly with wing staffers or anybody else available for odd missions. Small, like Avery Aughton, wanted his hundred counters as fast as possible so he could fly a second hundred from the front seat.

Truhaft and Avery had already teamed up—definitely aggressive/aggressive. Steve found himself paired with Major Bender, Virgil's front-seater on the ill-fated first mission. Steve was pleased—Frank Bender was a great pilot, cautious and stable—but he also fretted that this might be one of the strong/weak instances. He reviewed his encounters with Major Scott and could not think how he would have made a poor impression. He decided that the pairing was capable/ capable, but nagged anew at the question from time to time.

The day came for the move from the hootches to the new squadron BOQ (Bachelor Officer Quarters). Red and Blue Squadrons had moved into their own buildings the previous month. Steve looked around for a roommate and surprised himself.

"Mike, what do you think about rooming together?"

"I'd be honored." Mike seemed genuinely pleased.

They carried their meager belongings by foot the hundred and fifty yards from the hootch to the newly refurbished two-story plaster building. They lugged flight bags stuffed with clothes, flying gear, and a few favorite books; blue and tan uniforms on hangars; and flight suits slung over their shoulders up an outside stairwell on the east end of the building to the second floor and walked west along a long green corridor that swelled briefly into an alcove midway along the length of the hallway. Their room was off the north side of the alcove.

The building was "H" shaped. The two legs ran east-west, the west side facing the runway a half-mile away. The crossbar of the *H* was a hallway off the south side of their alcove which led past a simple, but spacious, latrine with a large common shower room and rows of wash basins, urinals, and stalls.

Their room was small and spartan. It came with a double-decker bed and two upright metal lockers. That was all. A fluorescent ceiling fixture provided light. There had been a window, but it was neatly boarded with plywood to keep the daylight out (for they would soon be sleeping days and flying nights). A small air conditioner protruded through a hole in the wall beside the plywood window and churned more or less continuously to provide adequate cooling.

After a few days, they collected enough odds and ends of lumber and plywood to build a makeshift but solid table, and they "liberated" two chairs, a small table, and a bench from a yet unoccupied building to fill out the cramped space. It was small, but it was theirs, by God, and they were pleased.

They cleaned the room thoroughly the first day, but neglected that chore afterward, and apparently the Vietnamese maids did, too, because there were always dust balls rolling around the concrete floor, inconveniently out of reach under the bunk or the table or in the small space between the lockers. The maids came in to make the beds, but that seemed to be about all they did other than clean the latrines. Steve was startled at a urinal one day when a girl came in with a pail and mop and nonchalantly began washing the floor as if he weren't even there.

One morning he was stirred awake from a sound sleep by another girl.

"Bed," she said.

"Uunnnhhh??" Steve wondered if he'd heard right.

"Make bed."

Steve shook his head groggily, stumbled into the alcove in his underwear, and plopped a sleep-crazed body not quite belonging to himself down in one of the chairs at the poker table. He folded his arms across the green felt of the table and laid his head down on them, dozing until the girl finished, then stumbled back into the room and into the bunk again.

Steve knew that Mike had played football at college. Thus he was mildly surprised one evening to find Mike stretched out in his bunk reading *The Oxford Book of English Verse*.

"You like that stuff?"

"Oh, yeah, I always have. Literature was my minor in college."

"What'd you major in?"

"Physics. And Poly Sci."

*Jesus Christ*, Steve thought. *A fucking Renaissance man. He probably had a four-point-oh grade average. And the son of a bitch is likable, too. I hate him.* But he didn't, really. He had discovered that Mike's appearances deceived.

Mike had been orphaned. By an unmarried, eighteen-year-old mother. His foster parents were loving and supportive people, but they were also poor, so that when it came time for college, he desperately needed a scholarship. Brilliance in the classroom and excellence on the playing field got him more than one, but when it came down to it, the football scholarship to a powerhouse college offered more than the partial academic scholarship promised by MIT.

He met his wife during his first year in college, and they married after graduation. Their daughter was born while he was in pilot training. Strongly conscious of his own lonely beginning, Mike fiercely devoted himself to his family. He'd worked hard for everything he had. Nothing had arrived on a silver platter.

Steve was ashamed of his initial attitude. There was no difficulty visualizing Mike as a senator. Or a friend.

One day Steve handed Mike a thin, paper clipped sheaf of typewritten pages.

"What's this?"

"Oh, just some stuff I wrote for my hometown newspaper."

The next day, Mike returned the packet with a smile.

"This is pretty good, Steve."

"Think so?" He strove mightily for a casual tone.

"You're a good writer. I liked your description of jungle survival school and the first mission, and the part about Avery's girlfriend was great …"

"Thanks."

"… but …" Mike hesitated. "Do you mind if I make some suggestions?"

"Not at all."

"Well, I made some corrections. I hope you don't mind. I think I see some ways you could make the writing even better."

Steve glanced down at the pages.

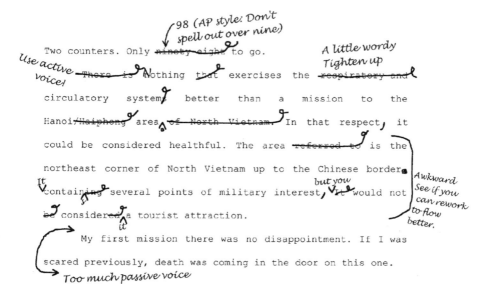

They were covered with penciled markings and notes in the margins. There was not one sentence that did not have at least one red mark or comment, and most had several: "Too much passive voice … A little wordy, tighten up … Awkward. See if you can rework to flow better … Use active voice …"

The comments went on and on, and there were scores of deletions and insertions and respellings and….

"You could punch it up by using active voice construction," Mike said. "I think you use passive voice a little too much. Instead of 'He was the pilot of the plane,' say 'He flew the plane.' Instead of 'We have been expecting a mortar attack,' say 'We expect a mortar attack.'"

"Umm hmmm," Steve murmured noncommittally.

"Also, it seems a little too formal sometimes. Maybe you could use contractions more; that would loosen it up. And you're probably using too many commas. It breaks up the flow."

"Hmmm."

"Your metaphors and similes are great when you use them, and that's when you come on best. It slows down when you get descriptive, so you need to keep it from getting too dry. Maybe by using more metaphors."

*Damn, damn, damn,* Steve thought, but he bit his lip and listened. They pulled their liberated chairs up to the makeshift table and went over the articles together. Steve picked back at a few nits, and Mike backed down on them, but he was right, mostly. Steve was surprised to realize that he agreed with and welcomed most of the suggestions.

"Geeze, Mike, do you think the editor caught some of this and corrected it? It's probably already been printed."

"Well maybe, but don't count on it. It depends on how busy he is and how good he is at copyediting. It's a tedious job. I know, because I took a course in it once. Best thing is just do it right yourself the next time. Then you know."

Mike smiled. "You really are a good writer. I hope you keep at it. I couldn't do this myself—I considered a journalism major for a while, but I'm just not a writer. But I'm not bad at critiquing. So now you've made me curious. Am I going to find myself in one of these articles?"

"Heh. Maybe. But only by first name. I wouldn't give anybody's full name, and the Public Information Office probably wouldn't let me anyhow."

"Can I read the rest of them?"

"Sure, as soon as I write them. Will you critique them?"

# 18

Steve checked the counter board. He had twenty-five total missions, but only sixteen counted. He checked his upper lip. Only marginally fuzzy.

It came Green Squadron's turn to fly nights. The three squadrons of the Phighting Phantoms rotated through this duty—two on days, one on nights. Steve had always hated night flying for the simple reason that you couldn't see where you were going or what you were about to hit. There was nothing to hit at altitude, of course, unless you were exceptionally unlucky and ran into another plane, but still it was discomfiting to drive headlong at four hundred knots into quiet still blackness, a blackness of Jell-O consistency with mountains of imagination embedded unseen ahead.

In combat it was different. He loved the nights. There was still the black Jell-O, but now it was friendly, cloaking, protective. They turned off the exterior lights, and the gunners couldn't see to hit them. The gunners heard a sound droning somewhere, a basso profundo mosquito flitting invisibly past the ears in the darkness waiting to bite. They were reluctant to swat because their tracers would give them away and bring the wrath of a twenty-seven-ton mosquito fully upon them.

"Got the gunner down there?" Steve would say.

"Got him," Frank Bender would answer, both of them watching a hose stream of tracers emanate from a pin point position on the side of a hill that was illuminated by flares. The hose stream would wobble generally in their direction. They could see it coming. They could even—yes—dodge it. Dodge bullets. And then they would roll in and bomb the living b'Jesus out of the gun site and look for another.

*They must be throwing a hell of a lot more at us during the day,* Steve mused, *and we don't even know it because the tracers are hard to see.*

Another benefit of night flying was that there were no far north missions. A day without a Package 6 was another day in heaven. The flip side was that counters accumulated more slowly. There were more in-country missions and sorties into Laos, fewer into Tallyho and Package 1. Less risk, less payoff. Less guts, less glory.

One night they flew a combat proof mission, which was like a radar-guided Ground Controlled Approach (GCA) to a landing, except that it was a ground controlled approach to drop bombs from altitude. They took off and staggered to twenty thousand feet with a full load of Mark 117 seven-hundred-fifty-pound bombs. At altitude, they switched to a radar controller's frequency and took his directions. The controller turned them northeast and headed them over Package 1. When they'd settled on a base heading of 343 degrees and a ground speed of five hundred knots, the controller guided them with minuscule corrections: "Turn left one degree. Twenty thousand yards and tracking slightly right of course, turn left another degree."

They were too high to worry much about flak, and there hadn't been any SAM warnings in this area for weeks. Steve slumped in the seat and tilted his head back to look upward. There wasn't much for him to do.

"Now turn right one degree, on course, twelve thousand yards."

The stars! There was nothing to kill his night vision, the outside lights were off, the inside lights were set to the level of a poker glowing dull red, most of the atmosphere above him was gone, and there was not a shred of clouds, cirrus or otherwise.

"… right one degree, six thousand yards …"

The stars were just crazy. They were steam and bright swirling snowflakes just above his eyes …

"… hold steady now. Two thousand …"

… they were peace and speculation—all the science fiction stories he had ever read …

Twenty thousand feet below was a truck-staging area that an astute intelligence officer had picked out of a jungle-filled reconnaissance photo taken the morning before. Less than two hundred yards farther along the flight path was a small hootch at the edge of a clearing. A grandmother, a father, a mother, a boy, and a girl lived there. Early in the morning, the father had helped arriving drivers camouflage their trucks with foliage. He had been a speck in the intelligence officer's photo. Now the family slept on grass mats beneath a bamboo thatched roof. They breathed slowly and dreamed peacefully as the quiet rumbling of a distant plane dragged overhead.

"Ready … ready.… Pickle!" The plane lurched as six thousand pounds of bombs departed and sliced through the cold, high air, arming propellers twirling merrily like spinners on beanie caps …

… all the wonders of the universe, and they made you think about creation, about God and the meaning of life and the purpose of existence …

Six thousand pounds of bombs in an eight-ship formation cut gracefully through cold night air that became steadily warmer, 2 degrees centigrade per thousand feet of altitude. Down they came, quietly, swiftly, in iron-jawed determination to execute the laws of gravity and drag, until finally the edge of the tip of the fuse of the lead bomb made first gentle contact with a solid object. While Steve wondered about the stars, a boy two hundred yards beyond a truck park dreamed of water buffalo, and the two remaining truck drivers of the two remaining trucks (broken, awaiting parts) in the intelligence officer's truck park glanced warily into the sky and also wondered.

Normally the accuracy was good—quite good, considering the method. However, a slight twitch of the stick could send the bombs dozens of yards astray, long or short, left or right. A blink-of-an-eye delay of the pickle-thumb on the pickle-button could eat up two hundred yards like nothing.

Halfway around the Phantom's long turn at twenty thousand feet altitude, the bomb formation checked in with rapid staccato enthusiasm ...

"Lead."

"Two."

"Three."

"Four."

"Five."

"Six."

"Seven."

"Eight."

That violently shouted roll call at ground level was ponderously silent at Steve's altitude, but bright. Ohh, bright! Steve's vision of stars was interrupted, and he wondered, but he never knew, and never could know, where the bombs landed, what dreams were terminated or what already broken trucks (awaiting parts) were further broken by those white flashes.

When they returned to the squadron, he wrote a red *1* with a grease pencil on the board in the row beside his name. Another counter. They marched across the board. Seventeen.

•        •        •

The next evening, Major Scott and Mike Ross took off as number two in a two-ship formation just as the twilight faded. As they broke ground, the last thing they heard on their radio for a while was an announcement on Guard channel. It was a SAM advisory for Package 1.

SAMs! There weren't many of those in Package 1. They were too vulnerable, too easy to pick off. The North would ship them down once in a while in a truck convoy, and a new site would appear in the morning—a little battery of fresh new mushrooms sprouting in the debris, waiting to be harvested.

SAMs in Package 1. Novel, but Mike and the major weren't going to Package 1 that evening. They were going to bomb Tchepone junction in Laos.

The reason the SAM warning was the last thing they heard over the radio for a while was that their radio was intermittently broken. It worked for a while, then it didn't, then it did.

They didn't realize this right away. At first, things seemed normal. After getting airborne with the gear in the wells and flaps up, Major Scott gave Mike the stick for the join-up. "You've got it."

"I've got it," Mike answered and rattled the stick. He cut into Lead's turn out of traffic, established a fast closure rate, and held it as they moved in smoothly. It was a quick, seamless join-up on the inside of the turn, with hardly a bobble as Mike moved in the last few feet. Coyote flight rolled out in close formation, climbing east over the Gulf.

They missed the channel change. They had to strain to see the hand signal from the Lead GIB in the hastening darkness.

"Two ... seven ... nine ... uhh, eight. No. Seven," Mike intoned mostly to himself. "They're on two-seven-nine point seven," he repeated for Major Scott as he clicked the dials on the UHF radio.

"Coyote Flight?" Lead's voice came over the newly functioning receiver.

"Two."

"Uhh, Rog, Coyote, let's go trail."

They slid rapidly back as briefed, and Lead was engulfed by the darkness, visible ahead only as a set of disconnected steady and blinking lights which soon merged together in the distance. Mike painted their blip on the radar. He saw them start a sweeping left turn around to the west, still climbing, and they followed in the turn after a little delay. Coyote Flight would go feet-dry (over the land) north of Danang and skirt along the DMZ, several miles south of it until they arrived over Laos.

They established a five-mile trail position and leveled off at sixteen thousand feet, heavy with bombs, just as they came inbound over the coast. Major Scott hummed a tuneless little tune to himself as Mike twiddled with the radar, and they both enjoyed the peaceful silence of a non-functioning receiver without realizing its non-functionality.

"Where the hell is he going?" Mike murmured as he watched the blip edge toward the side of the scope. "Looks like he made a hard left."

"Yeah, I can see him blinking way out there," Scott answered. "Looks like he turned south. He didn't call it."

"SAM," the receiver chirped, full of static and gaps. "This … on Guard … ssssss … all aircraft north of … sssssssss … out."

"Another SAM warning," Scott commented.

"Yeah, unless they're talking about Sam the Collie," Mike joked.

"Where the hell *is* he going?" Scott exclaimed again as he watched blinking lights dip below the horizon.

"… Flight, take it down sssss…."

"Who was that? Was that him?" Scott asked.

The hair on the back of Mike's neck, if it could have stood up under the flight suit, would have risen as an unpleasant possibility began to glow like slow dawn over the horizon of his brain. He jerked abruptly to his right in the seat.

There was a haze. Dark earth and dark sky blended together where the horizon would have been. There were a few scattered ground lights visible in the distance—probably small fires from someone else's sorties—and a couple of distant flares hung in the air. A few stars twinkled dimly.

One of the flares was actually not all that distant. It was noticeably brighter than the other one. As he watched, it seemed to grow even brighter, and then he noticed that it wandered slowly.

"OH, SHIT, SAM, SAM!" Mike screamed over the intercom.

"What …?"

"SAM, THREE O'CLOCK LOW, HE'S TRACKING US!"

Scott jerked the plane into a right climbing turn toward the missile as the tactics briefings recommended, except that the plane didn't jerk well at this airspeed and altitude with all those bombs. It crept into the turn and burbled on the edge of a stall as Scott pulled. The bright flare grew steadily brighter and "hunted" around a spot on Mike's canopy.

"Coyote Two copy?" the functioning, non-functioning radio spat.

"STILL TRACKING, MOVE IT!" Mike yelled as the stick slapped against his left leg.

"SAM launch, SAM launch, SAM launch! This is Mad Dog on Guard, all aircraft in the vicinity of Quang Tri near the coast, be advised SAM launch at Bravo Charley five."

"Thanks a lot."

"Coyote Two, check in?"

Now they were rolled over past vertical in a hard left diving turn, pulling gs away from the missile. This was better, the airspeed built quickly in the dive, and the gs came in harder and harder.

The sky flared for a moment.

"Oh, geeze."

It was somewhere behind them, maybe a mile away, maybe miles. They couldn't see the fireball, but Lead told them later that he had. It wasn't close, but if they hadn't seen it, if they hadn't maneuvered, it probably would have hit them.

They returned to Danang, not because of the SAM but because of the radio. After they landed, Mike greased up a black *1* on the counter board. He had learned an important lesson he wouldn't forget as long as he lived. He and the Major had relaxed and yawned in the face of the first rule of combat flying, which is "What you don't see will kill you."

•       •       •

Later that same night, Avery Aughton rolled over in his bunk. The wall-mounted air conditioner hummed, vibrated, and churned cool air into the room. His eyes darted behind closed lids. A helicopter moved along the beach. For some odd reason, he was aboard it, searching, searching ...

There she was! Avery pushed the gunner aside and stood in the open doorway, smiling, waving, the wind whipping his blond hair, crinkling his green eyes. She was just as he remembered, propped on an elbow, but this time she smiled. She rolled and sat upright, pivoting on her towel, legs together coquettishly, to follow the helicopter as it circled, kicking up white sand, *whup, whup, whup.*

Avery felt hands at his side; the gunner pushed at him. He wanted back into his doorway, back to his quad .50 gun mount. Avery resisted, pushed back, waved down to the girl. She waved up, her dark Asian eyes smiling, her black Asian hair blowing seductively in the wind. Avery ached, his heart pounded, and he was violently in love, for this enemy woman's every nuance was beauty, yearning, tenderness, joyous life itself.

The gunner stood in the doorway and swung an obscenely well machined assembly of blackness—cylinders, boxes, springs, sights, grips—in an arc toward the girl, turning to bear on an ancient Asian enemy in red bikini. Avery jammed him hard, hands against chest, and the gunner tumbled into a corner and lay still. Avery turned to look, and the girl stood now, arms extended upward in ecstatic welcome.

The gunner came up again and tugged at him while the girl danced and kicked her legs saucily like a Rockette. Avery and the gunner grappled with each other, jockeying for position at the doorway of the vibrating machine while the girl danced with ballet grace, legs arcing in slow motion timelessness above the sand.

The two men fell to the floor and punched, tugged, and pushed at the doorway until they tumbled out of the machine, clinging together and still flailing at one another. Bright blue sky and white sun whipped their eyes and a green forest canopy waited far below.

•     •     •

As Avery jerked and flinched in his bunk, two doors down the hallway Steve rolled over in his bunk. He didn't see Avery and the gunner fall by a hundred yards off his left wing, so intent was he on the action to the right.

There below, a stubby triplane Fokker DR.I putt-putted, red fabric surfaces blazing like a festive kite in the sun. Black German crosses shouted from the tops of the wings, from the body, and from the tail:

*Here, here! Come fight! Come tangle! Come play!*

Steve looked down on a tiny figure in the cockpit. It was a man wearing a leather cap and goggles. Was that …?

Yes! A white scarf fluttered in the wind. The Prince of the Air!

The Baron was down to the right, an easy-way turn for the Camel, and even better, he was in a right turn, his back toward Steve, left arm draped carelessly over the lip of the cockpit.

*Out for a Sunday stroll. He doesn't see me!*

Steve pushed the throttle forward, and the air rushing by his face smelt of burnt castor oil as the 110-horsepower Le Rhône revved up. Simultaneously, he jerked the stick right, and the Camel rolled fast and easy, aided by the torque and gyroscopic effect of the big rotary engine. It always turned right better than left—the Sopwith Camel, like a boxer, was famous for its flashing, slashing right. He reached forward to the grip of the twin Vickers machine guns perched ahead of the cockpit.

*He doesn't see me.*

Steve was over 90 degrees of bank, hauling around and down toward the Baron's six o'clock. His hand tightened on the grip. His finger touched the trigger.

*He still doesn't see me.*

The controls tightened with the speed, and the wire braces between the wings of the biplane howled in the wind, rising in pitch like a chorus of dogs.

Suddenly, the Baron whipped into a hard left turn.

*He saw me. The son of a bitch saw me all along.*

*How did he turn so fast?* The Fokker suffered the same limitation as the Camel. *He throttled back.*

The triplane whipped across Steve's nose too fast to get off a shot, and he jerked back his own throttle to idle, slapped the stick left, stood on the rudder, dragged the plane around to stand on its left wing, but it was too late, the Baron already had the angle and now rolled out level, falling back rapidly, already pushing up the throttle to kill the deceleration, getting ready to slide in on Steve's tail.

Steve looked left, which is to say that he craned his neck and looked up from his cockpit past the trailing edge of his top wing, and there—less than twenty yards away—sat the Baron, ensconced in his red office, left hand caressing the grip of twin Spandau machine guns.

Across a narrow chasm of air, the Baron grinned at Steve. He was horribly mustachioed. He slipped steadily back and disappeared behind Steve's tail.

*Oh, shit!*

# 19

At 0230 in the black of the night, Steve and Mike Ross slumped in their chairs in the small briefing room, legs propped up on the table. The Pistol Flight briefing was about to begin. All was peace and quiet. Sub-Lieutenant Sam wandered into the room, tail wagging, and visited them both in turn, wishing them luck.

There was a noise like two freight trains crashing head on.

•          •          •

*Clayton Daily Star*

### Danang attacked!

By Lt. Steven W. Mylder

Mortars attacked like a pack of furies at 2:30 this morning. The Wing Intelligence people had whined at us like a Greek chorus over and over "The mortars are coming." But we didn't believe them. Now we believe.

The "rain" of terror started while our small group of four pilots and Sam our collie mascot waited in the squadron building for a night mission briefing. *Whump-whump-whump-whump.* We wondered for about one second—but when the lights flickered and went out we knew. Four pilots and a dog dove under the table. Then we ran around the room in the dark stumbling over chairs and colliding with each other to get out the door.

We ran for the sandbag bunker outside the squadron building. Rounds hit near the aircraft parking area about a hundred yards away like a string of gigantic Chinese firecrackers erupting in a frenzy of white lights and staccato explosions, silhouetting planes against showers of sparks and illuminating the buildings around us like flash bulbs in a press conference or lightning in a thunderstorm. We ran for the bunker whose doorless mouth swallowed us like a sandbag giant popping hors d'oeuvres at a New Year's Eve party and huddled inside to digest the disaster that threatened to eat us alive.

The attack went on and on for four or five centuries at least, but probably not more that a minute or two, while we wondered if the sand bags over our heads could survive a direct hit or whether there would be a sudden shock of sound and fury and instant death at the hands of a searing fireball and ripping shrapnel.

·     ·     ·

They hunched down in the bunker silently, alone with their thoughts—four men and a dog. Steve pushed his back against damp burlap walls, fear and adrenaline pumping through his blood. He reached out in the dark and touched fur, then snagged and pulled Sam over to him. Despite his own turmoil, he felt Sam's warm heartbeat through the shaggy coat. Sam shivered.

"Easy, boy, it's all right."

Sam shivered harder as another freight train crashed nearby, and a snarl rattled deep in his throat. Steve thought the quaking was from fear until suddenly Sam struggled and kicked free from his grip and ran right out the door.

"No, Sam, no!" Steve lunged after him, stumbled and stopped at the doorway, then crouched halfway through, looking around the corner of the bunker toward the flight line. More shells went off while he watched and flinched. Silhouetted by the bursts, Sam tore across the tarmac, howling indignantly, straight to where he perceived the enemy to lie, straight to tear out the enemy's throat.

·     ·     ·

Sam ran fearlessly out of the bunker right toward where the shells rained down. He would put a stop to this but then the shells stopped falling and silence rolled in smothering everything like a heavy fog. Sam barked and growled at a cargo plane that burned on the ramp like a demon from hell. Maybe he thought that was where it had all come from.

We crept out of the bunker like mice nervous with silly laughter. The sky glowed red and black smoke billowed like clouds from Hades. The smoke came from the direction of our living compound. They had destroyed our quarters and killed all our friends sleeping peacefully in their beds in the barracks! Later we found out that the smoke came from a fuel tank burning on the far side of the compound and our quarters still stood although one of our buildings took a hit.

We drove the squadron truck to the hospital to help carry the wounded but a hundred volunteers had already beat us to it. Six wounded men lay unconscious on cots in the hallway inside the entrance covered with bloody bandages. Tubes ran into their mouths and noses and plasma dripped into their veins.

We took the truck out on the ramp to see the damage for ourselves.

Destruction.

A maintenance building took a direct hit. Two men died.

We found a nearly destroyed tow truck—a blast went off in front of it. Water leaked from the perforated radiator and three flat tires flopped on the ground. The windshield looked like it took a shotgun blast at ten feet. The driver may not live.

A fire had burned in a revetment behind our planes. We found a wreckage of gutted metal and foul-smelling foam—and a wrecked motorcycle in the middle of it all.

A brother squadron took a hit in its living quarters. They fly days while we fly nights and so their barrack was full of sleeping pilots when a round hit one of the rooms and totally destroyed it.

•     •     •

Will Styles, potential astronaut, future man on Mars, drifted up from a dreamless sleep and found himself in a darkened room in the Red Squadron BOQ. The base was quiet. A plane had taken off five minutes earlier, but the roar from jets rolling down the runway a half mile away no longer disturbed him nor any of the other pilots sleeping in the building—they had long since pigeonholed that particular noise as mundane.

He awoke not because of noise but because of a distended bladder. He lay still for a minute, balancing the immediate discomfort of getting out of bed against the long-term discomfort that would result from *not* getting out of bed. A dog barked far away under a blanket of darkness, and Styles imagined himself at home again, a child snuggled under warm covers listening with wonder to the dogs of the night.

He swung his legs over the side of the bunk and dismounted quietly, careful not to wake his roommate in the berth above. He slipped into slippers beneath the bed and softly opened the door just enough to get out, but not enough to allow the fluorescent light of the hallway to slap his roomie in the face. He padded down the hallway.

*Whump-whump-whump*

The distant noise came as he approached the latrine door, and his sensory Grand Central mechanism tugged and pushed idly at the problem of which track of consciousness to shuttle these particular sounds.

*WHUMP*

Will Styles gained considerable focus from this last disturbance, and cobwebs and childhood memories were cleared frantically from all incoming tracks. In a space of time measured in milliseconds, his sensory mechanism went high gain and dumped in a load of positive feedback, bringing the auditory loop to a point just short of squealing.

With incredibly heightened sensitivity, Styles did, indeed, hear a squealing from high above, stooping down, down, but rising in volume and pitch. A bird of prey descended with an explosive talon extended, wind whistling across steel feathers.

In slow motion, Styles dived, arms crossed in front of his face, body arching at a leisurely rate toward the concrete floor.

In slow motion, the latrine door six paces away—six seconds away from the turning of a knob—dissolved into a thousand fragments of wood and blew outward into the hallway, and in Styles's mind a singular event stormed track one into the headquarters of consciousness.

*KAA-WHUUUUUMMP*

A tiny sliver of wood impacted his chest just before he hit the floor.

•       •       •

It would have killed several people except that this particular room was the latrine—the only place in the building safe to hit.

My friend, Will walked down the hallway enroute to that very room just as the shell hit and he suffered a few small cuts and burns but nothing serious. A sliver of wood drew a little blood which makes him eligible for a Purple Heart. We joke with him about needing a microscope to find the wound.

Much later that night we went to the DOOM club. Everybody else decided to do the same because the joint was packed. Everybody laughed and told war stories and joked but I noticed that all of us seemed a little nervous and jumped at sudden noises.

We went outside when we heard about it: the Spookys—AC-47 gunships—orbited south-east of us across the runway and strafed the area the attack must have come from.

Picture this:

In the distance blinking lights move across dark sky. Then a thin solid stream of red tracers streaks from the sky and connects the plane to the ground. It's like science fiction and lasers and tongues of fire! It reminds me of the war machines in *The War of the Worlds*.

•       •       •

"That's great, Steve. You have a fresh approach; I wish I could write like that …"

"You think so, Mike?"

Mike Ross smiled. "You sure got rid of passive voice. And congratulations, I hardly saw a single comma. But I wonder if you might have …" He chewed on his pencil. "… uhh, gone just a little overboard, maybe? In places, I mean."

"Well, hell, Mike, you said I ought to punch it up, didn't you?"

"Hmmm …" Mike tapped the typewritten pages with his finger. "… there are a few things here you might just consider. And I found a bad problem. He held up one page and read from it: "Six wounded men lay unconscious on cots in the hallway inside the entrance covered with bloody bandages." Mike winked. "You do see it, don't you?" He lay the sheets on the table.

Steve winced. "Oh damn! How could I miss that?" He looked down. Penciled markings and margin notes covered the pages. Unfortunately, he had already mailed the dispatch. Well, maybe the copyeditor would clean it up.

# 20

Lt. Col. R. W. Gannis
666 TFW Public Information Office

Dear Col. Gannis:

Thank you for the tips on writing style. Your comments reflect appropriately conservative values and are well taken. However, I probably ought to move away from my pedantic style—make it snappier and inject a little more drama and human interest and maybe even a little humor. The previous dispatch might have gone a little overboard, but please consider it an experiment and thanks again for the advice.

Regards,
Lt. S. W. Mylder

• • •

*Clayton Daily Star*

## Pilots move to new quarters

### By Lt. Steven W. Mylder

Four days after the attack. We learned it was rockets that hit us—not mortars. More than 50 landed on the base and a nearby Vietnamese village. They killed 12 military men and wounded a lot more, but the villagers were hardest hit. Almost 40 Vietnamese civilians died.

Our base security people found the launch site—and a puzzle as well. The Cong must have goofed up, because only a few of the emplacements fired. If they'd all gone off, we would have taken a lot more damage. No one knows what happened, but here's a piece of the puzzle: found at the launch site was the hacked up body of a Viet Cong soldier, apparently killed by his own comrades with a machete. Now that leaves something to the imagination.

Our squadron moved into new quarters recently, two men per room. My friend Mike and I share a tiny 10' by 12' room, which contains a double-decker bunk bed, two upright metal lockers, a large table, a bench, a small table, assorted boxes, and a lot of personal trivia. We built the large table ourselves from the finest hand-hewn scrap pine boards available. It may be mediocre by most standards of fine workmanship, but to our undiscriminating eyes it's a work of art. Well, pop art.

The "hot" water in the building is no improvement over the hootch. It's lukewarm to lukecold, depending on the time of day and your mood.

The search for Avery's sunbathing girlfriend (the one he spotted on a North Vietnamese beach in a red bikini) continues apace. Almost every flight that goes near there does a low-level reconnaissance pass over that beach, but nobody has seen anything yet.

The DOOM club continues to improve. The front "lawn" has sprouted a white picket fence around the perimeter to enclose and protect the crab grass near the entrance, someone has painted the ash cans white, and the new bar thrives. Work continues on the new dining room.

It's very satisfying to come back home to the DOOM club after a hard day at the war, to cook a steak over an outdoor grill in the dwindling twilight and later sit under the stars and watch outdoor movies projected against the wall of the building.

Twenty down, only 80 more to go.

•       •       •

Cigarette smoke hung in the air of the new bar. A cigar reeked. Snoopy and the Red Baron continued their epic struggle in the skies of a jukebox which had moved to a new location but played the same old tunes. A carpet smothered the floor, and a magnificent new wooden bar stretched across most of the longer wall, but some work remained to be done—the walls were bare of decorations, and the new light fixtures were not yet installed.

Steve's watch read 0330. He and Avery Aughton stood in a puddle of light, an island of illumination that isolated the dart board and its environs from the rest of the bar. They'd parked beer bottles on a nearby table—six empties and two actives. The pilots did not stagger. Their brains were sharp, and their eyes were not dulled for they were fighter pilots. This was expected. To fly and drink (in that order) was part of the steely-eyed culture. Steve aimed and let fly. A tiny feathered missile flew through the air and buried its nose in cork, close beside the rest of its flock.

In another puddle of light, the nightly poker meeting chaired by Heck Sluder raged in raucous abandon. They were the usual sporting group, an equal mix of Green and Red Squadron pilots, front- and back-seaters combined. They argued and cussed, they smoked and joked, they drank and spit into an ornate brass spit-toon parked nearby, and so far no one had killed anyone or inflicted major dam-age to the premises other than break a few glasses—so far—and so they continued unabated and undisturbed every night, ignored by the management.

Heck Sluder's nasally contorted Southern accent rose above the din, and Steve pricked his ears to hear the word "Sam," but he couldn't say whether Sluder was talking about the missile or the dog.

Although one might expect to find the name Sluder on the side of a cinder block auto repair shop in a sleazy part of town, it was actually a respected name in the fashionable district of Birmingham, Alabama. Dr. and Mrs. Sluder were known for their liberal views, were patrons of the arts, frequented opera and bal-let, and contributed generously to charity. A building at the university bore their moniker. The Sluders were valued members of their community.

Their son, however, was trash.

Hector Payne Sluder had always been in trouble, always been a hell raiser, but he was nefariously smart—a ringleader. He was from the Frank Sinatra school of low-life gangsterism; he loved gambling, gotcha's, and getting-away-with-things.

In high school, he'd loved fights and hot, fast machines and bragged about playing chicken on dark country roads. When headlights swung around the curve ahead, coming his way, he closed his eyes and drove down the middle of the road. Nobody could outchicken him.

How did he become a fighter pilot? How did he sidestep a natural aptitude and avoid becoming a mob hit man or a John Doe morgue case? Because one day an F-86 Saber jet from the Air National Guard thundered fifty feet over his head, the pilot intent on impressing a girlfriend at the nearby college, and Hector Payne, after he'd ducked and wet his pants, looked up and realized that here was the hottest, fastest machine ever built and that nobody could play chicken against a machine such as this. He concluded that fighter pilots were the toughest of tough guys, and he decided then and there to become one. The idea lay fallow for a time until one morning he and his buddies went out drinking, got tattoos along the way, and ended the day by—"What the hell, why not?"—enlisting in the Air Force.

Hector quickly discovered that the only way he could become a pilot was to become an officer. And the only way to become an officer, if you didn't go to college, was to go to Officer Candidate School (OCS). So he worked hard, used his natural-born but warped intelligence, stayed out of trouble for the first time in his life, and—surprising everyone but himself—was selected for the school.

He liked the officer part of OCS. It offered status. But he disdained the gentleman part. He kept a Confederate flag in his room and went out drinking, gambling, and whoremongering with his buddies every chance he got. Heck Sluder liked to run with the crowd.

It was us versus them, white versus black, dog eat dog, our team against their team, the pack, the tribe, the mob, the crowd.

"Kill the sonsabitches," he often said, the sonsabitches being anybody on the other team.

"… Charlie …" Sluder's voice floated through the din of the DOOM club chatter, and the name bounced off Steve's eardrum, but he couldn't say whether the captain spoke of the dog or the enemy, Charlie Cong.

*Thunk* went another dart. Mental gears shifted.

"Heard any more about your, ahh … girlfriend?" Steve asked. He looked over at Avery and lifted an eyebrow full of meaning.

Avery was sorry he'd ever written the account in the Hero Book. There was too much traffic out there now, too much competition, a tour bus full of gawkers and potential rivals cruising over the beach every day looking for the beautiful, voluptuous enemy girl in the red bikini bathing suit. Avery worked best alone. A quiet, personal search was needed, but there was no opportunity because Green Squadron was on nights. He needed a plan, some way to first find her then meet her. If he could just meet her, put into action just a few words or gestures, then would come into play the natural combat seduction skills God had given him to charm the pants off beautiful women—to impale and impregnate.

Impregnate? No. She was impregnable. What could he possibly do? She was GU—Geographically Undesirable! It was a long, long commute to the Dong Hoi beach, and even harder to get back. He needed a plan. He'd racked his brain ever since he'd discovered her, but it was no use. There was no scenario that seemed even vaguely possible.

"Hmmph," Avery responded.

"Maybe she's out there at night, Ave. Maybe we could drop flares and look for her."

Avery's demeanor turned baleful, and his eyes flashed green. "Sunbathing at night? I doubt it, unless you can get a tan from the moon."

"Maybe it wasn't a girl. Maybe it was just a piece of driftwood with some red cloth snagged on it. Really! A girl? Sunbathing in a bikini on a deserted beach in a free-fire zone while F-4s pound the shit out of the countryside?" Steve smirked in his worst smart-ass manner. "Com'on, Ave, you gotta be shittin' me."

"I *saw* her, goddamnit! She wasn't my fucking imagination. I was close enough that I could almost see her eye color. Don't you call her a piece of driftwood."

This was the first Steve had seen Avery on the defensive. He was usually an attack kind of guy. It suddenly flashed—*he's in love!* After a quick date with an imaginary woman, after a fraction-of-a-second eyes-locked-together beach date with a scantily clad piece of jetsam, a hormonal urgency had kicked in. Love at first "site."

Steve should have let it drop, but a beer haze—maybe it did have a slight effect—made him continue along a thin line, skating the edge of pugilistic danger. Avery's fingers flexed into balls.

"What if she *was* real? She'd hate a Yankee imperialist dog like you, Avery." Steve laughed. "Oh! It's probably Jane Fonda down there! Jane Fonda came over to visit and catch a few rays."

"Shit." Avery threw a feathered missile. *Thunk.* It landed wide. "If that's who it is, I'll go down and drop a load of napalm." He laughed. "That'll get her a quick tan."

"Aww. Don't you like Jane?"

"Do you?" Avery glanced askance at Steve.

Steve made the mistake of a straight answer. "She's okay. Well, yeah, I guess I even admire her a little. She's gutsy."

Avery was aghast. "Like that bitch? What are you? A fucking communist?"

Steve couldn't tell if he was serious or joking. Suddenly, it was Avery on the attack, in his natural element, while Steve was on the defensive.

"No, I'm not a communist." Steve put strained patience in his voice. "Just because I like Jane Fonda doesn't make me a communist."

"Makes you goddamn strange, though." Avery brushed a lock of blond hair off his forehead and strutted the full length of his five-foot, ten-inch muscular physique. "I'm over here fighting the Commies, and when I go home, I'll probably fight the asshole war protesters and punk draft dodgers. What're you over here for?"

Steve suppressed a wince.

"Well … Well, I don't have anything against them. If I was drafted in a war I didn't believe in, I might do the same thing."

"You don't believe in this war? Fucking communists taking over yet one more country in their plan for world domination, and you don't believe in the war?"

"I didn't say that … but. Well, no, I'm not worried about communists taking over the world. I don't think it could happen."

*Thunk.* Steve's dart went wide.

Avery shook his head. "They walk into a village, take the leader, cut off his head with a machete in front of all his people. Make an example of him by killing him in front of his own family. People like that are not a threat?"

It was like an exploratory left jab to the head. *Get your gloves up! Move around!* "Oh, yeah, I know that happens, but that doesn't have anything to do with communism, that's assholes out of control. A lot of people have done that, communists, fascists, capitalists, …"

Avery drove straight ahead. "Why the hell are you over here if you don't think communism is a threat?"

"Well …"

"Well, well, well …" Avery taunted. Jab, jab, jab.

"Well, because of that brutality, for one. Doesn't matter who does it. South Vietnam is getting screwed over, I mean the people, and we're trying to stop it. We're trying to help them."

Avery stared with multifaceted emerald eyes.

"I mean there's too much nastiness in the world. And too many '-isms.' Capitalism, communism, socialism, patriotism, conservatism, liberalism, all the—isms—all those things people are always killing each other over. Including myself."

He got no feedback from Avery at all. A hard predatory beast stalked.

"I mean, I just can't credit the human race with enough maturity or wisdom to avoid wars, to plan around them so they don't kill themselves off. All those -isms are empty words if there's nobody alive to believe in them." Defensive crouch. Keep the gloves up.

Avery smiled broadly and genuinely through perfect, white, carnivorous teeth. "You're a liberal," he said, recognizing an essential, chasmic difference between himself and Steve. "You're a fucking fighter pilot liberal, soft in the head. I didn't think there could be such a thing."

He swung a violent right cross hook at Steve's nose, stopped a half-inch away, and gave it a little tap. A friendly tap.

Steve jerked back and spun around. "There are a lot of pilots who have brains and use them." He was still on the defensive. "There are a lot of pilots who have compassion and fight for the underdog."

Avery laughed. "Underdog be damned. I fight for the overdog. I kick ass for America and God and Right. I'm on the winning team. Kick the sons-of-bitches underdogs in the ass. Who needs them? And besides, where are those underdogs you're fighting for? Where are those poor, poor Vietnamese people? You've never even seen one except for the maids. And they're probably all Viet Cong. Do you trust them? I don't. One of these days when you're snoozing away in your bunk, one of them's gonna roll a grenade under your bed."

Steve was in a quandary. He couldn't say why he was fighting, and Avery was right—he didn't know any Vietnamese people. The pilots lived in their own self-contained world. They dropped bombs into blackness and returned to the amenities of fighter pilot civilization to tell their stories and sing their fighter pilot songs and chant their chants and celebrate their myths around the firelit darkness of the DOOM club cave. They never met a soul who lived in Vietnam.

# 21

It was a dark and sultry night as Steve struggled against time-worn clichés for the opening sentence of his next dispatch. Alone in the squadron building, he tickety-tapped the keys of the typewriter in McNish's office. The first shift of night fliers had flown the coop—ten Phantoms, twenty pilots—and briefings for the next shift hadn't started yet. McNish was out on a foray for office supplies and cornflakes for the squadron commander, and Steve held the fort all alone.

"Twenty-fvie conters, only seventy-fvie to go," he typed, then pulled the paper from the typewriter, crumbled it into the trash can and rolled in another sheet.

"Tewnty-five counters—only sventy-five to go." *Damn!*

He leaned back in the rolling green government issue office chair, took a sip from a coffee cup with the squadron's chicken hawk logo on the outside and a layer of fine brown moss on the inside, closed his eyes, nodded his head, and drummed his fingers against the top of the government issue desk. He drew a finger across his upper lip. *Hmmm?*

He went to the latrine to stare in the mirror and was disappointed because the protomustache was blond—all blond—and absolutely invisible to the naked eye from more than two feet away. *Maybe with a magnifying glass.*

He came back to the desk, ripped out the sheet and rolled in another. He sharpened a pencil and scribbled an abstract pattern on a yellow pad. Then he spent five minutes neating up the laces of his combat boots.

Oops—he was out of coffee. He took another trip to the coffee bar to drain the last cup and start another pot, then back to the desk. Then, it was time for a latrine visit. He leafed through a magazine in the stall, read an interview with Bob Dylan, and returned to the desk fifteen minutes later. He sat in the chair—fidgeting right, fidgeting left, drumming his fingers against the desktop, then he leaned forward and placed them on the keys.

"Twenty-five counters, only seventy-five to gi"

The front door opened, and Steve heard two pilots arguing as they came in.

"… not going there, man, I'm sorry, it's just one of those places I'm not going to mess with."

"I'm telling you, Karl, I'm short. I've got five crews gone to Clark, three people are down with flu, and two just finished their last mission yesterday. I don't have any choice."

Steve didn't need to recognize the voices or hear the name to understand that it was Major Jasper dickering with Sir Walter Scott to get out of a mission.

"I'm sorry, but I'm telling you I'm not going to Tchepone. Look, you can give me a combat proof over Package 1, or something down south, but damned if I'm going to fly over that hellhole. You sent me there last night. I went, and you could practically read a newspaper from the light of the tracers. No more! Never again to Tchepone."

There was a long silence.

"Well."

It was a resigned "well" from the throat of Major Scott. It was a "well" that would inevitably be followed by: "Maybe I can replace you with …"

*That's it?* Steve was amazed. *It's that easy? Scott didn't even put up a tussle. What if I said no?*

Suddenly, Steve realized that he *could* say no. It was within the realm of the possible, even the plausible and the probable, that he was free to choose. Free to refuse.

And if he did? What consequences sprang from the actions of a loner? What happened to pilots who refused to join the hunting tribe and celebrate the rituals and play the games and fight the fights of the brethren of the large flying mammals?

# 22

An argument flared at Heck Sluder's poker table in the DOOM club, one of several that broke out every hour. Steve heard a snatch from Farthington, one of the Red pilots.

"Damn dog couldn't fight his way out of a paper bag. He'd put his tail between his legs and run."

Jim DeWolf, the red-haired Green pilot, snorted derisively. "He'd rip that bastard a new bung hole. You can bet on it."

"Put your money where your mouth is."

"He'd kill him."

"Put your money where your mouth is."

Captain Heck Sluder hefted himself from the table, swayed and balanced his large, rawboned frame, then pushed off toward the latrine along a course that wove by the dart area. As he came by, Steve stepped aside at the last instant to avoid a collision.

"Pardon me," Steve called sarcastically.

Sluder stopped and turned, then stepped toward Steve until there was less than two feet of space between them. Sluder was tall—as tall as Steve and about twenty pounds heavier. Steve smelled strong beer breath, even though his nostrils were dulled by the several beers he had already put away himself.

"What's that you say, asshole?" Sluder's nasal voice dripped a brutal Southern accent.

"I said 'pardon me' for getting in your way." Steve's modulation was precisely neutral.

Sluder sneered, swayed a moment as if digesting the reply and processing it for impertinence. His beer-marinated brain apparently dismissed it as innocuous because he turned without a word and continued to the latrine.

"Real nice guy," Steve mumbled to Avery. "A milk-of-human-kindness type of guy. Makes you want to hug him, doesn't it?"

Avery shook his head from side to side. "Yeah, but you let him walk over you. Don't step out of the way like that. Next time the bastard does that, knock him on his ass."

It was Steve's opportunity to laugh. "You're a real hard-core conservative, Avery. A right-winger-dinger. That's your answer to everything, isn't it, bash the shit out of it?"

Avery looked thoughtful for a moment. "No-o-o. I'm a *rea*-sonable guy." He drew the words out and emphasized them. "I only beat the shit out of people that bug me, and that son of a bitch is one of them. Here, trade places." He pulled Steve out of the way and stood at the throw line. "If he comes back the way he went, he's going to wind up on the floor."

"You're an idiot. Not only is he twice your size, he's a captain and you're a lieutenant. They could court-martial you for striking a superior officer."

"He's also drunk, but it doesn't matter. The bastard could be sober and five times my size, he'd still fall." Avery's confidence was supreme. "And you think they'd court-martial me for striking an asshole? No, they'd give me a medal." They both giggled.

"You're an aggressive bastard, Avery. I bet that's the way you fly, too."

"Fuckin' A."

"I'll bet you and Truhaft are a real team. You probably make multiple passes on gun sites."

"Fuckin' A." Avery tossed. *Thunk*. In the center.

"You're gonna get yourself killed if you're not careful. It's not worth an F-4 and two pilots to take out a lousy AW site. Not cost effective."

"Yes, Mother. We do the job, whatever it takes to nail the bastards. I love finding them down there and going after them, like cleaning out rats' nests. It gives me a sense of visible progress, you know. To put it in terms a liberal can understand, it's my bag. If it feels good, do it."

"Right. Pissing contests with gunners—see who can piss the farthest. That's against wing directives. Single passes on single targets, drop your load and go. Right out of Sanger's mouth."

Avery snorted. "I've flown with Sanger twice now, and we blew the shit out of Triple As both times, two passes the first time and three the second. Don't worry about what Sanger says. Watch what he does."

"Don't you worry about getting shot down?"

"Naah." *Thunk*.

"Don't you worry about anything?"

Avery laughed. "You think too much. That's your problem, Mylder. You and your liberal ilk try to analyze the shit out of everything, talk your way out of ever doing anything. You can't fuckin' play Hamlet all your life." *Thunk*. In the center again.

"I just want to get at the truth. I just want to know what life's all about. 'The truth shall set you free,' you know."

Avery rolled his eyes and sneered. "Truth, schmuth. *Power* sets you free!" He paused a moment and launched two more missiles. They went wide.

"Shit, see what happened, Mylder. You made me think, and it screwed me up. Yeah, I worry sometimes, but I don't worry about getting shot down. I only worry about getting caught."

"What would you do?"

"I wouldn't *get* caught. If they got me in a corner, I'd use my little ole thirty-eight and take down as many as I could. They'd have to kill me, because they sure as hell ain't gonna capture me."

Steve shook his head. How could Avery value his own life so little? It was so goddamned puzzling and irritating that there was a breed or class of people who regarded life so casually. They pawned their own lives in a game. They were actually willing to die for their god and country and all those 'isms.' It was puzzling, irritating … and humbling.

Unless it was all braggadocio and macho talk. It might be that.

"I heard Truhaft got number ninety-five on your last flight. He'll be leaving soon. Are you looking around for a new AC?"

"Don't bet on it. He loves it over here. He's gonna re-up for a second hundred. He's planning to take two weeks R & R in Hawaii with his wife, then hop out of that saddle and into this saddle again."

"His wife?" Steve was astonished. "I didn't know he was married."

*Thunk, thunk.* The missiles flew. The wheels of Steve's mind turned slowly. "He's a good pilot. I flew with him once. But he probably has a bad opinion of me."

"Yeah? He hasn't mentioned it."

"Remember my first mission?"

"No. Why should I?"

"That was when Bender and Demopoulis got shot down. Remember how …"

"Oh. *That* I remember."

"Well. It was my fault."

"Your fault what?"

"That they got shot down."

Avery shot him a quizzical look. "How the hell did you do that?"

Steve told him about the arming switch he'd forgotten, the multiple dry passes with the gun.

"So how did that get Bender and Demopoulis shot down?"

Steve thought it was obvious. "Well, we made multiple passes. If the gun had been working, we probably would have got that sampan the first time, before he pulled into shore. They got a bead on Two the second time he came through."

"Bigus dealus. So he caught the golden BB. That doesn't make you guilty."

"Well, yeah, it does."

Avery slapped his forehead. "Oh. Right, I see. You fucking liberals are always guilty, aren't you? That's a way of life. You always have to confess something. Geeze! This is a war. That's what happens. People screw up and get killed. You just have to learn to screw up less and less."

"Hmmm."

"It's true, damn it. It's not that they're clever and they get you. It's more like you fuck up and hand them your head."

Avery held out his hand, palm up, a large imaginary lump on it. "Here, take my head, please. I'm stupid, I don't need it."

"Sounds like that's exactly what you're trying to do."

"Crap! Here we go again. You shifty fucking liberals. Rootless pansies, no sense of values."

"Fucking conservatives. Ruthless, controlling, no regard for the truth. No sense of compassion or community."

"Aww, shit!" Avery pushed the conversation away with his hands.

An argument flared at the poker table again. Heck Sluder's red-nosed voice joined the fray. Avery and Steve stared in amazement. Sluder was back at the table. They hadn't even noticed when he'd walked by.

They quit the darts and sat at the bar. Steve ordered another round of beer. "We're going off nights."

"I know."

Steve tilted his bottle up and drained it. "You can look for your girlfriend again."

Avery smiled at Steve and punched him hard on the shoulder. "I'll probably knock you on your ass some day."

•          •          •

The sun had filtered through a dreary Monday overcast for an hour before Steve, rubbing a sore shoulder, finally wove up the steps of the BOQ and along the fluorescent-lit hallway. In the alcove he found Ron Catarsis and Jaime Hornslug playing cards with two of the maids. There was a note scrawled on the back of an envelope tacked to the bulletin board:

*Tuesday morning go*
Dagger Flight
MIGCAP, 0425 brief

Phelps/DeWolf
Stanton/Demopoulis
Bender/Mylder
Camero/Taint

Spare: Luxington/Catarsis

•　　•　　•

Steve gave up trying to out-slow the Baron. He throttled up the big Le Rhône rotary, snapped hard right past 90 degrees of bank, and hauled back on the stick when he was nearly inverted, pulling the Camel through a skewed split-s maneuver. Halfway through, he looked straight down at patchwork farmland less than a thousand feet below. The smell of manure wafted upward to blend with the burnt castor oil in his nostrils. He kept pressure on the stick as the plane came out the bottom, and he felt the fabric of the wings vibrate as he neared the edge of a high-speed stall. He looked over his right shoulder for the Baron.

Not there!

He rolled ponderously left. Not there, either. He snap rolled right, 360 degrees, scanning, scanning.

Where the hell did he go?

*What you don't see will kill you.*

He jerked the little plane up and down, left and right, kept the stick stirring and the pedals pumping, but couldn't find the Fokker. The engine thundered and the bracing wires sang in his ears.

*Eighty men died tryin' to end that spree*

Oh, God, he couldn't find the Fokker. *The Baron is back there*, he knew, and braced for the inevitable. It was only a matter of seconds.

*What you don't see will kill you.*

# 23

"Dagger Flight, check in."

"Two."

"Three."

"Four."

"Ground, Dagger Flight of four to taxi."

The four warbirds gathered in echelon, engines roaring an idle lullaby while the last check ground crews fondled each plane, pulling red-tagged pins from the Sparrow missiles snugged under the fuselage and from the Sidewinders beneath each wing, pushing and tugging the external fuel tanks, tap-tap-tapping knuckles against access panels, inspecting underbellies and wheel wells for leaking hydraulic fluid. They fell back and stood in a line, eight fatigue-greened airmen, and saluted as the warbirds pushed forward. Steve raised a gloved thumbs-up to them as he lowered his canopy, and they waved back.

Dagger Flight assembled on the north end of runway one-seven right, Lead and Two on the left half of the runway, Three and Four on the right. The pilots pumped the brakes and ran the throttles up to 90 percent RPM. Lead released brakes and plugged in the burner. After a measured count to six, Two followed, then six seconds later, Three, with Frank and Steve aboard. Steve read 0631 on his clock as he punched the elapsed-time button. Finally, Four churned down the runway behind them all.

There was one more. Dagger Five charged down the runway, huffing and puffing, but Sub-Lieutenant Sam the Collie wasn't able to make it off the ground.

After the gear and flaps were sucked up, Lead rolled into a 30 degree right bank. Two joined on the inside of the turn, then fell slightly back and behind and slid across to the left wing. Three and Four joined on the right, just before the formation rolled out heading northwest.

Dagger Flight climbed to eighteen thousand feet, crossing over the border into Laos. There they met their KC-135 mother tanker, joined on her in a formation of large and small, and sucked, one by one, at the JP-4 teat until they were satiated. The tanker dropped them off heading due north, and Dagger proceeded toward North Vietnam.

•         •         •

*Clayton Daily Star*

## Clayton pilot in MiG fight

By Lt. Steven W. Mylder

There's always something new around here. We had a MiG battle today. Four Phantoms tangled with about eight MiGs near Hanoi. None of us is sure of the exact number—they were all around—but we are all agreed that it was a hell of a one-hour battle crammed into three minutes—a classic dogfight.

We flew a MIGCAP in the area just west of Hanoi. That means we were supposed to keep MiGs off the backs of other aircraft going in on bombing runs. We arrived about 8 a.m. and had just settled down, cruising at 10,000 feet, when we saw a strange looking plane all by itself. It was a MiG-17 at 10 o'clock, about a thousand feet higher, coming almost straight at us.

It looks like he's out for a Sunday drive! He passes to our seven o'clock, still going straight. We plug in the burners and our four-ship formation splits into two loose two-ships, Three (us) and Four pulling a hard right turn, and Lead and Two going left.

"This is easy," we collectively think.

"This is too easy!" we collectively realize about halfway through the turn. We roll level momentarily and look left.

It is too easy. There, coming from the same direction as the loner is a swarm of black flies in the sky—MiG-17s hell-bent on doing us in.

We've nearly been suckered! The Sunday driver was the bait, about five to 10 miles ahead of the pack. If we turn to fall in on his tail, they slide in behind us and a turkey shoot ensues.

We reverse hard left toward the pack, our wingman following loosely behind as best he can in the high g environment. The swarm of black flies breaks up, some of them going for Lead and Two, the rest coming for us. They're trying to get on our tails while we try to get on theirs. The after-burners stay on and we're loaded up continuously at four to five gs of force.

We're into it! There are planes all over the sky going all different directions, MiG and Phantom trajectories intertwined in deadly embrace. Somebody's going to get killed!

We're outnumbered, but besides that we have another disadvantage. Missiles. We've got them, but they've got guns.

Missiles ain't what they're cracked up to be. We have to lock up the tracking system on a target before we let fly, which is a complication you can't afford in a tight dogfight. All the MiGs have to do is point and shoot. Missiles need a minimum distance to work. If we're too close, they miss, but the MiGs can practically fly up our tailpipes with their cannons. What makes it worse is that the MiGs know our limitation and take advantage of it. They try to get in close where they're fairly safe while we're vulnerable.

At one point we're all traveling in a large circle like the snake who swallows his tail, Phantoms interspersed with MiGs, all shooting missiles and guns at one another.

•           •           •

"OKAY, I GOT A LOCK, I GOT A LOCK," Steve shouted rapid-fire staccato over the intercom.

"WHERE? WHERE? WHICH ONE?"

"TEN LEFT, TEN DEGREES LEFT. TWO MILES."

"DAGGER LEAD, THERE'S ONE COMING IN AT EIGHT O'CLOCK."

"… on guard, Bird Song on guard, SAM launch at Alpha Delta three, SAM launch at … three, Bird So …"

"… EIGHT, LEAD—AT—EIGHT!"

"Unhhhn." Frank Bender groaned from the gs. "WHICH ONE? THERE'S THREE, FOUR OUT THERE."

"CAN'T TELL. SHIT, DROPPED HIM. WAIT. THERE, THERE. FIFTEEN LEFT. NO. DROPPED HIM. SHIT!"

"I CAN'T TELL WHO …"

"… FOX-1, LEAD IS …"

"… Bird Song on guard …"

"Unhhhn."

"… COMING UP ON YOU, THREE, CHECK …"

"… Bravo Charlie two …"

"WHERE'D HE GO, YOU GOT HIM … EIGHT …"

"… Song out."

"COMING UP ON US FIVE O'CLOCK, THREE. DAGGER THREE."

"CHECK OUR FIVE."

•         •         •

We get a radar lock-on to a target out in front, but we're not sure whether it's one of them or one of us, so we hold fire trying to verify which it is, and meanwhile the lock is dropped and we can't get it back.

We're pulling four gs, grunting to stay conscious while the radio babbles away spilling confusion into our brains. I grab the two handholds at the canopy bow above my head and twist around in the seat as hard as possible, straining to see behind us.

•         •         •

"HE'S ON US. HE'S ON US. PULLING-LEAD, HE'S SHOOTING."
"WHAT? WHERE?"
"GODDAMN MIG FOUR O'CLOCK. I SEE HIS GUN."
"Unnhhhnnnn" The gs loaded up to five, and the plane burbled at the edge of a high-speed stall.

•         •         •

There's a MiG on our tail a few hundred feet behind. He's turning to the inside, pulling lead on us at a high angle of attack. I see his belly and his cannon flashes.

The MiGs will outturn us if we stay in a horizontal plane and play their game. Now it's time to play ours.

We roll out of the turn but keep the gs on and head for the sky. The F-4 may not be a pretty airplane, but when it comes to raw power nothing can stay with it. We pop up several thousand feet, pull over the top, and come down again toward the gaggle. The MiG can't climb with us and falls off. We'll be on his tail soon if he doesn't do something.

All the F-4s work in the vertical plane now, popping up to leave the MiGs behind, then coming back on them from above. The MiGs realize their game is over. They break off the engagement and head east "on the deck" (low altitude). We have time to get on one of them and fire two radar-guided missiles, but both miss badly.

About this time one of our planes is at a low fuel level that he announces over the radio as "Bingo," which means "Go home now!"

•          •          •

"NO SHIT BINGO. DAGGER FOUR IS NO SHIT BINGO. GET THE FUCK OUTTA HERE."

•          •          •

We break off the chase, regroup into loose formation, and head out of the area at 3,000 feet. On the way out, up come a couple of SAMs. They go ballistic and explode some distance from us.

That was the end of it. We fired four missiles from our plane, but all missed. Our wingman has the best chance of a kill, but we don't know if he really got the MiG. At the end, when they were running, he fired a Sidewinder heat-seeking missile at one of them. The Sidewinder was still homing at 400 feet out when the MiG went into a cloud. Wing saw no more of him or the missile. Infrared tracking doesn't work very well in clouds, but the missile was so close that it may have hit anyway. However, unless we find out definitively, the score for the entire engagement is 0-0.

Three *minutes*?! Is that all? No other human activity, including the obvious one, could match the intensity packed into each second of that time.

Well, that's 28 down, only 72 more to go.

•          •          •

Half of him hated it, and the other half loved it. The adrenaline had surged through his system, addicting as it went, pumping up his body, screaming "DO IT, DO IT, DO IT!" and he had become an automaton, out of control at precisely the same time that he was intimately *in* control, and it was good and bad and terrifyingly sensual.

Better than sex. Worse than sex.

They gathered in the large squadron briefing room, an excited flock of large flying mammals—hunters back from the kill even though there had been no kill, no corpus to roast and tear apart limb by limb. They joked. They shook hands and slapped backs. They drew curving, intertwined lines on the blackboard, with arrowheads at the tips, with streams of hot lead coming from the MiG arrowheads and curlicue lines of smoking missiles coming from the Phantom arrowheads. Their hands went around in the air, one following the other, diving, looping, vying for position. They said, "Did you see …?" and "That son of a bitch was down running ..." and "I could see the tracers come by the cockpit ..." and "You nearly stuffed a Sidewinder up his ass ..." and "Those goddamned Sparrows aren't worth ..." and "If we only had fucking guns...."

After the hubbub had cleared and the squadron truck had hauled most of the hunters off to the DOOM club to drink and dine and fight again ... after the party was over and the bunting was down and Steve sat in a glow of self-congratulatory introspection, Sub-Lieutenant Sam hobbled into the briefing room.

"Oh, Sam. Not again."

This time, Sam had gone to the enemy. He knew where Red Squadron's BOQ was. He had trotted a mile along the road and gone loping into the enemy camp looking for Charley. Sam's dogfight had happened simultaneously with Steve's, and despite the hobble, despite the nasty gash on his foreleg, he was animated, vital. He pranced, proud and happy, around Steve.

"You liked it, Sam! You son of a bitch. You *liked* it, didn't you?"

•          •          •

Lt. Col. R. W. Gannis
666 TFW Public Information Office

Col. Gannis:

I don't see how my reference to guns and the fact that we don't carry them on our far north missions can help the enemy in any way, since they already know we don't have them and take full advantage of it. Missiles just don't cut it in dogfights, sir.

I have left it in. I hope you will reconsider and let it stand.

Lt. S. W. Mylder

# 24

Steve and Frank Bender ferried a plane eight hundred miles across the South China Sea to Clark Air Base in the Philippines. They checked into the Hotel Royale in Angeles City, just outside the main gate, the same place Steve had stayed during jungle survival training a few months earlier. The hotel was a new construction with wooden scaffolding still up along one wall, built especially to cater to the influx and outflux of Vietnam fliers. It combined urbanity and garishness in strange juxtaposition. The rooms were quiet and well appointed, but the exterior plaster glowed obnoxiously pink, and odd rococo growths jutted from the walls here and there like small malignancies.

For the next two nights and days, while their plane was modified with new missile warning equipment, Steve and Frank sampled the quiet cheerful environment of the sprawling green-lawned air base.

The first morning, Steve enjoyed a lazy late breakfast in the dining room of the officer's club. Back at Danang two hours earlier, Virgil Demopoulis had pulled on his flying gloves. Now, while Steve absently forked the remnants of a ham and cheese omelet, drank his third cup of coffee, and read the newspaper, Virgil's plane entered the traffic pattern at Danang and—*whack, bang*—took automatic weapons fire from somewhere off (or on) the base; no one discovered quite where. A few minutes later, while Steve sat grunting gently in an elegant wooden-paneled, white tile-floored stall in the men's room reading the Sunday funnies, Virgil's plane pitched up 30 degrees on a long, shaky final approach, rolled right 120 degrees, and Virgil and the aircraft commander punched. A little after that, Steve smiled up at the barkeep who had just placed a tall Bloody Mary before him, Virgil gave a thumbs-up to a descending rescue helicopter, and a junked plane sent a column of black smoke into the air a mile south of Danang. It was a good life after all. Maybe everything would come out all right in the end.

•　　　•　　　•

That afternoon, First Lieutenant Lewis Luxington III raised his canopy to the tepid outside air and breathed deeply. It was good. Moisture condensed clamily

115

on his skin. A trickle of warm sweat ran down his nose and clung to the end before being absorbed into the sleeve of his flight suit.

Luxington would normally have been uncomfortable, except that now he was too numb to feel and too tired to complain. But he was also elated. It had been a good mission. A superb mission, and very hazardous as well. He could read in his mind the citation for the medal. A Silver Star, at least.

> Disregarding his own personal safety, First Lieutenant Luxington, in spite of withering ground fire inflicting numerous hits to his aircraft, delivered his high explosive ordinance on target, resulting in several secondary explosions and sustained fires. Lieutenant Luxington exhibited extraordinary courage … heroism … repeatedly rolling in … maximum destruction … (etc., etc., standard closing sentences).

That was roughly the way it would go, for being Green Squadron's Awards and Decorations Officer, he would write it himself. In fact, he would even write up Lieutenant Ron Catarsis, his back-seater, for a Distinguished Flying Cross—a juicy tidbit—even though he was a loser.

Catarsis had begun whimpering as Luxington began the third roll-in on the target. Indeed, he had even grabbed the stick in the backseat and tried to take control of the aircraft until Luxington authoritatively told him to let go and punctuated the command by snapping the plane into a bone-crunching six gs. After that, Catarsis had been obedient, although he had mumbled to himself and hadn't been any help on the way home.

Catarsis had an inordinate number of personal problems and was always trying to slickey out of dangerous missions. Luxington thoroughly mistrusted and disliked him, although he refrained from expressing this, for they were paired together and—much as Lux hated it—they had more than forty counters to go before they were each free of the other. At times Luxington even went out of his way to be nice.

He was elated, until he saw Colonel Sanger approaching the aircraft.

The colonel approached with calm and massive authority. He approached with an inscrutable smile on his lips, an expression that was rarely absent. Colonel Sanger smiled when he got out of bed in the morning. He smiled when he went to bed in the evening. He smiled when he was climbing into the cockpit for a combat mission and when he got back. The same smile he used while playing poker with his colonel buddies at the DOOM club was present when he was hanging a subordinate from the yardarm. Colonel Sanger's face was frozen into a perpetual smile which had the effect of terrorizing subordinates for it was sadistic and predatory. Some said it was the result of an old Korean War wound that had paralyzed certain muscles of the colonel's cheeks, leaving his face asymmetric—the left side immobile, leaden and jowly, and the right side slightly more relaxed and expressive.

Luxington's elation turned to horror as Sanger approached, for not only was Sanger regarded with dread by all the pilots in general, but for Luxington in particular Sanger was a man for whom he could do no right. He was a cause of awe and, yes, even idolatry—but also a cause of agonizing self-appraisal. Lux was guilty in his presence without knowing why. Luxington wanted to emulate him and be as like him as possible. He even practiced Sanger's careless and powerful gestures in private in his room when no one was around.

But he could not talk with the old man. He was obsessed with the desire to demonstrate wisdom and integrity to the colonel, but he was struck dumb when the colonel's penetrating blue eyes turned on him. Everything he said was exceedingly foolish or stupid. He sank into a staccato of "Yes sirs" and "No sirs" each time he found himself in the colonel's presence. Luxington lived an ambivalence of worship and fear of the old man.

Sanger's eyes smiled up at him now as the colonel waited patiently at the foot of the ladder. As Lux nervously unstrapped, he wondered to himself, "Did I do something wrong? Did another tool chest go over the revetment wall? Why did he come out to meet me?"

He was a frightened young rabbit, an innocent bunny frozen in the trance-inducing stare of a predatory beast. He had a quick vision of the colonel popping the eyeball from a bunny's head, putting it in his mouth, and biting down.

Lux started out of the cockpit, a noncommittal mask over his face, and stepped to the ladder when he nervously dropped his clipboard and made a lunge for it as it floated in subjective slow motion toward the concrete. He would have been all right had the dangling leg strap of his parachute harness not caught on the ladder rail and yanked as he lunged. The yank made his foot lose traction on the first step, and he felt himself falling, pivoting around the anchored strap, until the point of his nose and forehead brought him up short, after 180 degrees of rotation, against the side of the aircraft. As he hung there, huge white stars circling his vision, his nose bleeding profusely, blood running down the camouflage paint of the F-4 and dripping onto the ramp, the perverse strap dislodged and let him down for a three-point landing on the back of his head and shoulder blades.

Sanger, who had watched impassively, strolled to his staff car and instructed the Wing Command Post to send an ambulance. Then, as Luxington lay moaning and bleeding on the ramp, comforted by Catarsis and Crew Chief Thornton, the colonel drove off in his big blue station wagon to another part of the base to watch the rest of the afternoon's missions land.

•          •          •

Later in the afternoon, a crew chief crossed his arms above his head, and a Phantom jerked to a stop, nose wheel centered on a yellow painted spot on the tarmac. A fire truck idled in front of the plane, red lights blinking violently, two crewmen atop it with hoses at the ready. Harold Kamsky climbed down from the front cockpit, Jim DeWolf from the rear. The squadron commander, Lt. Colonel Parsons, waited to greet them, as did Major Scott, Airman McNish, Mike Ross, Ron Catarsis, Harry Taint, and a few other ACs and GIBs.

Twin streams of water hit the pilots when they stepped to the ground, instantly soaking them and almost knocking them down. They twirled in twin streams of giants' piss, hands above heads with Vs at the ends, big grins glowing from happy faces.

One hundred counters. One hundred missions over North Vietnam. Colonel Parsons handed them a bottle apiece of Cook's Champagne.

Several hours later, Jim DeWolf staggered home from the DOOM club bar, red hair frizzed out, drying strangely from the hoses. He ritually counted the money stashed in his locker from poker winnings—$1,800 in tens and twenties—and went to sleep a happy man. At that moment, eight hundred miles away, two Philippine girls walked on Steve's back as he lay groaning on the lush carpet of his hotel room, naked except for boxer shorts. *So this is a massage*, he mused. *I wonder what else comes with it?* He was too shy to ask, the girls didn't volunteer, and he would ponder that question the rest of his life.

•          •          •

Late that evening, Avery Aughton rolled over in his bunk. As it did every evening—a prelude to the dream state—the wall-mounted air conditioner hummed, vibrated, and churned cool air into the room. His eyes darted behind closed lids. Trucks moved through the jungle.

They had followed him for hours, interminably, doggedly—big Soviet military trucks, four, five, six of them, he didn't know. They were many, simply many. They were great gray stodgy things with yellow stars on the doors, open-backed and filled with troops in heavy combat gear who crowded forward so they could point and shoot over the cab. Earnest youthful faces glared with slanted Asian eyes as Avery plunged through the jungle.

He heard the burst of an AK-47. Too close. He dodged left on a narrow path through dense undergrowth. That would slow them down. He ran fifty feet, then stopped to empty the last three rounds from his revolver—*pop, pop, pop*—at the nearest truck. He grabbed a fistful of shells from his survival vest, reloaded, and plunged forward again.

The path led east into the morning sun, and he was over and across a long, narrow dune before he realized where it was taking him. Suddenly, the jungle was gone, and sand scrunched beneath his combat boots. He stopped abruptly and gazed ahead.

Out beyond smooth white sand heaved a shining green sea. Waves crested, rolled into long tubes, and glided ashore in strings of white foam. The sun smiled down on a holiday beach.

*Oh, God!*

He knew what he would find, and he turned slowly to look north along the sand.

*Yes!* He broke into a run again, and his heart pounded, but not from fear or fatigue. Even though he had run for hours, he was still fresh and strong. Now his heart pounded from exhilaration, from hope, from …

He ground to a halt thirty feet from it.

*Damn, damn, damn!*

Driftwood. It was a piece of driftwood, vaguely human-shaped, with red cloth snagged on it. That was all. A fucking chunk of wood.

Wait. He came closer. It wasn't just a piece of red cloth.

It was *two* pieces. They lay draped over the wood, spread neatly to dry in the sun. One was the top of a bathing suit. The other was the bottom.

He jerked around and his heart jumped. Yes. He had run right past and didn't see. There. On a towel on the sand.

She stretched casually on her back, squarely facing him, elbows out with hands languidly behind her head to tilt it upward gently so that she could cast ancient Asian eyes on him.

His hormones churned as Avery gazed at his prize—the girl in the red …

No. There was no bikini, either red, white, or blue. There was instead, an expanse of smooth skin flowing all around, covering every last tempestuous square inch of a beautiful woman's body. Light cocoa skin without tan lines dipped inward here, rose outward there, rolling with subtle, gut-wrenching nuance across valleys, crevices, canyons, trim ripples, ridges and other interesting outgrowths, rising finally to gentle mountains topped with chocolate-drop nipples. Coal-black shiny forests accented her landscape—long hair flowed around the face, graceful eyebrows adorned a broad forehead, and a tuft of thick undergrowth mounted the head of the canyon between legs that were stretched out, propped up, and spread slightly toward him in invitation.

She gazed steadily up at him with ancient enemy eyes—with slits—with no trace of expression on her face, no smile, no merest hint of either encouragement or discouragement, nothing but a mask, but her body and her legs invited, exuding moist hormonal urgency.

The blanket. Now he saw it. How could he not have noticed?

The enormous blanket was solid red except for a five-pointed yellow star at the center. The North Vietnamese flag. She luxuriated across the enemy flag!

The yellow star framed her buttocks. The black tuft of undergrowth at the head of her box canyon of legs was centered in the star and pulled on Avery's eyes, sucking them into the center of her sex. The folds of her vulva pouted at him, beckoning, inviting, daring, challenging, while her eyes, cold and distant, invited something else, something unknown and unfathomed.

An AK-47 sounded distantly. Avery looked down at his revolver. He looked down at the tent in the crotch of his flight suit.

•        •        •

The next morning, while Steve enjoyed his second breakfast at Clark, Phil Stanton and Rich Small ejected from their burning F-4. Rich was Karl Jasper's GIB—they were a hawk and a chicken joined unnaturally by Major Scott—and out of desperation, Rich searched out every opportunity to fly with other aircraft commanders. This was such an occasion. Now he was on the ground in North Vietnam, maybe dead, maybe not.

There were chutes and two good beepers on Guard, but they were well inland in Package 1 in a forested area where there had been a lot of traffic. A Jolly Green rescue chopper accompanied by two A-1 Sandys tried to pull them out, but the chopper was hit and staggered out empty-handed.

In the afternoon, while Steve and Frank drank and flirted with two cute airline stewardesses at the O-club bar, a blonde and a brunette, the search resumed. There were two Jolly Greens, three Sandys, and two flights of F-4s from Green Squadron. Major Jasper respectfully declined to join the search. No beepers were heard, and no pilots' voices came up to the would-be rescuers from RT-10 survival radios. Both Steve and Frank came away dry also.

The next morning, while Steve strapped into his office for the return home, the search party went out again with fading hopes. Again, Major Jasper respectfully declined. By noon, the search would be abandoned because the pilots had not been seen or heard from.

•        •        •

On the way back from Clark, Steve looked down into the ice-gray ocean thirty-eight thousand feet below him and spotted a tiny island, probably not more than a few hundred yards in diameter, parked atop a beautiful platform of shallow turquoise waters. What would it be like to punch out and go stay on that island? It was small—no trees, no nubile women to share the time, no fruit or wild pigs to pick or hunt. But still ...

He swam through cold water, through the coral breakwater, through the surf, to the sandy shore, stripped out of his flight suit and underwear, pitched naked onto the beach, and warmed in the sun, watching the contrail of a long-past jet crawl sidewise against the sky.

# 25

Steve and Frank landed and parked. They walked in together, garment bags over their shoulders, helmets dangling by chin straps from their hands. They found Sam outside the front door of the squadron building. He wanted in.

"Hi, Sam. What're you up to?"

Sam wasn't in the mood for socializing. He just wanted to be on the other side of that door. He growled at it, rose up on hind legs, and pawed at it, raking his nails across the five wooden MiGs screwed into the front of the door.

"Jesus Christ, guy. Glad you're so happy to see us. Hold your water. I'll let you in."

As soon as Steve had pulled the door open a crack, Sam slithered in and ran straight through the operations area to the ready room. Steve and Frank followed, laughing, until they saw the crowd of flight suits through the ready room door. Sam had already plunged in and disappeared among the pilots.

"Oops. Squadron briefing," Steve said quietly. They propped their bags against the operations counter and came to the ready room door, but there was standing room only. Pilots overflowed into the doorway, and Steve and Frank had to crane their necks over and around flight-suited bodies to see what was going on.

The room was not exactly full, although it seemed that everybody in the squadron, about seventy pilots, had been summoned. It was not full because they crowded into roughly half the available area, surrounding a large open space at the far end. They drew back into the semicircular periphery of an arena in which a single individual seemed the prime focal point or feature attraction.

Major Karl Jasper stood ramrod straight, with his chin tucked in and his chest thrown out, and around him paced Colonel William D. Sanger. The major was the only man in the room not in a flight suit. He wore Air Force blues, with a light blue shirt and dark blue, almost black tie. His shoes were meticulously spit shined to a mirror finish, and he wore a wheel cap, bill pulled down two finger widths from the bridge of the nose. He looked more like a fourth class cadet at the Air Force Academy than an officer, Steve thought, like someone who should have fuzzy boards on his shoulder with the heraldic wavy line of a grunt cadet instead of the gold oak leaf insignia of a major.

Jasper was a slight man, about five feet six, and the colonel towered over him by a full eight inches. Sanger wore his flight suit liberally open at the neck, chest hair flowing out around the zipper like black jungle undergrowth, and his head was topped by a flight cap that gave him a casual, almost jaunty air. He didn't seem angry, merely thoughtful, if a little sardonic. He paced at leisure in a circle around Jasper, hands clasped lightly behind his back.

He didn't *seem* angry, but if he wasn't, why did Jasper stand up so stiffly?

First Lieutenant Luxington was there, adoration for and fear of the colonel battling for control of his facial muscles. A large bandage covered his forehead. Steve wondered what had happened to him. Sluder was there also, beaming in sadistic pleasure. *The hyenas are out*, Steve thought. They slavered at the mouths because a wildebeest had been cut off from the herd. Never mind that it was their own herd.

The colonel paused behind a hapless Major Jasper, out of his field of vision, leaned forward and whispered quietly into his ear.

"Yes sir," Jasper answered.

"What was that? I had trouble hearing you."

"Yes sir!"

"Woof!" Sam barked. The hyenas laughed.

"Good," the colonel replied. He ambled around to Jasper's front and stood toe-to-toe with the major, gazing peacefully down into his face, a hairy leviathan contemplating a shrimp. He frowned and stepped back.

"May I touch you, mister?"

Jasper hesitated a moment. "Yes, Colonel."

The colonel grasped the knot of Jasper's tie delicately between stubby thumb and forefinger and centered it. He smiled. "That's better."

Sam growled, and the pilots around him snickered. Suddenly, he jumped out into the arena.

"Sam!" Steve called him back, but the collie didn't listen. He circled the major like Sanger, but tenser, crouching low and snarling.

"Woof." *I'm a colonel, too.*

"That's right, Sub-Lieutenant Sam," Sanger beamed, standing back with his hands on his hips. "I'm giving you a temporary field promotion. You're a colonel for the rest of the day, Mister, so I expect you to take names and kick asses." He looked at the pilots. "You assholes better do everything he says."

The pilots guffawed. Even Jasper cracked a smile. Sanger looked at him. "Pretty funny, huh?"

The smile left Jasper's face immediately. "No sir."

Sam circled tightly around Jasper, snuffing at his legs. An image leaped into Steve's mind. He saw Sam raising his leg as if to a fire hydrant.

Apparently, everyone else imagined it too, because they all cackled again, and Steve laughed with them. He caught a glimpse of Avery just a few feet inside the door, almost hysterical, tears running down his face. There was Harry Taint, chuckling, and there was Mike, a little farther in, but Mike was not laughing. He was frowning, and Steve suddenly wondered if he ought to be frowning as well. Despite Sam's comic relief, this was not a pretty sight.

Finally, Sam sat back on his haunches in front of the major to keep a sharp eye on him, to see that the major obeyed the colonel. His tongue lolled out of a panting mouth, and his tail began to beat the floor.

Sanger turned back to the major. "Everybody should be here to see this, hmm?" He was reasoned, soft-spoken.

"Yes sir." Jasper's face was a mask.

"I'll bet Lieutenant Small would like to be here. I'll bet he'd love watching this. A lot. Don'tcha think?"

Silence.

"Or don'tcha?"

"Yes sir."

"Where do we think Lieutenant Small is right now, Major? Hmmm? Even as we speak, he is undoubtedly somewhere in North Vietnam wishing he was right here. He'd give a lot to be here at this very moment to see his good buddy, his aircraft commander, don't you think?"

"Yes sir."

Sam snarled.

"Colonel Sam thought he detected a note of insincerity, lad. We're not insincere, are we?"

"No sir."

"Tell that to the colonel."

The major hesitated.

"Tell Colonel Sam over there that you're not insincere."

The major shifted uncomfortably.

"Go ahead, tell him," Sanger urged gently.

"I am not insincere."

"Sir."

"Sir?"

"You forgot to say 'sir,'" the colonel reminded the major with patient good humor. "I am not insincere, *sir*."

"I am not insincere, sir."

"Woof."

The flying mammals jostled and howled.

"That's better. We'd fly on a mission to rescue Lieutenant Small if we had a second opportunity, wouldn't we?"

"Yes sir."

The colonel paced again. He came up to the major's left side, leaned forward and whispered into his ear, but loudly enough this time that most of the pilots were able to hear it.

"Your chin is beginning to stick out, Major. Pull it in a little. Tha-a-at's right. A little more." Wrinkles deepened at Major Jasper's chin-line as it began to disappear into his neck. "A little more."

Sam snarled.

"Now push out the chest and get the shoulders back and down." The colonel put out an open palm in front of Jasper's chest as a target.

"That's right, touch it, touch it." Sanger smiled. "Now hit it for a hundred, mister."

"Sir?"

"Hit it for a hundred push-ups, Major. You need the exercise, you're a little on the puny side."

Jasper dropped to his knees, extended his hands, and began. It was obvious that it had been a long time since the major had done push-ups.

"Count, lad," the colonel exhorted.

"One sir. Two sir. Three sir."

"One, one, one, major." Sanger clucked. "Those are all terrible, mister. Straighten that back. My grandmother does better push-ups than that."

"One sir. Two sir. Three sir."

"One, one, one ..." It was obvious that the major would have difficulty getting past fifteen of his own push-ups or beyond one of Sanger's. The colonel got down on all fours and slid his hand across the floor under Jasper's chest. He leaned forward, lips inches from his ear. "Hit my hand with that puny chest, Major. One, one, one ..."

Sam jumped up and took a post at the other ear. "Woof, woof, woof ..."

The pilots were in stitches. Tears rolled down their faces. Sluder, nearly doubled over, seemed to be having trouble breathing, and Truhaft was obviously enjoying the entertainment immensely. But Virgil Demopoulis looked a little thoughtful.

Jasper's face turned red, not entirely from exertion.

"That's a lad. You got a good one. Two, two, two ..."

The major stayed stuck on two for a long time, but finally got to three before collapsing on rubbery arms.

"Ohhh," the colonel commiserated. "A little out of shape, aren't we? Well, we'll just work on that a little. No, no, we can't relax just yet. Push up on those arms; let's get into the ready position." Sanger stood and pulled on Jasper's belt, tugging him up until he was supported on locked elbows. "There. Now get that butt down." He placed a combat boot on Jasper's rear to push him down from an almost jackknifed position to a straight position.

The colonel paced again while the other colonel watched and thumped his tail against the floor.

"My, my, my, what are we going to do with you?" Sanger stopped and turned thoughtfully, then paced the other direction. "I could probably get you assigned to Leavenworth for a decade or two, but we'd have to go through a messy court-martial to do that. I'm pretty sure I could bring it off, though. Let's see ..." The colonel scratched his head, stopped, and paced around behind the major. "How about dereliction of duty? And maybe failure to ... no, refusal to follow direct orders. How about insubordination? There are a lot of possibilities. What do you think about those, hmmm?"

The major sagged in the middle. "Yes sir."

"Get your butt up. Your belly's dragging the floor." Sanger inserted the tip of his boot under Jasper's stomach and lifted. "Oh, I know!"

The colonel had an idea. He got down on his hands and knees again, and purred into the major's ear: "How about cowardice? How about yellow-belly? How about running dog? Ooops, sorry, Sam, no offense. That's all good court-martial material isn't it, Major?"

Silence.

"But I'd miss your smiling face around here, and I'd miss the chance to get you into better shape, so maybe we'll hold off on the court-martial for a while, hmm? What do you think?"

Silence.

Softly, the colonel said, "I can't he-e-ear you, Major."

"Yes sir."

"Besides, that's a little dull. It's sort of fun to have you here, Major Jasper, right under my watchful eye. It's a little like roasting a rabbit on a spit, you know." Sanger's voice was syrupy sweet. "I'll be here for a long, long time. I'm not counting counters. Wouldn't you like to do time with me, too, Major Jasper? We'd work well together, lad, don'tcha think?"

"Yes sir!"

"Good! Well, let's just set up a little training program, why don't we?"

And he did. The major would report to the colonel once a week at his trailer for posture inspection. And he would jog seven times around the Air Force compound every day in full uniform. The colonel posted the major for the first jog, called the compound guard post to keep tabs and report the count to him, and then departed himself, leaving behind a gang of very entertained and satisfied pilots.

A few hours later, after sunset, after everyone else had departed, while Steve sat in the squadron building tickety-tapping at McNish's typewriter and Sam slept in the corner of the office, Major Jasper returned to the squadron building huffing and puffing in a sweat-soaked crumbled blue uniform covered with dust, looking like he was about to die.

Sam growled.

"Quiet, Sam." Steve followed the major into the ready room. Jasper must have expected the colonel to be waiting for him, but the colonel wasn't there. The major's eyes were haggard, and his breath came hard.

"Can I help you with anything?" Steve asked sincerely.

The major looked at him through weary, but unflinching, eyes.

"No." He sat for a minute or two while his breathing slowed. Steve watched circumspectly.

"I'm sorry," Steve said.

The major got up without responding and walked slowly out the door.

Steve expected something terrible to happen. He wondered if the major would commit suicide. Or if he would punch out on his next sortie, leaving a surprised GIB behind to bring back the plane. Or simply disappear one day with no trace, AWOL into the jungle or anywhere else far from the confines of Danang.

But the next day, the major was still there. And the day after that, and the day after that, and after a while things seemed to be just the way they had always been, and Steve began to think that maybe Jasper would survive intact after all.

# 26

*Clayton Daily Star*

## Danang attacked again

By Lt. Steven W. Mylder

They have surrounded us. For the first time in this war, the enemy has abandoned guerrilla tactics and amassed to press a swarming, coordinated attack, frightening in its audacity. We've spent the last of our ammunition and cannot hold out much longer. The bug spray is gone, leaving person-to-insect combat with fly swatters as our last recourse. The Viet Cong mosquito is a formidable enemy.

On the other hand, maybe we'll just retreat to our netting-enclosed bunks and leave the field to the mosquitoes. One learns to sleep through their Kamikaze attacks and ignore the dull thuds as they bounce off the netting and spiral down, trailing flames and smoke, to crash into the floor.

Meanwhile, flares light the darkness off the end of the runway like giant street lamps, artillery bangs away, and the more dangerous enemy—the human kind—lurks somewhere in the night. Will they, or won't they?

We had another rocket attack two weeks ago. It was smaller than the first one, and lasted probably less than a minute, although I don't think anybody timed it with a stopwatch. Four or five rounds went off in the space of just a few seconds, there was a long pause, and then another string went off, about the same number. After a few minutes our own artillery began firing.

I was at squadron ops again, the same as for the first attack, and this time I made it to the bunker in under five seconds. If we could get some timing officials here, I think we could set some new records for the 100-yard dash.

Nobody was killed, and injuries were confined to the self-inflicted kind caused by irresistible forces running into immovable objects such as closed doors, and person-to-person collisions between less than calm individuals taking less than leisurely strolls to the bunkers in the darkness. Harry, one of my contemporaries, still walks around with a splint on his pinkie, victim of a hasty dive from his bunk to the concrete floor.

Damage was light. A rocket exploding beside the runway punched shrapnel through one of our F-4s on take off roll. The pilots aborted and stopped in the barrier unharmed, but the plane was not nearly as well off. They got a fuel truck too, about a half-mile from us. It burned like hell for a few minutes and then went out.

Since then, Dong Ha was hit heavily with rockets and artillery from across the DMZ. Another post near the DMZ got worked over, too. Last night we had a fire fight about one and a half miles off the end of runway 17. What's going on? The big push?

Virgil, my friend who was shot down during our first mission, "punched out" for the third time yesterday. He and the aircraft commander were rescued safely, except that the aircraft commander went to the hospital because of a few cracked vertebrae. Virgil, who has become the local expert on flying without an airplane, now casually congratulates his front-seater on each successful landing. He has three more takeoffs than landings, which is quite possible as he has demonstrated, and a good deal more feasible than having more landings than takeoffs.

We had a squadron party recently and did a number of skits. It was a good event, complete with guitar ballads and a Greek Chorus. Though it was intended to be a tragedy, everyone laughed, so I suppose it should have been termed a comedy. Or a farce? We tried.

We're flying nights again. This evening I got the shakes pretty badly before climbing into the plane. I was sure this was *it*! All I could think of was dying young. By the time we got airborne though, I felt better—like being back in the saddle.

As it was, we got about 400-500 rounds of automatic weapons, probably .50 caliber, shot at us. There was a smart gunner down there who knew how to lead. He didn't lead quite enough, but his tracers nipped at our tail.

There's something strange and hypnotizing about watching those tracers come up. Besides the obvious fear factor, it's an unworldly sight. They spurt out of the ground ahead of you like bright-red vomit, then because of your speed they sweep up and around in long, graceful arcs. It's actually pretty in a perverse way. Just out of the muzzle the shells move quite fast, but then they visibly slow down. If the gun is turning, they spray out like water from a hose. They usually pass behind. Occasionally, when the gunner is on target and leading properly, they seem to speed up again and whip by like crazy on all sides. Then you cringe. After they pass, you watch until they intersect the earth from whence they came. You've been shot at.

One mortar round landed in the compound tonight about two hours ago, just behind the non-commissioned officers club. No one was hurt or killed.

It's amazing how the rocket attacks and other strange noises in the night have improved our senses of hearing. (Every misfortune has its compensation.)

To our now hypersensitive ears, the sound of a sneezing gnat becomes a medium-sized rocket landing nearby. A gently slammed door is a nuclear explosion. Should anyone want to become unpopular, he would only have to go outside and set off a string of firecrackers. Meanwhile, a certain amount of dynamite blasting is going on across the runway, and the people who run the show are undoubtedly sadists. I woke up this morning from underneath my bed after a particularly loud blast.

The water is out in our quarters. Laundry goes unwashed and teeth unbrushed. We still have electricity, and I knock on wood.

So curse this stupid war with its mosquitoes and cold water and loud noises, and curse you too, Red Baron.

# 27

He went through the forest canopy. He folded his arms over his face, clamped his legs together, and hit the first layer. It wasn't bad. A mass of green screeched by, vines and tiny branches slithering across the flight suit, and he was through, floating through pencils of sunlight, and then the second layer came up, hit the back of his helmet—*bonk*—and a hundred tiny hammers quickly pounded him all over, leaving bruises but nothing more serious. He worried about the chute snagging, hanging him up a hundred feet above the floor where he'd be an arcade gallery target for the hunters.

It *did* snag momentarily and then came through with a ripping sound, and he ran the gauntlet at the third level of growth, broad clubs battering his arms and legs painfully.

He hit the ground with flexed knees, twisting as he fell forward so that he caught the impact not on his chest and chin but rolled it across his right hip and shoulder. He was on his feet in a second, untangling from the risers, throwing off the helmet, and unbuckling and dumping the harness. It was a textbook landing.

But the chute was caught. He grabbed a handful of nylon cords and strained against them until pain cut through his gloves. He bundled them methodically, wrapped them once around his right hand, clasped his left hand over his right and pulled, straining. He found a small tree trunk to push against with a cocked left leg, but the chute was caught solidly in the third layer. He couldn't budge it, and he lay back, gasping for breath, on the leafy floor.

*Damn! It's an advertisement.*

X marks the spot. They'd know exactly where to start the hunt. They'd know the origin, the root location, the epoch state from which he radiated outward, a rippling circular probability density wave diffusing through the brush, a random walk-leap-jump as fast as his legs would move him.

He checked to make sure he hadn't lost anything vital. The RT-10 radio was securely there in his survival vest, two baby bottles of water zipped into a pocket, emergency rations, and …

The gun! It was still where he'd tucked it into the vest.

He plunged into the undergrowth, legs pumping. It was important to get immediate distance, to get as far away as possible as quickly as possible.

He'd gone only a few hundred yards, wheezing, the air cutting a dry painful channel down his throat, when he saw them ahead in the distance coming right for him.

A rifle exploded and something *WHIcked* by his ear.

He turned. He ran. Another two hundred yards passed beneath his feet. Another river of air seared his throat before he saw the second group across a clearing, coming out of the trees and down the side of a hill. Toward him.

North. They were there. South. All around, hunters came.

He waded through thick undergrowth into a tangle of tree trunks. When he could no longer go upright, he got down and tunneled through the growth. His heart pounded. Sweat poured from his face and flooded his flight suit.

He heard them coming, yelling across the distant damp air to one another in ancient hunting language. They were tribe. They were pack. They were hyenas come to kill a large flying mammal that had lost its wings.

He lay forward against the ground, breath raging through his chest. He rolled over onto his back inside the tiny green cavern. Leaves and twigs matted his body, clinging tenaciously to his soaked flight suit, wet hair, and damp skin. A large stilt-legged insect crawled across his boot.

He pulled the revolver from its holster. He turned it around and around in both hands above his face, fondling it, communing with it. The blue metal was velvet to his touch.

He flipped open the cylinder. Six bullets, he counted: one, two, three, four, five, six. He flipped it closed. He spun the cylinder: *Clickclickclick ... click ... click.*

Use it or not? There was a trade-off here; he had to decide quickly.

Don't use it. Consequence: a brutal, nearly life-snuffing beating with rifle butts and boots and an infinity of time and torture in the Hanoi Hilton. Live. Maybe. Marginally.

Use it. Kill a few of them. Consequence: a brutal, *certainly* life-snuffing beating with rifle butts and boots and a bullet in the brain at the end. Die. Like an animal.

But that assumed capture. He didn't have to be captured. He didn't have to leave it in their hands. Salvation lay like the metal velvet in his own hands. The pills were sugarcoated, sweet. He could save one for himself. It would go down fast, would soothe and numb instantly, and would kill all the sorrows and all the pain. A mocking child's song played in his head.

*No more suffering, no more death,*
*No more smelling Chester's breath!*

Those were the options. He weighed the gun in his right hand, pushed the heel of it into his palm, closed his fist around it, and slid his finger tentatively across the trigger.

He heard a droning above the forest canopy. Not a helicopter but something steadier. He rolled back and forth to see through the leafy cavern. An A-1 Sandy already? One of the angels of the sky come to redeem, to succor the fallen? Was there another option, after all? He'd been down for less than twenty minutes.

Another song played. *The Sandys are coming so soon, so soon, the Sandys are coming so soon.*

He rolled in his bramble bunk, searching the sky. He reached out, way out, fumbling, fumbling, until his hand touched the alarm, stopped the buzzing.

0300.

"Oh, God, oh, God."

He sat up in the bunk panting. Leaves and twigs fell away slowly with the cobwebs of sleep, the Sandys droned gradually into silence, and the gun melted in his right hand until it was an emptiness, a dying memory.

Fifteen minutes later, he ran through darkness, boots clopping across the asphalt road, to catch the van before it pulled away from the front of the DOOM club. Virgil Demopoulis drove.

"Red Squadron lost a plane," Virgil announced mildly.

# 28

*Clayton Daily Star*

## Danang flier shot down, lost

By Lt. Steven W. Mylder

They got one of my friends yesterday. I knew Will at the Academy, and we were at the same base in England.

Will was number Two in a four-ship formation up north, near Hanoi. The aircraft commander was a major whose name I ought to know but don't.

Nobody is sure exactly how it happened, but here's what I've pieced together: the flight spotted several MiGs behind them. They did a fast barrel roll except for Two, who slid way out ahead. Two MiGs slipped in on his tail while he was straight and level, and shot him down. The plane exploded and began a spin. The flight saw only one chute and heard a single beeper. Whoever it was, he landed right in the target area. Almost sure capture.

They never seemed to realize the MiGs were behind them, even though there were several radio calls. Maybe they had a problem with the engines, or controls, or communications. Or maybe it was the inexperience of the aircraft commander, who was on his first mission in that area. Will told some people that he was nervous about this particular flight.

Will wanted very much to come over here. He had a good assignment waiting in the States, and couldn't have had more than a month to go. He said he'd be an astronaut some day. He wanted to walk on Mars.

I heard about it after getting up early this morning to brief for a mission to the same area. We went over to Intelligence to hear reports of intense anti-aircraft defenses. How did it feel when the mission was canceled for weather? I confess. It felt great.

I plan to get back to Clayton alive and in one piece. I'm not particularly interested in dying in this rotten little war. It would be a worthless death.

All death is worthless, but I can't credit the human animal (with the emphasis on animal) with enough maturity, judgment, or wisdom to ever realize this and plan itself around wars. Freedom is an empty word if there's no one alive to believe in it, as is communism, capitalism, socialism—and all the other '-isms' and things that people are forever killing themselves in the cause of. Myself included. Enough philosophy.

Forty-one counters.

•        •        •

Lt. Col. R. W. Gannis
666 TFW Public Information Office

Dear Col. Gannis:

With all due respect, no sir, I am not inclined to change it. Maybe I HAVE gotten a little emotional about this, maybe I WOULD reconsider after sleeping on it a few more nights, but Will Styles was my friend and this was my immediate, honest reaction to his downing, and I feel strongly about it. My hometown friends have a right to know what I think. Changing what I wrote would amount to putting out a bunch of propaganda, and I don't think I want to be a party to it.

Respectfully but adamantly,
Lt. S. W. Mylder

# 29

"What're you talking about, Avery?" Steve was astounded.

"Communism. The theoretical perfection of communism. It's really a great system, you know." Avery winked at him.

Steve turned incredulously to Harry Taint and Mike Ross. "Has something happened? Is this the Avery we know and love?" He recognized the put-on as such, but he wondered at Avery's motivation.

"It's true." Avery grinned an insufferable grin, flaunting an intolerably superior attitude. "Communism is the better system. Capitalism sucks. It's uneven. It doesn't serve society. It meets its own needs and always leads to excesses because capitalists are greedy. Look at the Great Depression! Look at the industrial rapists. Look at the recessions we have every few years—people losing their jobs and homes and going hungry. On the other hand, communism …"

"Full'a shit." Harry mumbled in his soft Southern accent while Avery enthusiastically droned on. A dark cloud shadowed Harry's usually pleasant face. "He's full of shit." He tugged at a bottle of San Miguel and leaned his beanpole frame back in his chair, his eyelids drooping half-mast. Mike leaned sanguinely over the table, toying with the dice cup and not actively participating in the debate.

"… care about society. There's always a safety net, people don't lose their jobs, they don't get hurt."

Communism versus capitalism: best not to be thought a communist in a capitalist fighter squadron. Wasn't done—not copacetic, even in jest. Avery wasn't worried. He didn't care. Avery was pugnacious.

Harry brushed unruly hair back. "Why don't the fucking communists just leave us alone?"

"They're just trying to help. They just want to convert us to a superior system, Harry. It's beautiful if you think about it." Avery's face glowed with an unchecked love for humanity. "The common good, the unity of the people in one living being—the state. *Everybody* should be a communist."

"Ri-i-ght. They want to help us by killing us. And their own people. If the communists are so fucking wonderful, why do they kill so many of their own people? Why did Stalin have purges if the state and the people are one?"

"He wasn't a true communist. He was a deviant, a dictator." Avery smiled condescendingly. "But a true communist state doesn't have Stalins. Everybody works for the common good."

"Su-u-re. *From* each according to his ability, *to* each according to his needs. I went to college, too, smart ass. That's freshman political science, make that high school freshman. But that's not the way the world works. Somebody is always ambitious, wants more than just sharing. They do the work, they get the reward. *That's* the way the world works. *That's* the way it is, and that's the way it ought to be." Harry sneered, threw Avery's name back at him as a taunt. "That's the way it oughten to be, *Aughton!*"

Avery laughed and mocked Harry's accent. "Taint, Harry. Taint. The world ain't like that a-tall."

"'Tis!" Harry simmered with whimsically righteous indignation.

They played a game of Liar's Dice. Steve lost. He ordered a round of beer for breakfast, then settled back in his chair to listen. He ran his finger over his upper lip, the upper lip he hadn't shaved since the first day at Tan Son Nhut. There was the barest hint of fuzz, just discernible to the touch, not visible from more than three feet away. He'd checked it again in the mirror this morning, as he had every morning since arriving in Vietnam, leaning close, nose a looking glass Mount Everest, and sure enough, there it was, still. The faintest hint of delicate blond fuzz. No—fuzz is too definite, too visible. This was less than fuzz. It was sub-fuzz. It was humiliating. No one had even asked if he was growing a mustache. If someone would just *ask*, at least that would be something.

"I'd give my left nut to upgrade to the front seat." Harry swigged from a fresh bottle. Apparently, the communist war was over.

"Not me," Avery responded. "I'm saving *my* nuts. All you gotta do is come back for another hundred." He swaggered even though he was seated. "Only forty-three more counters and bingo ..." He swayed, danced a little imaginary soft shoe, and flourished his hands: "F-r-o-o-ont s-e-e-e-at!"

Harry's left eyebrow lifted. "Yeah, and you're nuts, Avery. You're gonna get killed."

"Nahhh. Only happens to the other guy. I'm gonna fly, fight, fuck, and kill Commies."

"Shit. Who you gonna fuck? The maids?"

"Naa. Hornslug and Catarsis are already dipping *them*. Their peckers will probably fall off."

Mike leaned slyly over the table. "How about your girlfriend, the sunbathing beauty?"

"What about her?" Avery's smirk disappeared, and there was a sudden edge to his manner.

"Well. How you ever going to get into her bikini?"

Steve spoke up. "I heard somebody in Blue Squadron got a tally yesterday."

"Who? Where?" Avery refocused.

"Package 1. Dave Snyder. On the beach near Dong Hoi where you saw her."

"Really? What'd he see?"

"Somebody walking on the beach."

"A woman?"

"Maybe. Maybe not. He couldn't tell. They were too high. They went down and flew along the beach, and whoever it was was gone."

"He couldn't see any details? Anything red?"

"Aww, com'on, Ave. She's probably got a bikini for every day of the week. She was wearing her black bikini that day."

Mike nodded. "Picture that. Uummmm!" They all drooled while a black cloud formed over Avery's head, sheet lightning flashing ominously.

"She's all yours, Ave." Mike laughed. "I'm married, anyhow. But what are you going to do about her? I mean, it's hopeless. You'll never meet her. The best you can ever hope for is to see her once in a while from the air. Unless you punch out and go down there to talk communism with her."

"Yeah," Harry drawled. "That'll get her nice and hot. Tell her how good communism is, and she'll wrap her legs around you and fuck your brains out."

Avery ignored the jibes and shook his head, puzzled. "I just ... she ... I just don't want anything to happen to her. Be careful around there, will you?" He admonished them earnestly, sincerely. It was the first supplication of any kind that Steve had seen from Avery. "Don't hurt her."

They played another round of Liar's Dice. Steve lost. He ordered another round of beer.

Harry was getting "short." Eighty-six counters, only fourteen to go. Major Scott had begun working him into some of the easier missions, flying him with new ACs to break them in. He'd just gotten his next assignment. In a few more months he would become an instructor pilot at Williams Air Force Base.

"Whoa! Willy, hunh?" Avery's zeal returned. "That's where I went for pilot training."

"But hell, that's more dangerous than Vietnam," Steve added. "Here they try to kill you from the ground. In pilot training, the student tries to kill you from the other seat."

Harry yawned, rubbed his eyes. "My AC tries to kill me from the other seat sometimes. Tries to kill us both. He rolled in three times on the same gunner in Tallyho yesterday. Tracers were going by everywhere. This was daytime, but I could see every one of the suckers—*zip, zip, zip*—they were so close, and my zip-head AC, he's a new major from Wing, kept going for more. He *likes* it, he gets that adrenaline pumping, and he's wired. He's ready to kill …" Harry raked a laconic eye over the other pilots. "*Me!*"

"But you said you wanted the front seat, Harry."

"I do, I do. So I can be careful. So I can fly, fight, kill Commies, and not kill myself. I can take pilot training. At least I'm in control. If the student gives me trouble, I rap him with seven gs. Maybe after three years of teaching dumbshits, I'll get another fighter, maybe a Thud. Anything with a single seat. Then I do what I fucking please."

"How about a bomber? Or a cargo plane or a tanker? How about a B-52 or a KC-135?"

"You gotta be shittin' me. I'm not a truck driver."

They played another round of Liar's Dice. Steve lost. He was out of cash. He borrowed $2 from Mike and ordered another round of beer.

They got onto the perennial subject of what to do when they grew up. Steve didn't want to talk about it, but it came around to him finally. They pestered him so much that he had to say something just to get their attention away from him. He wanted to be alone, but he didn't want to be alone; he wanted the comfort of friends, but he didn't want to talk, not this morning. It was beginning to eat on him. Vietnam and Danang and Package 6 and Styles getting shot down and all the things he didn't want to think about that he was thinking about, and they were eating on him.

"I want to be a test pilot," he said to get them off, to pass the conversational baton.

"How about a writer?" Mike asked. He explained to the others, "He's writing articles for his newspaper back home. They're pretty good. Maybe you could be a war correspondent, Steve. Then you could come back for three or four more tours."

"Yeah, Stevie boy, why don't you write about us?" Avery playfully punched him on the arm.

Steve shook his head, but he didn't shake it hard enough because even as it shook, a seed connected to one of his gray cells and anchored itself with a tiny root. Meanwhile, he blew some obfuscating smoke. "I want to go to test pilot school at Edwards."

"Sure. Good luck." There was an expectant beat of about three seconds while they waited for him to elaborate, but he didn't, and the conversational baton was passed.

# 30

Steve checked the board. Seventy-eight missions, but only fifty-three counted. His next flight was a Package 1. Mike Ross was in the other airplane.

•       •       •

*Clayton Daily Star*

## Lt. Mylder's roommate downed

### By Lt. Steven W. Mylder

I'll write a little about Mike now. Mike was my roommate. What happened today was incredible. It wasn't pleasant.

We were in a two-ship mission on a daytime counter, going across the DMZ to an area about 150 miles north of Danang. Mike was in the lead aircraft and I was in wing. We took off from Danang, flew out over the Gulf, then turned northwest paralleling the shoreline from about 10 miles out. Near Dong Hoi we turned west to "coast in."

We loosened formation and started jinking coming over the beach at about 10,000 feet. It was a good thing, too, because they were busy down there. The flak started coming up, and it was close. We got several bursts all around, then Lead called that he was hit.

It was lucky that it happened so soon. Both of us made a 180 and were back out over the Gulf in a minute or two heading for home. We rejoined on lead and looked him over top, bottom, and sides.

Not too bad—a few holes here and there but nothing major. The problem was that they had low hydraulic pressure and the flight controls were jerky. The plane bobbed up and down and side to side. They might not be able to land, but at least they could get back to base before bailing out. We moved away from Lead, about 50 yards off his left side just to be safe.

It turned out that this was a very good move. I put my head down in the cockpit a moment, and when I looked up, Lead had rolled up onto his left wing in nearly 90 degrees of bank and was coming right at us!

We popped down so hard that cockpit debris rained upward onto the canopy, and Lead came screaming overhead, continuing the roll until the plane was inverted, nose dropping down to about a 60-degree dive. One of the canopies flew off, and an ejection seat came out right behind it and started tumbling. A few seconds later the other seat catapulted out.

The plane continued almost straight down, probably supersonic after a few seconds, and exploded into the sea. We started a left descending spiral around the two chutes, following them down to the water.

Somewhere in the ejection sequence, Mike got snagged momentarily. He came loose from the seat, but in the process something happened. Nobody knows for sure what it was. Maybe he collided with the seat. Maybe he got tangled and jerked around by his parachute lines. Whatever it was, it was pretty violent because it broke his right arm in three places. Mangled!

As Mike descended in agony toward the water, 10 miles from shore and 100 from home, he looked down for the life raft that should have been swinging below him on a line. It wasn't there. He looked above him and saw his wingman circling, unable to help him in the slightest degree.

With his right hand dangling uselessly by his side, Mike used his left to pull the lanyard that should have inflated his life preserver. Nothing happened. He fumbled for the tube to inflate the preserver with his mouth, but he was either unable to find it, or having found it, couldn't get air into it.

He hit the water and went under. No life raft and no preserver. He struggled back to the surface against the 30 pounds of equipment he wore, stroking with his one good arm and kicking with his combat boots. As he got to the surface, his parachute settled into the water and the lines came down on top of him, tangling and trying to drag him under again. A thousand feet above, Wing circled, having no idea of the terminal survival struggle going on below.

Mike wanted very much to live. He had a wife in the States and a three-year-old daughter. He'd been here for six months of those three years. He might have thought about them as he flailed with his left arm, barely able to keep his mouth above the water. Mike was strong. He'd played football in college and was very good at it, an All American I think, but that kind of strength only goes so far against the forces trying to drag him down.

One more unusual thing happened, the only one that really counts in the end. The thing that happened, the thing that keeps this from being a sad story is that, against all odds—out of a thousand square miles of empty sea, in a deus ex machina totally unacceptable in literature—Mike didn't miss by far landing right on the deck of an American warship steaming below him.

The ship had been damn near hit by his airplane as it crashed into the sea, and now he landed less than a quarter of a mile from it, as did the aircraft commander in another direction. The ship had boats down and out to both of them in about five minutes.

Mike is no longer my roommate. He's in the hospital, going home tomorrow for medical treatment. He's not feeling particularly good, but he's feeling a hell of a lot better than dead, and for that I'm glad. I'm not sure he wanted to come here in the first place, but he came, and now his war is over, and he's going back. I don't think he'll need to worry about returning to Danang to finish his tour.

Mike's a strong guy—he's a smart, tough, gentle, stubborn, kind, and very likable fellow, and he'll heal quickly. He says he's going to be a senator when he grows up. I believe he will.

This story doesn't have a moral. It's just a story. It ended all right, and I'm glad I'm telling it.

•       •       •

"I don't have a roommate anymore, Avery."
"Neither do I."
"Want to move in?"
"Sure, Liberal."

# 31

*Clayton Daily Star*

## Danang hit again!

By Lt. Steven W. Mylder

Attack number three.

I had gone to bed at midnight. Avery, my new roommate, shook me awake 20 minutes later. "Rocket attack," he said quietly. I didn't believe him until there was a muffled explosion, at which moment I beat him under the bunk.

Silence for a few minutes. We decided to investigate, and had just sneaked out of the door and down the hall when another explosion sent us scurrying back. I dove under the table. Avery took the bed. A siren began. For the next 10 minutes, the rockets rained down near and far, several close enough to shake our building. This was a bad one!

Then there was a lull. It got longer and longer until finally we realized it was over. We crept out of our rooms one or two at a time until there were fifteen or twenty pilots milling in the hallway who had just had the b'Jesus scared out of them. We ventured out onto the second-story landing and stairway on the west end of the BOQ to survey the damage. It was like a small grandstand packed with sports fans except that nobody cheered. The home team was losing.

The entire southern half of the base seemed to be on fire, and to the west, across the runway, not quite a mile away, the Marine ammo dump blazed brightly, sending up belching secondary explosions every few seconds as something new—a bomb or a napalm tank—cooked off. Good Lord, the home team was losing badly!

We watched the south end burn. Smoke filled the air and obliterated the sky, filtering the light from the fires through an eerie haze. Several large secondary explosions went off, reflecting off the smoke—like lightning from thunderheads, and then after a few minutes, the Marine ammo dump got our attention again. It blew up.

I've never seen anything like this. Everything in the dump went off at once like a nuclear chain reaction. Standing silently in our grandstand, as if from another world, we watched an awesome fireball grow and grow and grow out of the pit of the dump, above the earth embankments surrounding it, high into the sky until we had to crane our necks back to see the top of it. Brilliant red light bathed the landscape. The fireball alone must have gone a thousand feet high, and the mushrooming cloud went much higher. The word "mushrooming" is no misnomer. It looked exactly like a nuclear explosion.

There was no sound yet. It had a distance to travel. All was silence except for a few quiet "Je-sus Christ"s and "Ohmygawd"s swallowed by the stillness of the night. A few empty moments ticked by until suddenly everyone realized what was about to happen. I flattened myself against the wall of the BOQ just before the concussion hit. The building shimmied and trembled against my back like a boat rocking on the ocean.

The door at the landing faced the dump, and the hallway behind it ran directly toward the explosion like the long bore of an oversize rifle barrel. The shock wave went straight into the open door. It traveled down that long hallway like a bullet going the wrong way and branched off left and right into individual rooms, blowing out the boarded up windows, shattering lights, and causing general mayhem everywhere—this from an explosion nearly a mile away.

We ran inside, all of us sports fans, just before debris began raining onto the roof. Our room was a mess. Glass covered the floor. Dust filled the air.

In the morning, Avery and I went down to the south ramp. General mayhem everywhere. In the revetments F-4s had been pitched over onto their backs and blown to bits by their own bombs. Part of one, a gear assembly, was lodged in the wall of a building 200 yards away.

The six-foot-thick reinforced concrete revetment walls were blown completely in two in places, and massive sand-filled steel walls had been blown over. Cannon shells in the gun pods mounted on the planes had gone off like popcorn, and 20 millimeter empty casings littered the ground. There were some sandbag bunkers nearby with bad hits on them. Pock marks and brutal gashes and holes were everywhere in the tarmac.

Two fire trucks stood before two completely destroyed revetments. Or rather, their gutted frameworks slouched there. Five firefighters had rolled up in their trucks and begun spraying the planes from 20 feet away when the bombs exploded. All five died. A few tiny flames still flickered in the interior of the charred remains of one of the trucks.

Three two-story barracks were completely destroyed—burned to the ground—and the top half of another was gone. Left standing in the smoldering ruins were neat rows of charred and partially melted metal lockers, like gnarled soldiers at parade.

How many were killed? Besides the firefighters, only three more. Incredible.

Debris from the explosions litters the whole base. Cleanup crews are already at work. All of Blue Squadron's F-4s were damaged or destroyed, but ours were unscathed since we're all parked on the north ramp.

How long until the next one?

Sixty-four counters.

# 32

Steve took a latrine break at the DOOM club. While he was there, Avery came in, and they stood side by side whizzing into the urinals, gazing blankly at the wall, alternating small grunts of relief. Avery laughed and backed off a few feet, keeping the stream centered. "Wanna have a pissing contest?"

"Avery, I'm warning you, if you splatter me …"

Avery moved back in. He smiled a friendly smile. "Not very talkative today."

"Just thinking."

Avery hummed a little tune, then added, "Loosen up, Mylder. You're thinking too much. I can see the wheels goin' 'round in your head."

"Yeah."

"We oughtta go on R & R together, you and me."

"Yeah."

"Find some girls and get laid."

"Hmmm."

"Say, have you ever had two girls at once?"

"Hmm, no." Steve felt lucky to have occasionally had one girl at once.

"Well, you ought to try it. In fact, three at a time is even better. It needs a little juggling, though."

Steve had to laugh.

"We could go to Bangkok. Or Hong Kong. Or Tokyo, or just about anywhere. It's easy to get laid anywhere, so you just want to pick a place where they're unusual or exotic. Gourmet screwing, y'know."

"Hmm, yeah. Well, how about your girlfriend up the coast? Have you given up on her?"

Avery was suddenly thoughtful.

They rejoined Harry Taint at their table in the bar, and the conversation turned to dogfighting.

"Gawddamn missiles ain't worth a shit," Harry said. "Wish we had guns. The gawddamn MiGs *know* we can't shoot them down, they just screw around, they don't give a shit if we get in close because they know the missiles won't work there. We ought to carry gun pods instead of that worthless gawddamn tank."

Steve couldn't get interested. He floated about eight feet above the table and the conversation, locked into his own internal dialog: to fly or not to fly, to fight or not to fight, to be or not ...

From the second table away, he heard the names "Sam" and "Charley" drift over the poker-playing banter, but he hardly bothered to prick his ears any more when he heard those names, they were two dogs, or a missile and an enemy, or two guys, but he didn't care. Right now he was thinking gloom and doom, and nothing else mattered.

Harry and Avery went on about tanks and guns. Avery's reply was like cold water, patient and condescending. "Don't have the gas, Harry. If we mount the centerline gun instead of the six-hundred-gallon tank, we don't have enough gas to get back."

"Shit, we don't need the tank. It adds so much drag it only extends the range a couple hundred miles anyhow."

"So then what? The gun adds drag, too. We mount it instead of the tank, and we run out of gas a couple hundred miles earlier."

There was a verbal explosion two tables away.

"Put your fucking money where your fucking mouth is, or shut up!"

It was Sluder, and his face had gone purple with rage. The argument was apparently with one of his Red Squadron compatriots, Ras Farthington, because Ras stood glaring down at Sluder while Sluder glared back up. He rose heavily, menacingly to his own feet, fists clinched at his side, and dwarfed the smaller man. The bar came to a screeching halt for a moment while all ears cocked in gleeful anticipation of some spontaneous entertainment.

It was not to be. Cal Smythe at the table cracked a joke; Ras laughed, pulled his wallet from his flight suit breast pocket, plopped it onto the middle of the table, and sat down again. "There's *my* money, Heck, where's *yours?*"

The spell was broken. Sluder still glared, but nothing would come of it. He sat slowly, heavily down again, and all eyes and ears swiveled gradually back to their own orbs of interest while the background noise of voices and laughter and clanking glasses and rolling dice and scraping chairs and clattering beer cans slowly built up from zero again.

Avery and Harry talked guns and dogfights. Steve worried about his four-ship to Package 6 in a few hours. He really ought to get to bed. He'd be seriously hurting in the morning.

What if he refused to fly? Or more gently, what if he argued Major Scott into taking him off that flight? Think of an excuse, any excuse—he was sick; he'd been on too many Package 6s lately; it wasn't fair; he'd just like to fly some non-counters for a while.

Why did he need counters anyhow? Why did he put his life on the line for a war he didn't love? Let the pilots who begged for counters take his place. There were plenty who'd jump for the opportunity. Yes! He could make that argument and get away with it. If Jasper could, he could, too.

But what a price! Jasper had paid a tub of blood in humiliation in front of the whole squadron.

But maybe it wasn't that bad. Steve had gone through verbal abuse in spades at the Academy. The only difference was that he hadn't been singled out. All the fourth class dumbsquats had been equally chewed on, day after day, month after month, for a year. It was tough, but at least they hadn't individually been pariahs like Jasper.

Yet Jasper survived well enough. Steve had seen him yesterday jogging around the compound in his uniform blues. It was three weeks now since the chewing out by Sanger, and the little guy was actually getting into shape, not huffing and puffing any more. And he seemed almost contented. The guard at the front gate had saluted him as he jogged by, and he'd snapped a salute back in mid-stride. He could do this. He could do it for another year or two and survive.

Steve headed for the latrine, but when he saw Sluder moving toward the same destination, he turned off and walked out of the bar instead. He pushed through the door to the outside, and the heavy night air deposited an immediate layer of moisture on cool skin. He shook his head to clear his brain. He paced out to the sidewalk and back again and then slipped around the corner of the club into the dark area shaded from the street lamp.

Steve unzipped his flight suit. While he steamed the ground in front of him, he looked up at the stars.

*Will Styles wanted to go out there. He wanted to walk on Mars.*

Will Styles had been a counter.

*A counter is someone who deserves respect.*

Major Jasper wasn't a counter. He lived his life by inches and died by inches.

*A counter is something you want and you fear. A counter is when you put something on the line, your life or career or reputation. You play the game of terrible consequence versus marvelous payoff. You skirt the edge of disaster, flirt with it, blow kisses and pump your adrenaline, exuberantly alive and terrified at the same time.*

Jasper chose the safe, the sure. Maybe Sanger thought he roasted Jasper on a spit, but Jasper didn't see it that way. He wasn't particularly upset. He just went on and on, dying by inches, never all at once.

*A counter. You have to decide. Stand still or go forward!*

•            •            •

They *still* talked about guns and dogs when Steve returned to the table. Avery had warmed to the possibility of carrying the Gatling gun pods. "We could get some of the range back by dropping the wing tanks as soon as they're empty. They're worthless after that anyhow. That leaves us clean except for the gun."

"And the missiles," Harry added. "We could dump those, too, and get a little more. The Sparrows for sure."

They smiled and nodded. There were no friends of missiles at this table.

"Ahhh! They'd never let us drop the tanks. They probably cost three fucking thousand dollars apiece." Harry was indignantly sarcastic in his soft-spoken way. "Mister Secretary of Defense McNamara would shit—*all* the bean-counters would shit. 'Can't waste the money.' A three-million-dollar plane, and probably more than that on pilot training and experience, but they're not going to dump a three-thousand-dollar tank to save a pilot's ass."

"And that probably still wouldn't do the trick." Avery went negative again.

They argued back and forth, Harry and Avery, pro and con, con and pro, but Steve mostly stayed out of it, lost in his own thoughts.

"The tankers!" Avery had a revelation. "Get refueling after the mission."

"We already do, oh Wise One."

"Yeah, but only as an emergency. Sometimes we don't even need them. We get home without refueling. I'm saying put the tankers right up there on the border waiting for us, instead of the middle of Laos. Every time! Drop us off at the border. Pick us up right there at the border."

"They wouldn't take the risk. KC-135s are even more expensive than wing tanks."

"That'll do it." Avery's face glowed. "That'll get us in there with guns. Then we can have a turkey shoot."

"Right." Harry was unimpressed. "Why don't you tell that to Sanger next time you fly with him. He's sure to go along."

"I will." The answer was smug.

"Su-u-ure! Scratch one problem. Next problem."

•          •          •

Wind sang through the brace wires between the wings of the Sopwith Camel. Steve looked down on a tiny Fokker at two o'clock below him.

*He knows I'm back here. What do I do? If I roll right and go in on him, he counters hard left, and maybe I can't stay with him. But if I roll left? If I turn away and keep going …*

Steve raised his gloved left hand into the slipstream and rested it on the grip of the twin Vickers machine guns.

*A counter or not a counter. You have to decide.*

# 33

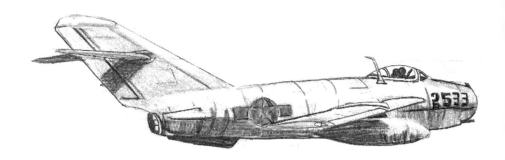

Colonel William D. Sanger had already thought about the gun pod problem, or maybe his omnivorous ears had picked up the conversation at the DOOM club. Whichever the case, about six in the morning of the second day after the gun conversation, Avery Aughton strapped himself into the seat behind Pat Truhaft. They were Buckshot Lead ("... flight of four, number one for runway three-five left") on a MIGCAP mission. Hanging beneath the white belly of the F-4 was a large ugly gun pod, a four-thousand-round-per-minute 20 millimeter Gatling cannon mounted on the centerline station. Besides the gun, there were two wing tanks. And that was all.

A few revetments away, Steve and Frank strapped themselves into Buckshot Three. Beneath their plane was the same ugly baggage as Lead's.

On their walkarounds, all the pilots had tucked several chaff packs, like slender boxes of Christmas tinsel, into the red painted interior of the partially open speed brake wells beneath each wing. When the engines began their deep-throated whine, a fresh surge of hydraulic fluid sucked the large speed brake slabs up flush with the under surface of the wing, trapping the cardboard packs inside. It was an odd way to store and dispense the radar-deceiving clouds of tinsel, but the F-4 had no approved method, so this was the pilots' practical work-around.

Buckshot taxied. Lead and Three had "the gun." That was daring. But Two and Four had a full complement of missiles and no gun. With true military conservatism, Sanger had hedged his bet.

Steve had decided, just like Sanger had. Or had he? Maybe he'd hedged his bet, just like Sanger. *One more counter. Just one more.*

Four Phantoms roared off the runway. Buckshot Five, engine howling, leaped into the air behind them but went only a foot or two before coming down again, and had to abort down the runway, paw brake pads sizzling from the friction.

On the way to the tankers, the four planes flew in tight fingertip formation, Two on the right of Lead, Three and Four on the left. Steve jockeyed the F-4, still marveling at its power after an intimate relationship of more than a year and a half. A tap, a tweak of the throttles, walking them up or back a quarter of an inch, or fingertip control at the stick brought instant response. It was a good plane. A *damn* good plane.

The tanker dropped them off right at the border and promised to pick them up at the same place. Buckshot turned due east toward Hanoi and spread out in combat formation, fifteen hundred feet of air between each of them. After a while, all the wing tanks had emptied and were jettisoned en masse. Now, except for the guns and missiles, they were clean machines. As Buckshot Flight made a shallow turn at fifteen thousand feet over a verdant jungle on a painfully clear blue morning bursting with sunshine, Steve looked back and saw the silver tanks tumbling far below, eight tiny fluttering things, a diminishing swarm of twinkling sun motes. Karst formations dotted the jungle, sharp jagged geological skyscrapers thrusting violently hundreds of feet above otherwise smooth, rolling land.

Buckshot descended to ten thousand feet and wheeled and circled thirty miles north of Hanoi while four flights of Thuds dropped sixteen loads of bombs on the Thai Nguyen Steel Works thirty miles farther north. Buckshot watched orange explosions and quick black clouds on the ground and smaller black puffs among the Thuds as they darted around the target. Buckshot kept a wary eye on Phuc Yen airfield five miles away, from whence cometh MiGs, and an even warier eye toward Kep airfield forty miles farther east, from whence cometh even more MiGs. And yet—like the never-boiling watched pot—the MiGs came not. Or at least not from Kep or Phuc Yen, because Buckshot was looking in the wrong direction.

It was incredibly quiet and easy. There was no flak for Buckshot. They had their own radio channel and heard only occasional interruptions from Guard. Buckshot Two picked up a Fansong Radar signal on its newly installed warning gear, but no missile could be seen. As a cautionary measure, Truhaft called for chaff. Buttons on throttles clicked, hydraulic pumps churned, metal slabs cracked momentarily into the airstream below the wings, and wind ripped into the speed brake wells tearing out clouds of Christmas tinsel. Peace. Peace on Earth.

Avery saw them first—a swarm of angry black hornets coming from above, out of the sun.

"BUCKSHOT, BANDITS AT FIVE HIGH. BANDITS AT FIVE!"

Buckshot was lucky to see them. Most kills happen because the pilot doesn't know what's coming. Buckshot was nearly blindsided.

There were six planes spread loosely a few thousand feet higher and maybe two miles back. They could have been any model of MiG: 17, 19, or 21. It was impossible to tell at this aspect angle against the glare of the sun. Whatever they were, they were in good position except that they'd rather have been at six o'clock on Buckshot, and the crossing angle was a little high.

Burners on! The Phantoms were relatively clean, had kept speed up while cruising, and they popped into five gs immediately. Steve grunted to keep from passing out while they made a hard climbing turn to the right. Now Buckshot split into two elements just as planned. Four slid behind Three, Two behind Lead.

The MiGs banked right to stay inside Buckshot's turn and fired their cannons, pulling lead on the Phantoms against g-forces which made the tracers fall rapidly away from their line-of-sight aim. Buckshot's hard turn made the angle too large, and the closure rate too high for a good shot. Two MiGs flashed over Steve's head less than fifty yards away—*zip-zip*—racking up in a hard turn. MiG-17s!

He saw both pilots! Clearly. They wore black-ridged leather helmets, the old style from flying days long past, and black flight suits. A flamboyant white cravat was tucked into the collar of each pilot. They looked down at him. For an instant, *people* were involved in this. For an instant, scarves flew in the wind, and Snoopy and the Red Baron entwined their wakes in mortal personal combat. And then—quickly—they were black dots in the sky again.

It would have been natural for the Phantoms to reverse turn to the left into the MiGs and the MiGs to continue their right turn into the Phantoms. They would have crossed, reversing again and again like two threads intertwining, until one or the other, most likely the MiGs, got the advantage and came out on the tail. Instead, both elements of Buckshot pulled into the vertical dimension, going up instead of around, going over the top in an exaggerated left barrel roll while the MiGs turned right. It was a beautiful move, Steve thought from a rational, nonparticipating corner of his mind—beautiful because it did so many things at once. It made them harder to see by bringing them behind the MiGs' tails (now *they* were lost in the glare of the sun) instead of out to their three o'clock. It traded off speed for altitude while keeping the total energy up so that they could play the turn at the top for position, and it used gravity to help them pull inverted tightly through the top of the roll loop so that as they came out the bottom, it brought them around on two MiGs from behind and above. Lead and Two rolled out on two others, splitting off to the left. In one slick trick, Buckshot had gone from inferior to superior position.

The MiGs didn't mind. After all, these were Phantoms. These were the planes that had no guns, the gang with the radar missiles that wouldn't hit the ground if they aimed for it, the gang that couldn't shoot straight. The MiGs turned this way and that, but they weren't really worried; they'd have their chance shortly. They had superior turn capability. When it came to tail chasing, they were kings. The Phantoms had other advantages, but they had no teeth in a tight dogfight.

"HOT DAMN!" Steve heard himself yelling to Frank. "LET'S GET THE BASTARDS!" The small rational corner observed, *They're people,* and was ignored.

They went for the hindmost of the two, the calf that had strayed from the herd. They were practically in close trail, less than a hundred yards behind an airplane that rolled right, rolled left, bounced through jetwash turbulence, loaded up gs, unloaded gs, and all the while Steve saw the details of the plane, the rivets in the wings, the yellow star in a red circle with yellow bars on the side, the ailerons flapping up and down, the rudder whipping nervously left and right and left and ...

Buckshot Three stuttered and vibrated. The cosmic fart!

It was only a two-second burst, but at four thousand rounds per minute, 133 1/3 cannon shells, more or less, ripped from the spinning barrel of the Vulcan Gatling and spanned the distance between the two planes. Of these, 131 1/3 missed. Completely! Of the remaining two shells, one passed harmlessly through the horizontal stabilizer and fell nine thousand feet to the ground. The remaining one shell flew into the tailpipe of the MiG. There it passed through the turbine wheel, clipping off three blades near the axle, hit the outer hull, and exploded a thousandth of a second late, leaving a jagged, but nonvital hole in the skin of the plane. The three turbine blades came out, tearing another hole. The turbine wheel, grossly unbalanced now, wobbled once in its mad spin, wobbled twice, then came unhinged and tore itself apart in fifty different directions, sawing off the entire tail section of the plane from the inside.

The pieces nearly hit Buckshot Three. A fragment of a blade *did* hit the front of the canopy, leaving a deep gouge three feet in front of Frank Bender's head, making him blink violently. The rest passed to all sides. Red flame and black smoke erupted from the truncated tail of the MiG as the plane pitched up uncontrollably. Smoke washed past their cockpit. The Phantom inhaled it, sucked it through its intakes and hungry engines, and blasted it out the ass as carbon monoxide.

The MiG's canopy came off.

"HOT DAMN. HOT DAMN. WE GOT HIM. WE GOT HIM." Frank and Steve alternated exultations over the radio. "THREE GOT ONE. THREE GOT ONE. THREE GOT ONE!"

The pilot came out riding a pitching, bucking seat. The wind tore off his headpiece, ripped the cravat from beneath his flight suit, and now his black hair shone in the sun, his white scarf whipped in the wind. He whisked past their canopy, clearing it by less than fifty feet, and his junked plane followed.

"HE'S ON YOUR TAIL, THREE, BREAK RIGHT, BREAK RIGHT!"

"Unnhhhhh." The gs slapped in again just as Steve saw tracers streak by. He braced for impacts that never came. He grabbed the handholds on the canopy bow, adrenaline pumping, and hauled himself around against the gs to see out behind. The MiG was there inside their turn, but Four was back there, too, behind him, trying to move inside.

Four had missiles. Only missiles. Four selected a Sidewinder. It growled an electronic growl through the headset, telling the pilot "Yes, I have an infrared target, launch me, *launch me!*" Never mind that dogs growl and not snakes. The missile bared its teeth and strained against the leash to get at a warm-blooded target.

But for whom did the missile growl? Which target? Phantom or MiG? They were both in the field of view. If Four weren't careful, he'd send it right up Three's ass—not good form.

"BREAK LEFT, THREE. BREAK LEFT, BREAK LEFT."

The plane whipped beneath Steve, almost cracking vertebrae in his neck as his helmet was snapped to the side and hit the canopy.

"SONOFABITCH, SONOFABITCH, WE GOT HIM, WE GOT THE BASTARD. WE GOT HIM, SONOFABITCH!"

The voice was unmistakably Avery's. Three miles away, the score had jumped to two-zip.

As Three hauled left, the MiG was left hanging by himself momentarily in empty blue sky. The Sidewinder growled, and now it was clear for whom the growl tolled. The missile leapt off the plane and charged.

*Too close, we're too goddamn close*, Four realized. It missed! Four hauled back on the throttles, cracked the speed brakes down for a second to get more spacing while he selected the other Sidewinder.

This one didn't growl at all. Nothing came through the headset. A dud! A goddamned pussycat. Meanwhile, the MiG had seen the missile come by and decided he'd had enough. He rolled inverted and split-s'd toward the ground. Four started to follow—he could use the Sparrows, but he thought better of it. *We'd never get a radar lock. He'd be lost in the ground clutter.*

"HOT DAMN, WE DID IT AGAIN, WE DID IT AGAIN!"

It was Avery. Apparently the score was three-zip.

"TWO IS NO SHIT BINGO."

The MiGs were running. It was time to go home.

•          •          •

They entered the traffic pattern in four-ship echelon left.

Aileron rolls on initial were strictly forbidden. The regulations were very clear on this: No aerobatics of any kind. Colonel Sanger had reiterated this and drawn his line across the sand. Just two weeks earlier, a pilot had disregarded this dictum, metaphorically pissing in the sand by rolling his airplane fifteen hundred feet above the runway before pitching out to the downwind leg.

Sanger had met him at the airplane and debriefed him personally. The hapless pilot was taken off flying status. An entry was made in his permanent record. His photograph took up semi-permanent residence in the Anus Award display, framed between the laurels of a toilet seat. He would receive a bad officer evaluation rating in a few months, and most likely his Air Force career was effectively over.

"Want the roll?" Frank asked.

"Oh, yes, yes! Goddamn yes, thank you, sir, I've got it." Steve rattled the stick.

They entered in finger-tight formation, clearances of inches, proud, precise, full of themselves—the wolf pack—gunfighters back from the kill. Eyes on the ground turned upward, not knowing why but understanding somehow that this formation was different, was special, was the reason the Air Force existed.

Buckshot Lead rolled right, 360 degrees in place, while the remaining three planes maintained perfect unwavering position. Without pausing, the plane continued 60 degrees farther right, snapping precisely into a two-g pitchout.

It was an amazingly dangerous and stupid maneuver.

Four seconds later, Two repeated the ritual, then Three, then Four, until they were all in a line on the downwind, smoking proud black Phantom smoke behind them, landing gear hanging like dangerous talons beneath feather white bellies. Lead began the turn to final.

Sanger met them as they pulled into the chocks and shut down: one, two, three, four. Sanger smiled. He always smiled. But he also carried a bottle of champagne.

# 34

Sanger was ebullient. He hugged Truhaft and Avery. *Hugged* them, practically lifting them from the ground in a bear embrace. Amazing. Steve wouldn't have been surprised if the colonel had kissed them each on both cheeks. He shook hands warmly with all the rest of the crew members. This was only the third time Steve had spoken to the colonel.

A table sat on the tarmac almost under the black bulbous nose of Buckshot Lead. A lace cloth covered it, topped by nine fancy glasses. Sanger worked the cork on the champagne bottle, angling it toward the plane. *Pop.* The cork flew fifteen feet through the air, bounced off the inside of the open canopy and rebounded cleanly into the front cockpit. The pilots cheered. Sanger poured.

He raised his glass.

"I'm very, very proud of you today." He sniffed. Would a tear roll down his cheek?

He glared. "And I'm pissed. Anybody who does a roll in my traffic pattern better damn well have a MiG to back it up. You did four rolls, but you only got three MiGs. You owe me another MiG, and you damn well better get it soon."

It did—yes—a tear rolled down his cheek. On the paralyzed side.

"You people gave a new name to the Wing today. Say good-bye to the old Phighting Phantoms." He pointed toward the placard hanging along the side of the Wing Command Post a hundred yards away. "Tomorrow that goes away, and a new name goes up there. Lift your glasses to yourselves. Here's to the Gunfighters!"

They cheered. They laughed. They buzzed among themselves and slapped one another on the back.

"Champagne is too dainty for men like you. It's all right for ceremony, which is clearly called for this morning. It's symbolic. But I know that you men are thirsting for substance, so we brought a little of that along, too."

Major Scott and Lieutenant Colonel Parsons waited, smiling in the background, beside an Air Force blue pickup truck. Sanger motioned, and Scott threw aside a tarpaulin. Underneath was a keg of beer.

•       •       •

Steve and Avery walked home together. They could have ridden, but there was a whole, wide, blue afternoon ahead of them. It was too pleasant to hurry along, so they sauntered in high spirits down the dusty trail beside the road, kicking with the exaggerated grace of ballet dancers at dandelion puffballs, arms thrown expressively wide, jaunting as only fighter pilots can jaunt when they've conquered the world.

They heard the commotion a hundred yards from the BOQ. Steve's ears perked up. It was a snarling, ripping dogfight. He walked faster, then broke into a run.

They were between the two eastern *H* legs of the BOQ: seven or eight laughing, boisterous pilots spanned the legs, closing two dogs off from exit on the enclosed grassy playing field. One of the pilots was Heck Sluder. One of the dogs was Sam. Steve had never seen him before but knew that the other dog must be Charley. He was rugged-looking, black with white spots—the quintessential junkyard mongrel—a little smaller than Sam but more muscular. On the grass between the pilots and dogs, weighted down by a brick, was a wad of green bills large enough to wallpaper a room, probably well over $2,000.

Steve didn't hesitate but waded straight in to try to separate the dogs, grabbed Sam's mane but couldn't hold him. He kicked at Charley, connected a glancing blow at the rump, but the dog wasn't intimidated. Steve chased them around like a Keystone Kop while they snapped and snarled at each other, and the pilots alternately snarled and laughed at him, cheering the dogs. Every time Steve came at them, Sam and Charley moved the fight over a few feet just out of reach. They tried to get at each other's backs and legs for a crippling bite. *Just like a real dogfight, get on his six.*

Finally, he got between them, arms spread wide, facing Sam to cut him off in either direction. Charley was somewhere behind, but didn't come around. The pilots jeered and booed.

Sam backed away in a crouch, eyes wild, tracking Steve's face like a radar antenna, ears and tail laid low in a fighting configuration. *Clean!* Steve flashed. *No tanks, no missiles.* He reached for Sam. Grabbed.

The reflex was incredibly fast. Sam caught the hand in his jaws in mid-swipe, bit down. Hard! Steve saw stars, jerked away, fingers welling blood from serrated wounds. There was raucous laughter.

"Damn you!" Steve yelled at the collie. "Goddamn you, you bastard! That's the hand that feeds you. That's the goddamn hand that feeds you!"

He looked straight into the animal's eyes, and suddenly he saw wildness, saw with the clarity of epileptic vision the reason for the world, the secret of being, the unity of the universe. He saw himself, saw a soul down deep inside those soulful brown collie eyes, saw a wild naked boy ...

Someone slapped at Steve's shoulder from behind, slapped again and spun him around. Sluder! He saw a face contorted with rage, the pockmarked nose even redder and more bulbous than usual.

"You son of a bitch!" Sluder yelled. "You son of a bitch, this is none of your *fucking* business!"

Abruptly Steve found himself on the ground looking up at a dazzling blue sky with a black hole in the middle of it, not knowing how he got there. A fluffy white cloud shaped like a toad floated on the periphery, surrounded by flashes of light—fireflies in the daytime, flashbulbs, muzzle flashes, sheet lightning. His face was numb and ached at the same time, and warm fluid ran from his nose across his cheek and down his neck. Boots stood in front of him, but there was a hole in his vision. There was nothing above the boots and two disconnected legs except a hole, black with shimmering red curtains which slowly came apart. The hole weakened, diminished, evaporated, and he was looking up at Sluder standing over him, fists clenched, face evil.

Steve didn't think. No thought crossed his mind. It required no rationality, no cerebration of violence, no analysis or trade-off of benefit versus consequence. There was no preparation, no delay, no premeditation, plotting, arrangement, conspiracy, sense, logic, or rationale.

The adrenaline flowed. Copiously. Vengefully. Naturally. It felt good, it felt right, it felt ...

He struck. Hard. Steve's combat boots ascended through the air, hard caps at the end of viciously straightening legs. One boot caught the midriff, the other the groin. It was a murderous, savage, grinding blow, with the full force of his body lifting from his shoulders from the ground, following behind the legs.

Sluder lifted from the earth and stopped in a time-frozen moment in midair, eyes wide and rolled up in the sockets, then he fell backward in slow motion, his mouth in an *O*.

Steve was on top of him almost before he hit the ground, smashing his fists against Sluder's face, slashing knuckles against teeth, making red, wet spots at the cheekbones and nose, while his own nose gushed blood onto the enemy and stained the green grass beneath the enemy's bulk.

Too soon, hands pulled at him, enfolding and constraining him. Too soon, they pulled him from a contorted, convulsing body. His fists were wet and slippery with red. His face dripped red. His flight suit, arms, legs—all were soaked red.

He struggled and shook involuntarily against the hands, but they held him, five pilots, for a long time, for a minute or longer until he began to settle.

"Jesus *Keerist!* You were going to kill him! You were …"

"Sluder? Sluder? Are you all right?"

"Shit, man he's not talkin'. He's gonna need an ambulance. Somebody better call …"

"God damn! Did you see how he lifted up when …"

"Hot damn, that was even better than a dogfight, that was …"

Avery came around from Steve's peripheral vision to the center. He cocked his head and put his face up close to Steve's.

"Hey." Avery said it softly, gently, genuine admiration gleaming from his face. "Not bad for a liberal."

•          •          •

"I didn't do anything."

Avery was ecstatic. "Yeah, you did. You stopped thinking and acted."

They were in the BOQ. Steve had stopped the nosebleed with ice wrapped in a T-shirt while Avery wrapped the middle finger of his right hand with gauze and tape. Then Avery had taped a big wad of gauze over the nasty gash near the bridge of Steve's nose. When Avery finished, Steve looked in the mirror. It looked like a bunny tail grew between his eyes. He thought that it somehow enhanced his appearance, made him look funky and rugged at the same time.

"I *reacted!* He handed me his head on a platter. He said, 'Here, take my head, I don't need it, I'm stupid.'" They laughed.

"It wasn't his head. It was his nuts. He invited you to kick him in the balls."

It was hilarious. they laughed on the way to the DOOM club, nearly doubled over, tears running down their faces.

They drank and played darts and drank some more, and slowly the room filled with drinking pilots until there was standing room only.

Frank Bender was there, and Pat Truhaft and all the other members of the eight-man hunting party, and they became the nuclei of little clusters of tribesmen who welcomed them back to the council lodge. There was Virgil Demopoulis, Harry Taint, Sir Walter Scott, Harvey Camero, Art Hoppovich, Jake Phelps, Phil Stanton, Jaime Hornslug, and on and on. Almost all the members of Steve's squadron and a lot of members from Red and Blue Squadrons too. Altogether, a hundred or more large flying mammals jostled into the layered, hazy air of a room intended to hold much less. A heavy bass beat flowed out from the jukebox into the dimly lit bar, and the sounds of rotary engines ripped the air as Snoopy and the Red Baron mixed it up again.

Sub-Lieutenant Sam was there, and he wandered and wiggled—slightly hobbling, his tail wagging prodigiously—socializing and making merry with the crowd. Someone would have given him a drink, but he had no opposable thumbs to hold it with.

Captain Heck Sluder was not there. Major Karl Jasper was not there.

The tribesmen came to Steve and Avery and slapped their backs and shook their hands and said, "You guys really brought home the buck today!" They stroked Steve's ego, admired his big bandaged nose, and brought him beers.

They touched his bandage, like a talisman, and said, "Sluder! That sonofabitch had it coming …"

"He was always an asshole …"

"… surprised somebody hasn't killed him."

"I would'a done what you did …"

"Nobody can blame …"

"Blah blah blah blah blah blah."

Steve drank, and the noise came into his ears and plunged down inside a dark echoing well, a steady, dull roar of voices indistinguishable from one another. A sea of faces came, with eyes that looked into his eyes, with mouths that told him things that someone inside him understood, because that someone said things back to them, but *he* didn't know what either he or they were talking about. The words simply flowed. He went to the latrine after a while, and found that he was bleeding again—the bandage was turning red.

They went a little silly. Silver-headed lieutenant colonels and salt-and-pepper majors wiggled their butts in time to the heavy beat of Grace Slick and the Jefferson Airplane on the jukebox.

They went a little nuts. Someone shouted, "Anybody who can't tap dance is queer," and all hundred or so pilots did a five-second rigmarole with their boots on the floor. Someone jumped up on a table and did a clog dance of sorts with heavy combat boots to the beat of the music. The table wobbled, tilted, and began to fall over, but at the last moment before being dumped onto the floor, the dancer dived out into the crowd, arms spread wide, and took down several revelers with him, causing a ripple of falling bodies that went to the far wall. The far wall crowd pushed back, and another ripple went to the other wall, then back it came, again and again, growing in amplitude, a pumped wave in a resonant cavity, until it broke up into disorganized eddies and whorls, tribesmen reeling, teetering on their feet, laughing, singing, screaming, and cursing.

It was abandonment of thought but unity of purpose, a re-bonding of hunters. They reaffirmed their creed, elegant and powerful in its simplicity:

US against THEM!

We are the WE, the righteous and the worthy. We are the tribe with the purest hearts, the best planes and guns. Our sexual organs are large, and our faces and asses hairy. Our women have big breasts and firm butts.

That was the song they sang, not precisely in those words, of course, but in words that came down to the same thing:

THEM against US!

They are the enemy, evil and unworthy to live in this land or even on the same earth with us. Their sexual organs are stunted. Their women are ugly and have bad teeth. They are damned while we are worthy and blessed. God help us to kill them.

They went a little berserk. Someone picked up a chair and tossed it into the air. It went up and down in a sea of arms, not quite as lightly as a beach ball, and soon slammed into a wall, punching a hole in the plasterboard and breaking off a leg. Steve brought his beer bottle down hard over the edge of the bar for no apparent reason other than that it seemed the right thing to do, and shattered glass tinkled across the floor. Another hunter's bottle smashed, and another and another, and soon their combat boots crunched over broken glass. A chair went over the bar, narrowly missing the young airman standing behind it, and smashed into the mirror, shattering it and most of the row of bottles in front of it. A brief Niagara of liquor cascaded off the small shelf.

A few years later (but probably no more than five minutes), Steve found himself retching over a toilet in the latrine. When he'd finished, he roamed and stumbled through the rest of the club, pushing through doors into the empty kitchen, into the silent dining room, while the sounds of laughter and singing and chaos and breaking furniture emanated from the bar. He accidentally stumbled against the wire screen which fronted the large room and felt it give, ripping loose at a corner. This was funny! He backed off a few feet and wobbled into it again, and the screening unzipped along the base. He ran against it with outstretched arms, and the entire bottom came loose. Funny! He punched at another large panel of screening. More ripping, more gaps around the side.

Steve had wandered outside just before the Air Policemen arrived. They waded into the crowded bar. They were burly, uniformed fellows with steel helmets, fondly called Apes by the rest of the Air Force population. Steve lay in the dark, flat on his back on the grass around a corner of the building looking up at a full moon punching into clouds while inside one of the tribesmen swung a misguided punch at one of the Apes and got cut out of the pack and brought down real fast. You don't mess with Apes, especially if you're drunk and can't swing straight.

Steve found himself walking into Squadron Ops, although he couldn't remember getting there. He stumbled, laughing, over chairs, ran into walls, pulled down a large wall map of Vietnam, pushed over the coffee bar because it got in his way, peed on McNish's typewriter because it misspelled words, …

•        •        •

Steve woke curled up in the front seat of an F-4 parked in a revetment. The moon hung over the western horizon, and the eastern sky glowed pink. He shivered. He was cold and his joints were stiff. He pushed cobwebs out of his mind. *Finally made it to the front seat. How the hell did I get here? Is this my reward?*

# 35

"You're on my shit list, mister."

The summons had come late that afternoon. Now Steve stood at rigid attention in the living room of Colonel Sanger's trailer, chin tucked in, chest out, shoulders back and down.

"You screwed up a perfectly good pilot, an aircraft commander, a superior officer."

Thank God, Steve hadn't been caught at the O-club or Squadron Ops.

"Yes sir. I'm sorry. I intend to visit the hospital and apologize ..."

"Shut up! I don't care about apologies. I don't care about reasons. I don't care about aileron rolls in the pattern and all the other chickenshit regulations. The only thing that counts around here is a good war and a smooth operation. You pissed in my beer, and you're going to pay for it."

Steve's tongue found a large ulcerated spot inside his cheek for the hundredth time. A fresher, neater bandage had replaced the earlier blood-soaked wad that had grown between his eyes. The new one grew across the bridge of his nose, covering the cut Sluder's ring had made. There was another smaller cut on his right cheekbone, and a yellow and blue bruise spread rampantly under his eye. A fresh bandage covered his middle finger. Iodine stained the other fingers that Sam had bitten and the knuckles that Sluder's teeth had cut.

*You look battered,* Steve had thought when he checked the latrine mirror earlier in the afternoon, staring into penetrating blue eyes that stared back. *Wonder if there'll be scars? Still, it's not bad. They're almost like adornments. Tattoos. You even look ... well ... sexy.*

"The only thing that counts is fighting this war, and you just made a ripple in my operation by taking one of my pilots out of commission for at least two weeks." A ham-size fist came down on the colonel's well-manicured desk as he paced by, and a coffee cup, a lamp, two pictures, and a well-thumbed copy of Machiavelli's *The Prince*, right beside an anthology titled *The Best of de Sade*, jumped into the air.

"There's paperwork involved in this, lad. There's already a general wants to know what it's about, and pretty soon there'll be a shit-nosed congressman from Alabama calling me." The colonel smiled. It was exactly the same smile he'd smiled yesterday when he'd congratulated Steve. Yesterday, it was friendly. Today, it oozed with malevolence. "This takes time away from my war, lad. I don't like being distracted from my war."

Sanger's eyes seared Steve from head to toe, compelling him to tighten his brace more effectively than if he'd been shouted at. A drop of sweat started down Steve's forehead. His neck turned warm. Out of the corner of his eye, he saw something move across the beige carpet.

"I could court-martial you."

Sanger ambled the room leisurely. To and fro in front of Steve, and around behind Steve.

"I could terminate your career," he whispered invisibly, inches behind Steve's right ear. Steve felt warm breath against his neck and smelled a faint odor of garlic. Out of the corner of his eye, something moved again. Sort of "hopped." It was small and white.

"Yes sir."

"Take you off flying status. Keep you here for the next two and a half years on a shit job."

*Oh God, is he going to do a Jasper on me?*

It looked fluffy. Steve swiveled his eyes. *An Easter bunny!* A warm, white, cuddly Easter bunny with long silky ears and cute, twitchy, pink nose. It hopped again and again, stopping at a bowl of carrots and lettuce at the foot of the colonel's desk. It twitched its nose. Sniffed. Nibbled.

"Yes sir." Steve had a sudden suspicion.

Still out of sight behind Steve, the colonel whispered in the other ear. "There are a lot of possibilities. What do you think I ought to do?"

A mirror, a mirror, was there a mirror? Yes, there *was*. On the wall to his left. He turned his whole body ever so slightly and strained his eyeball muscles as hard as he could to gaze into the mirror without moving his head.

*Yes!* There, in the mirror, standing behind Steve, the colonel cuddled and stroked another bunny. More than cuddled, he performed an unspeakable act—the colonel puckered up and kissed the little critter full on its cute bunny lips.

*Oh my God*, Steve thought. He had become privy to a terrible secret. *The colonel kisses bunnies!* Thus was a myth destroyed.

"What should I do with you, lad?"

"Sir, I ... sir, I do not know."

The colonel came around to Steve's front. The bunny was gone. The smile was gone. The face was pleasant.

"I'm sending you on R & R."

"Sir?"

"You're leaving tomorrow. Tokyo. Be at travel at zero eight hundred sharp to get your orders and tickets."

"Sir?" Steve was struck dumb.

The colonel frowned and put his dark face in close to Steve's, only inches away. He scrutinized him closely, curiously.

"Are you growing a mustache, lad?"

"Yes sir."

"Hmmm …"

# 36

He met her near the Ginza, near the neon-crowded beehive of Tokyo's downtown district. Her black hair, bubbling manner, dark Japanese eyes, intelligence, slim body, sensitivity, and large breasts intrigued him from the first moment he saw her. It was in a bar called The Playhouse. A blinking neon martini glass teetered above the entrance.

Actually, it wasn't exactly a bar.

He'd gone in by himself. The girls, two of them, descended on him as soon as he walked through the door at the top of the red carpeted steps. They guided him through a dimly lit—no, a *dark* room to a private booth. They sat with him, one on each side. Puzzled, he ordered drinks for the three of them.

"Name is Midori," the girl on his left said. She leaned close and smiled. "Midori." She was cute. Pretty, actually. Very pretty.

She continued smiling, her eyes locked onto his. "You?"

"Oh! Oh, yes. Steve. I'm Steve."

"Got last name, Steve?"

"Mylder. Steve Mylder."

She gently touched the bruise under his eye. She laughed. "Milder! *Wilder* Milder."

He asked for her last name. She told him. It was unpronounceable. He forgot it immediately.

The drinks came. He gagged at the bill. He nearly rose from the seat to leave.

Midori leaned over and whispered into his ear. He felt her breast against his shoulder. "Wait, Steve. Two more drinks, Hon-eee." Her hand was warm on his arm. The other hand touched his knee. "Two more drinks. Just two and I go with you." She blew into his ear. Instant erection. The drinks were expensive. Horribly expensive. Steve suspected that the girl's drinks had no alcohol at all—that they were colored water or soda.

The other girl was pleasant enough, but superfluous to Steve. From the first, he'd set his eyes on Midori. Hormones heaved and tugged at his body and brain, inducing stupidity.

Midori kept her word. She pulled him from the table after he had paid—*how much? A hundred dollars? A hundred fucking dollars on nine drinks, six of them col-*

169

*ored water!* She pulled him from the table protectively. He was hers! The other girl faded away.

He worried. He was completely dependent. This was her world—her friends, her connections all around—she could lead him into anything. He could end up rolled into the gutter on an unlit Tokyo street without a wallet, without anything of value left on his body including his life. It could be a total disaster.

She led him down steps to a taxi waiting at the back entrance. How long had it waited? Just for him? She gave instructions he couldn't understand. They drove streets he didn't know, in directions he couldn't compass. She snuggled against him, pulled his arm around her, and cupped his hand over her breast, chattering at him, with him, giggling like a girl on a first date. After a long drive, maybe thirty minutes, the taxi pulled over to the curb on a dark street. The driver got out, a black hulk in the night, and opened the back door. *Is this it?* Steve wondered. He braced himself for the worst.

She had to translate the amount for him. He paid the driver. They went through the front door of a building into a vestibule. Bamboo mats covered the floor, delicate paintings hung from the walls, and sensuously carved bare wooden benches and small tables graciously invited them to sit and rest. An old woman in a kimono came in. She and Midori talked pleasantly, unintelligibly. Midori translated the amount for him.

They were shown to a room. It was comfortable, spacious, and well equipped. There was a large and luxurious bed. Midori undressed quickly and hopped in, teasingly pulling the covers over her body, up over her breasts. She smiled fetchingly.

The first time was much too fast. The second was a little better; she straddled him on top and tried to control the pace, tried to slow him with only a little success. The third was much improved, and the fourth was an infinity in heaven. They lay back exhausted.

She woke him nearly every hour, and he was surprised to find himself renewed and ready.

She was only his third woman. She had sensed this—it was one of the things that attracted her to him. That and his battered warrior's face, a face scarred by life, by combat, by the vicissitudes of existence. She ran her fingers caressingly over the bandage across Steve's nose, pulled him down to kiss it, then resumed teaching him wordlessly, showing him where to touch, where to kiss, where the tip of the tongue brought painful pleasure. She helped him discover that motionlessness can be far more erotic and mind-blowing than rhythmic pumping. They quivered at the edge for long minutes, eyes locked together—Asian black and

American blue, strange race into strange race—before tumbling screaming together into the abyss, singing, exulting—souls twined harmoniously, sensually, sexually together.

His hands pulled fervently on her warm bottom, snugging her firmly against him, and he began to harden inside her again. Her face was fevered, damp—a lock of black hair lay matted against her cheek. Her eyes were half closed. She moaned in pleasure, pulling him into her, snaking her warm arms and legs around him. She coaxed him gently, warm hands caressing his back. She pressed wet, grateful, hungry, satisfied lips against his.

•          •          •

"Have no work two days."

It was eleven in the morning. They breakfasted and lunched on the contents of the small refrigerator in the room.

"No what?"

"Don't have to work two days. Time off. Want to see Tokyo?" She giggled pleasantly. "We stay together. Busman's holiday? Yes?"

"Yes, yes."

They did Tokyo. They fed pigeons at the Meji shrine. Midori drank holy water from a wooden cup at the fountain but couldn't convince Steve that a heathen would be welcome to do the same. They rode the subway, toured the Olympic stadium with its vast cathedral swimming pool, came back by bus and walked near the Royal Palace, plied exotic teeming streets at dusk as the lights came on, and visited coffee bars. They window-shopped, and he bought her a dress that she admired.

In the evening they checked into the same room and exhausted themselves again.

The second night, he invited her to dinner at the Tokyo American Officer's Club. He wore his suit. He waited nervously in the reception area. She was late. Would she come?

She came. She was lovely, dressed conservatively in a black strapped evening dress—the one she'd chosen, the one he'd bought for her the day before. They drank wine and talked and ate scallops and spooned dessert into each other's mouths and danced to live music and spent another ardent night together, this time in Steve's hotel room.

The next morning before he had to leave for the airport, they lay on the grass together, propped on their elbows in a small downtown park, a green island in the middle of a busy street.

"Make love to me."

"Are you serious?" He looked around.

"Yes. Make love to me here. Right here in bushes."

She tugged at his arm.

They were surrounded by bushes, but still … Busses went by yards away. Above, he could see into the windows of buildings.

Visions of hidden cameras played through his mind. Did he really trust her this much? Was it a setup? Would he be caught in a web of intrigue, made to divulge military secrets through blackmail?

"We have very interesting picture of you in downtown Tokyo park, Reutenant Mylder. You rike to see? You want to talk?"

Or what if they just plain got caught. By anybody. Jail in Japan. His imagination churned. Headline:

### Lt. Mylder busted on morals charge
### Caught with pants down in midtown Tokyo

End of flying, end of career, end of everything.

She had his zipper open and put her mouth around him. He had no choice. He pushed his hand along her leg, under her skirt, beneath her panties. She was wet, ready.

They lay gasping on the grass after they'd finished. "Wilder Milder," she laughed. "If I have baby, I send him to you in box."

Steve was horrified.

"Joke, joke," she laughed again. She laid her head on his shoulder.

"You write me?" she asked plaintively. He made her write down her name and address in English so that he could transcribe it exactly to an envelope. He looked at the unpronounceable last name. He looked at the first name.

"That's not Midori!"

"Ha ha. No. You don't think Midori my *real* name? Like John or Mary in English. Common. But you call me Midori. I like it."

•      •      •

"Take care," she said. "Fly good." She kissed him good-bye. He felt her tongue in his mouth.

He returned to Danang rested and refreshed. A few days later, he wrote to her. He never received a reply.

# 37

When Steve returned, there were three shiny new red MiGs on the squadron door diagonally crossing the old echelon of five. Inside, Sub-Lieutenant Sam hobbled to greet him, wagging a ragged tail behind him.

"Sam, oh Sam." Steve hugged him. "War is hell, isn't it." He grinned and ruffled the dog's dilapidated coat. Sam was spotted with bandages, one in the center of a shaved spot on his neck, another around his front leg just above the right paw, and a large one on his left hind rump. There was a patch of raw skin behind his left ear where McNish had shaved the fur to clean and dress a fresh wound.

Steve's own nose bandage had come off the day before. Midori had peeled it away gingerly, curiously, touching the war wound with gentle fingers, kissing it. The cut was nearly healed, but there would be a scar.

There was a subtle difference in the way the other pilots dealt with Steve. It was hard to put a finger on it, but the symptom was that he seemed to have more authority. People listened a bit more closely when he talked. It wasn't much—barely detectable. In fact, maybe it was his imagination.

But maybe that wasn't it at all. Maybe it wasn't that other people listened more when he talked. Maybe it was that *he* listened more when he talked. *Am I a counter?*

He checked the board. Seventy.

# 38

*Clayton Daily Star*

## Clayton flier's R & R
## Found Japanese girls charming

By Lt. Steven W. Mylder

I have just returned from a week's R & R in Tokyo. It was unbelievably good! Tokyo was quite a change of pace from Danang, and it's also quite a bit different from downtown Clayton. This was my reward for being such a wonderful person and exceptional fighter pilot. R & R works: I am rested and recreated!

The Japanese people have so many wonderful qualities: hospitality, friendliness, confidence, competence. I like them very much.

And the women! Graceful, with a quality of lovable cuteness. I met one of them, a very pretty and intelligent girl who was also on a holiday. She graciously took the time to show me around town and introduce me to some new concepts, and we got to know each other reasonably well. Her English was broken, but my Japanese was nonexistent. I learned a lot from her, but when she tried to teach me a little Japanese, I lapsed into pidgin English out of confusion.

Back to reality. My friend Virgil was shot down and rescued for the fourth time yesterday. This tops the previous squadron record holder by two shootdowns. Both Virgil and his aircraft commander were promptly picked up after about 30 minutes in the water. When they ejected, the plane was in a steep dive and had gone supersonic. The air blast ripped their helmets off and gave them both black eyes (Virgil looks like a cuddly panda bear). Supersonic ejections are not to be pooh-poohed. The only thing that saved them from being killed was that they were at high altitude where the air is less forceful at that speed.

Last week while I was in Tokyo, Lux and Ron went down in Package 6. Hit by 85 millimeter anti-aircraft shells. Their flight had just pulled off target and was rejoining when they called, "We're hit." The plane pitched up, and both pilots ejected immediately. Two good chutes and two good beepers. The chutes landed right at the edge of a hill in a bad area. Very populated. They were probably captured immediately.

The remainder of the flight, including Avery, my roommate, returned okay except that Avery's plane took a hit. Frank, my usual aircraft commander, was also on the flight, and he says he counted nine holes in the plane when he walked around it after landing.

The squadron had a beach party two weeks ago. This was the first time I'd been there. We beered, barbecued, and played Frisbee most of the day. Danang's beach is magnificently beautiful by any standards. Maybe someday a long, long time from now, this will be a resort area.

Today is a Buddhist holiday. The sentiment of nirvana, the calm peacefulness, the supreme repose, the impassive all understanding serenity of the religion is nowhere evident. Maybe in the villages and temples far away from Danang. This is a bustling military base, and just being here imparts a sense of nervous activity and restlessness to us as well as the Vietnamese workmen and maids who commute to the base.

I don't know any Vietnamese people. I see the maids each day and occasionally speak to them and listen to their replies in broken English, and yet I know them even less than I know their language, which is not at all. Their customs are strange, but I wonder what they think of ours. Maybe if there were time, or our jobs different, we'd be able to learn the language. But there isn't, and they aren't, and we don't. So I continue without really knowing anything about the inhabitants of the country we fight for.

The DOOM club is finished! It had taken a little damage recently, but that's all been repaired, and the new combination dining room and theater has been completed as well. We had our first USO show in there two nights ago—Don Ramble and his Guitarists of Renown hot off the Clark, Tan Son Nhut, Udorn circuit.

Thank God for small improvements. Long live the DOOM club!

# 39

*Clayton Daily Star*

## Pilots complete missions at Danang

By Lt. Steven W. Mylder

Eighty-five down, only 15 to go.

All the old heads are leaving. Harry, our resident Georgia cracker, flew his last mission yesterday. It was near Hanoi, and he brought back a going away present from the folks in that part of the country—two holes in his airplane. I flew on the same mission. To drop our load, we had to dive through flak so thick that it was like an evil black undercast beneath us. Frank and I got 10 holes drilled through our plane in the process—didn't even know we'd been hit until after landing.

Stu got his 100th last week, and had a bang-up party in the BOQ. John flies his 99th today on a Package 6. Jaime, Stan, and Rich departed for the States early this morning, and Smitty left last night.

Virgil, the ejection king, somehow got way ahead of me in the counter department and finished up last week even though we both arrived about the same time. He's on an R & R trip to Bangkok. His last mission was an easy one, but that evening there was a little excitement. We had another rocket attack.

Avery and I had taken our usual defensive positions under the bunk and the table. While we crouched there listening to the rockets go boom in the night, waiting for one of the damn things to come through the roof and make a mess of our room, we heard someone singing. It was surreal! While some loonies out near the base perimeter tried to kill us with rockets, one of our own loonies down the hall tried to kill us with a lousy rendition of a Mamas & Papas song. During a lull, I crawled along the floor on my stomach to the door and peered around the frame down the hallway.

Virgil! He lay nonchalantly on his side in the middle of the hallway with a drink in one hand and his head propped up in the other.

Virgil, "The Prince of Punch" as we call him, was supremely happy! He sang because he'd flown his 100th counter. He sang because this was his lucky day and *none* of those rockets, by gawd, had his name on it. It was just not in the nature of an essentially optimistic universe that such a thing could happen. Vir-

177

gil also sang because he was less than completely sober. Later he claimed that the attack was a fireworks celebration for his 100th counter.

The squadron continually changes. New pilots arrive each week, and older, grayer heads leave at about the same rate. The "Hundred Counters" party is a frequent and welcome occurrence. It begins with a bottle of champagne.

When the old-timer lands, he's met at the plane by a contingent of well-wishers who watch him step down from the ladder for the last time and cheer as he gets soaked by a fire truck hose. Then they hand him the bottle. With a flourish, it's uncorked, swigged from, and passed around with a lot of hand-shaking and backslapping. After this comes a triumphant ride through the compound to the sound of sirens, and open bar at the DOOM club with a second series of handshakes and backslaps. The party ends, as often as not, with a bottle of champagne. This is one of the few places in the world where friends are happy to see friends leave. Another one has made it.

Meanwhile, the rest of us are stuck here looking for ways to make time go faster. We all love to speculate. It's one of our favorite entertainments. Anyone bringing up a new rumor always finds a ready ear. There are stories about rocket attacks, pay cuts, extended tours, more hazardous missions, water shortages, reduced BX privileges, canceled leaves, ad infinitum. The worse the news, the more avid the attention—it's the adult equivalent of ghost stories. The rumors are almost never true, but it doesn't matter; they entertain, producing in the listener an exquisite sense of exuberant gloom:

"Did'ya hear we're being extended to 150 counters?" Shades of Catch 22.

# 40

The weeks flew by. One day, Secretary of Defense Robert Strange McNamara came to visit the air war. He swept up from Saigon for a few hours with a plane-load of aides to learn about the wonderful new use of guns in air-to-air combat, a revolutionary new concept to the wizards of the McNamara Pentagon—a technique that threatened the centuries-old practice of downing enemy aircraft with high-technology, radar-guided missiles.

The party was red-carpeted at the foot of the boarding steps by a contingent of sycophants and other toadies who interminably *yes-sirred*, *no-sirred*, and *three-bags-full-sirred* Mister Secretary up, down, sideways, and inside out while Steve and Avery, among the other unwashed and uninvited hoi polloi, watched in amusement from the crabgrass front lawn of Green Squadron Ops. The contingent disappeared from view into the heavily guarded barbed wire-wrapped confines of the Wing Intelligence Building, and emerged thirty minutes later, enlightened and entertained. The hoi polloi smiled to watch a one-starred brigadier toady run to hold the secretary's car door as the contingent made ready to repair to the DOOM club to snack on shrimp and avocado salad.

"Now that's power!" Avery exulted. "They'll do that for me someday."

"That's sick." Steve remarked, laughter echoing through his brain. "You're a sick man, Aughton. You oughten to have your head examined."

That evening just before sunset, the two friends picked choice cuts of steak from the DOOM club cafeteria line and carried them into the pleasant outside air to cook them on barbecue grills, dribbling beer from the can over the sizzling meat for flavoring and flame control. They sat and ate outdoors in large white wooden chairs while a rosy gray twilight faded to black and the movie of the day began—a rerun of "Dr. Strangelove" projected against the white clapboard wall of the club. They had a dessert of ice cream and popcorn while Peter Sellers and George C. Scott danced a military ballet that led to the end of the world. After the world was destroyed, they joined the happy throng milling in the freshly decorated DOOM club bar, basking in the glow from old friends and the dim light of large frosted glass globes hanging from the ceiling—tired, weak suns glowing gently through a twilight haze of smoke.

"How many you got?"

"Ninety-three, babe. Seven more to front-seat land."

"You've only got three more than me, Aughton, and I'm gonna catch you."

# 41

The squadron had one more Package 6 mission to fly before going on nights again. Steve and Avery were on it. Steve completed the flight. Avery didn't.

They were Cactus Flight: Avery and Truhaft in Three, Steve and Frank in Four. They came to bomb the northeast railroad running from Hanoi up into China. The target was a junction forty miles northeast of Hanoi and five miles northeast of Kep airfield, home of swarms of MiGs. Cactus came in from the east, refueling over the gulf before heading into the group of islands just off the coast that crews had renamed "Newfoundland." From there the formation turned inland.

They'd been one minute early at Newfoundland. This threw the timing off and cast the flight into a space-time continuum just different enough to trash the well-laid navigation plans of the nominal mission. That and the clouds. There were a lot of clouds, and because of them, Lead missed a critical checkpoint, saw a small lake shaped like a wine bottle through a canyon of clouds and mistook it for a larger lake that looked like a beer bottle. Consequently, Lead distrusted the inertial navigation system, which was working perfectly, and led the flight along a track that was a little south of the intended run-in, thinking he was on course and back on time instead of early. As a result, they flew past the target, smack over Kep airfield.

The gunners were superb! The 85 millimeter shells tracked them all over the sky at twenty thousand feet, popping like black popcorn. They couldn't get away from it. The black popcorn followed them when they jinked left, when they jinked right, when they climbed, when they descended. It stuck right with them. On another day in another war, Steve might have congratulated the gunners.

They'd gone ten miles beyond the target when they figured out where they were. They made a sweeping right turn and came at the railroad junction opposite the intended direction.

"It's a right roll-in, Cactus." They'd planned a left roll-in.

The target area was clear of clouds except that there was a layer of flak undercast at twelve thousand feet, the kind of stuff you can get out and walk on. The gunners knew the planes would come through that altitude, so they lofted 37 and

57 millimeter rounds, thousands and thousands and thousands of them. *Remarkable, really*, Steve thought. *They parked a cloud there just for us.*

They rolled in and started down. Steve played the throttles for airspeed while Frank wove their flight path until the gunsight tracked the target.

"Seventeen thousand, sixteen thousand ..." Steve called at one-second intervals. "... fifteen, fourteen, thirteen, twelve, eleven, ready ... ready ... pickle!"

"They're off." Eighteen thousand pounds of bombs from the four planes began a short and spirited journey.

Cactus Three, four hundred yards to Four's left, rolled awkwardly on the pull-out. He trailed smoke.

"Three's hit, Three's hit," Avery's voice came over the radio.

"You're trailing some fire from your right engine, Three," Frank called. "Use the left throttle."

"Bring it on up, Cactus," Lead called.

Three didn't come up with them. Lead terminated the climb, and the formation came around to the left, descended again, chasing Three, who marched north to his own drummer.

"Check him out, Four."

*Click-click.*

"Three, your right engine is on fire. I think you better shut it down."

"I can't," Avery snapped back. "Can't shut down the goddamn engines from the backseat. Remember?" There was a hurricane of wind behind his voice.

"Why doesn't Pat do it?"

"He's not ... He's ... I think he ejected."

"Get your right throttle back to idle. Turn right. Right toward the coast. Let's get out over the water."

Three banked right. Four turned inside to cut him off and close. From a distance, Steve could see that the plane had taken a hit in the nose, on the right side near the front cockpit.

They didn't need to get much closer for Steve to see that the hit was *at* the front cockpit. The front canopy was gone, and at first it looked as if Pat Truhaft *had* ejected; the top of the seat was not visible above the canopy rail, but as they moved into the last hundred yards, they could see that he had not.

*Oh, shit!*

The hole was just forward of the intake ramp, centered on the fuselage. It was nearly round, about three feet in diameter, with jagged, ragged metal edges peeled back here, pushed in there, bundles of exposed broken wiring vibrating in the wind. The explosion had taken a nick out of the intake ramp, peeled back a foot's length of metal which fluttered precariously in the airstream, begging to be sucked in and gummed by the engine.

Something moved near the top of the hole as they closed. Something green and red hung out the hole and fluttered in the airstream. Steve watched in horror as they moved in, for he knew what it would be, and he was confirmed.

It was a leg. Or some of a leg, extending from the cockpit through the hole, caught by the violent eddies and whorls of air moving through what was left of the front cockpit and forcing this limb out of the hole to dangle and flutter helplessly like a flag on a pole. The lower half of Truhaft's right leg fluttered, the green material of the flight suit ending in a red pulpy mess somewhere around where the middle of the calf would have been.

They moved forward and in, against their inclination, against churning stomachs, against a tide of horror that swept into their brains whispering in tiny expulsions of breath "no, no, no," until they were abeam and then slightly ahead of the other aircraft and could look right through the hole up into the wrecked cockpit.

*Oh God, oh God, oh God!* Why did they have to know? What difference could it make?

None! The end was ordained, there was nothing they could do to change it, but they had to know, it was required for them to know so they could live the experience, pass the experience to others, wonder the rest of their lives how to turn back time five minutes so that the outcome was voided, so that the future was not fixed.

For the moment, Patrick Truhaft was alive. He shouldn't have been, and a merciful God would not have let him be, but he was, and his nearly uncomprehending but not totally uncomprehending eyes stared out at Frank and Steve from a helmetless, undamaged, pristine head atop a ravaged green and blood-cloaked body. The ejection seat was pushed askew across the cockpit, broken from its moorings to lie slanting across the wrecked interior, and it cradled what was left of Captain Patrick Allen Truhaft.

Shock undoubtedly balmed his pain, smoothing his mind with cobwebs and memories of childhood and cherished cadet days. Steve hoped he had lived good memories and that a loop of salvation and redemption played through his mind, for he should and would soon be dead. Living dead eyes stared out at him, spoke to him, told him of loneliness, of friendless helplessness, of the bearing of a cross so totally alone, so totally alone …

For the first time in his life, for the first and only time in the seven months that he had tossed like a feather in the violent currents of a tumultuous thunderstorm of combat, Steven Mylder beheld in Patrick Truhaft the naked face of war.

It was a visage unforgiving, final, haunting, damned. Its eyes stared at him closely, personally, across a chasm deeper than their fifteen thousand-foot altitude, much wider than the furious river of four hundred and fifty knots of screaming wind pouring between them. The chasm was deep, wide, and final. It was death.

There was nothing to do but pull out, pull away from the bucking plane and a lifetime of memories and save what could be saved and let pass what must pass. Steve and Frank were the injured now. They were the wounded, the walking casualties who would wake screaming in the night. Truhaft was gone. Avery was redeemable, marked in innocence with the blood of the lamb.

"Don't tell him. Don't mention it. It won't do any good."

It was a miracle that the controls weren't wiped out, that Avery was able to fly the plane at all. It was nearly out of control, its hydraulic surfaces chattering, vibrating up-down-up-down. The plane had a bad case of delirium tremens. Shrapnel holes dotted the right engine and wing. A mist trail of fuel drew out in a long stream from the wing.

"Is Pat out?" Avery screamed into his microphone through the wind noise.

"He's gone. Yeah, he's gone."

"Roll out, roll out." Avery had continued the turn past east, past south. Now he was headed back toward Kep and Hanoi.

"Turn left ninety degrees. Left ninety." The plane leaned slowly, very slowly into a left bank and eased out of the turn heading south.

"Good, good, Three. Turn left forty more. Left forty for the coast."

The plane jerked, danced Saint Vitus's Dance, but continued south, drifted a little more to the right.

"Turn *left*, Three. Head for the coast so you can punch."

Avery continued resolutely south-southwest. They passed east of Kep. Some flak came up again, but not heavy. Steve prayed that MiGs didn't come up. Their airspeed was low. They'd be sitting ducks.

"Push it up, Three, push it up. Let's get a little more airspeed." No answer came.

They passed almost midway between Haiphong and Hanoi headed southwest, about fifteen thousand feet altitude, drifting farther right in heading.

"Cactus Three, are you injured?"

"Naw, I'm okay." Avery's voice came back almost bored. "But it's hard to see, there's a lot of air blast in the cockpit, I can't hear you very well, and I can't keep the plane level. Other than that, everything's fine." A small finger of flame had taken hold at the root of the right wing at the trailing edge.

"Turn left."

"I've got full left stick already, and I can't trim it out. My arm's getting tired. Stay clear. I'm going to roll."

The nose came up a little, and the bank drifted right, more, more, and then it coasted around fast, nearly 270 degrees, while the nose fell. He ended in a slight left turn with the nose way down.

"Pull it up, Three."

"I'm tryin'." The nose rose slowly, slowly, until finally the altitude bottomed at nine thousand feet, and the plane climbed again. The wings came through level and began to bank right. He'd come up heading south, but now he was drifting west again. Avery was in a plane that would only turn right.

Far ahead, the coast came in from the left and curved around to touch their projected flight path and run tangent to it for a distance. If he could ride it out, keep it airborne another five or ten minutes without drifting farther west, he might make it to the water. Of course, he could try a 270 degree right turn, but the odds of completing that maneuver successfully seemed much worse than just keeping it nearly straight and level.

Avery kept it together another seventeen minutes. He rolled the plane again and again, trying to spend more time in a left bank than a right bank, but the net effect was discouraging; they were at the coast now, but it ran underneath, not off to the right as they'd wanted. Meanwhile, the flames slowly crept along the wing and up the aft part of the fuselage, feeding on fuel that leaked from a few small holes in the body. If he could just hold this course another minute or two, the coast made a jog to the right just ahead before turning permanently southeast to run down toward Danang. Another minute or two, and he'd be five miles out to sea.

"I can't hold it. It's going." The plane heaved ponderously to the right, faster, then faster, and a few seconds later began wrapping itself into a tight roll. Avery punched. There was a good chute at eight thousand feet. The beeper was loud and clear on Guard channel. Steve said a silent good-bye to Pat Truhaft as the Phantom twirled toward oblivion.

Avery was actually over the water by a hundred yards when he ejected. However, a perversely brisk wind caught him, and he began drifting west. The rest of Cactus Flight watched glumly while the parachute drifted over the breakers, over the sand, over a low line of sand dunes, over a heavily cratered Highway 1, and over a small hill. The chute settled out of sight into a wooded area.

# 42

Avery came down near the westernmost incursion of the Gulf of Tonkin into Indochina, 120 nautical miles due south of Hanoi, forty miles north of the city of Vinh. Danang was 270 miles farther south along the coast.

Cactus Flight circled overhead, four talonless hawks searching for a hawk child. They heard his emergency radio squawking loudly. After a few minutes, there was a voice.

"Cactus Flight, how do you read Cactus Three Bravo?"

Avery!

"Loud and clear, Bravo. Are you all right?"

"Rog. I'm in good shape; I have my chute down and hidden. I'm in the jungle. I can hear you overhead, but I can't see through the overgrowth."

"Anybody chasing you?"

"Not yet. But they'll be sorry if they do."

*Ever the swashbuckler,* Steve thought. He pictured Avery with drawn pistol, determination illuminating his face from within.

"Copy that, Bravo. There's a Jolly Green on the way, be here in about fifteen minutes and the rest of the cavalry behind him. We'll hang around a while, but we've only got ten minutes of gas to spare."

Just as Lead spoke, flak began to dot the sky a hundred yards to his left.

"Whoops, Bravo, they just started shooting. We're going to move it out over the water."

"Where am I, where am I?" Avery called. "Where did I come down?"

"You're just inland a mile or two, about thirty, forty miles north of Vinh," Steve heard himself call. He checked his map again. "About halfway between Vinh and Than Hoa. Lead, Four, we can take on gas from the tankers and hang around longer."

They'd forgotten, all of them, about the tankers, two KC-135s orbiting above the gulf. They usually weren't needed on these missions; they were just there for emergencies.

"Rog, Four. There's no need for all of us to stay, we're out of BBs, we can't do anything but provide moral support anyway. Cactus Two, you go on home by yourself. Lead and Four will refuel and hang around a while longer."

When Lead and Four returned from the tankers, the Jolly Green rescue heli-copter had arrived, but Avery couldn't be raised on the radio.

"Cactus Three Bravo, this is Cactus Flight on Guard, how do you read?"

Silence.

The Jolly Green called.

Silence.

The A-1 Sandys arrived, four of them, escorting another Jolly Green.

Silence.

One of the Sandys went down to reconnoiter. There was a lot of AW fire, tracers coming up on both sides of him. The A-1 was hit in the wing and limped away, escorted by one of his companions.

The two helicopters droned in circles over the water while Cactus circled over-head at fifteen thousand feet out of range of the Triple A and AW. Two more Sandys arrived and flew inland to draw fire. They succeeded. They wheeled on one of the AW sites, came in at a thousand feet, strafed.

"Give 'em shit, guys. Kill those fuckers."

Avery!

"Cactus Three Bravo, where are you?"

"Dunno. Been running." Avery's voice came in jerks. He was gasping for air. Still, he sounded almost cheerful. "I can hear the Sandys and their guns, so I can't be far from them. I must've gone about two miles west of where I started. They're after me. I'm up against some sort of cliff or real steep hill. I can't get up it." There was a popping sound behind his voice. "They're close, less than a hundred yards away. Shooting."

"Hang in there, Avery!"

The Sandys had him transmit the beeper for thirty seconds so they could get a radio fix. He was deeper into the jungle, near a long, rocky ridge running north-south. There were no roads or clearings nearby, no holes in the jungle canopy to see down through to shoot at the bad guys.

Ruby Flight, two F-4s from Red Squadron, arrived on the scene.

"Hello, Cactus. We heard you could use a little help up here. We've got six Mark 82s and a gun apiece."

There was no need for Cactus to stay. They'd done all they could. The Sandys and Ruby would take it from there.

"Frank, I want to stay. He's my roommate. He's my friend."

Frank offered no resistance. "Sure, he's my friend, too. Take it a while, will you? I need to use a baby bottle."

Cactus Lead departed, leaving Four behind.

"They're real close now, *real* close." Avery's voice came across in a hoarse whisper. "Seven or eight of them less than fifty yards away. If I play it right, I think I can take a few of them with me." The popping sound was louder.

"Avery, don't … Avery, don't …" Steve called, but he couldn't complete the transmission. He wanted to say, *Don't get yourself killed.* But he couldn't. And shouldn't. If he fought them, he was sure to be killed, but if he didn't, he was likely to be killed anyway, slower and tortured in the process. It wasn't Avery's way to go out like a lamb. It wasn't Avery's way to roll over and say "Do me." It was Avery's way to scream and fight and kill and never give up. Avery's way.

"Ruby Flight," Avery called, "I want you to lay your bombs right down on top of me."

"Can't do that, Bravo. We're not even sure exactly where you are."

"I'm up against this ridge. Ripple them right along the ridge. And hurry."

One of the Sandy's called. "He's near that second little peak in the ridge, Ruby, the little one south of the bigger one. Why don't you put yours in about fifty or a hundred yards away, along the ridge right there. We've got four two-fifty pounders apiece. We'll follow you in."

"Put 'em right on top of me. Right on top." Avery laughed. "You'll miss anyhow."

"We'll put them as close as we can, Bravo." Ruby Lead rolled in. "Get your head down."

"You're a real son of a bitch, Avery," Steve called. "Give 'em hell."

"I will, Liberal. I love you guys, all of you. Give my regards to Broadway. I can't talk anymore."

# 43

They heard no more from Avery. Ruby Lead had twitched on the way down, had run into turbulence, had been hosed with 37 millimeter flak and AW fire coming right at his eyes, and his Mark 82 five-hundred-pound bombs, all six of them, had landed not fifty yards from the ridge but right at the base of the ridge, in a line right below the second little peak, the little one south of the bigger one. He had aimed to miss, but missed his aim.

"Oh, shit!" That's all that was said as Ruby Lead pulled off. It was all that *could* be said. Everyone saw it. Every crew member of the nine aircraft at the scene groaned inwardly, but nothing else came over the airwaves, not even over the intercoms. A deafening silence of the mind ruled completely—a silence of dejection overwhelmed the sparse and perfunctory radio calls made while the rescuers mechanically delivered the rest of their bombs and bullets. They called and called again.

Nothing.

And nothing was expected, really. They were all done.

They departed in pieces, reluctantly, first Ruby, then the Jollys and the Sandys, finally Cactus Four.

Later in the day, late afternoon, another rescue armada arrived, Sandys, Jollys, and two F-4s, Steve in one of them. They called and called again.

The next morning a third attempt was made. Nothing. After that, the search was abandoned. Steve wrote a letter to Avery's parents. He felt guilty. He should have ejected and gone down to help. The next day, he tore the letter up and tried again. The day after that, he put his fourth effort into the mail.

That same afternoon, an electronic warfare aircraft, a single EB-66 flying along the coast, picked up a weak beeper for about twenty seconds. There was a short, garbled voice transmission at the end, which the crew captured on tape. It was played, replayed, and re-replayed later that day after the aircraft landed at Tan Son Nhut. Only one word could be unambiguously picked out of the hash of noise. "Cactus."

The direction-finding cut that the crew got, when extended through the coast, put the transmission south of where Avery had gone down, somewhere along an east-west line that passed just five miles north of Vinh.

The Seventh Air Force intelligence analysts were skeptical. If it was indeed Lieutenant Avery Aughton, he had gone thirty-five miles through hostile territory in just three days. That was the straight line distance through rice fields and mostly open land. Not believable. That would have been easy under peaceful conditions but impossible under *these* conditions. If he'd tried to follow the jungle around part of the way for cover, it would have amounted to almost fifty miles.

*They have his transmitter*, the analysts decided. *Or any transmitter. They got his call sign by monitoring the rescue attempts.* It was a well-known and occasionally practiced trick to set a trap. But still, thirty-five miles south? *They'd know we'd know he couldn't have gone that far*, the analysts puzzled, practicing their crafty craft. *They'd know we'd know they'd know, so why did they bother with such a transparent deception?* Thinking.

Steve had a theory but didn't voice it. It didn't involve thinking, only motivation. He couldn't really believe it himself.

The next morning a two-ship formation was targeted to a location near Vinh. They had auxiliary instructions to listen for a beeper, and they were given Avery's authentication questions and answers, just in case. They heard nothing unusual.

Four days later, another radio call was heard, and a scenario almost identical to the first one played itself out. This time, though, the signal was thirty miles farther south, between Vinh and Ron Ferry. The analysts repeated their conclusions. This time, no special activities were scheduled, and the incident was forgotten after a day. Except by Steve. He wondered again.

A week after that, Blue Squadron had a flight of two up near Dong Hoi, twenty-five miles south of Ron Ferry. Both crews were relatively new and inexperienced. This was a teething exercise.

Opal Two called, "Lead, check down low at four o'clock on the beach."

Lead checked. Four thousand feet below, off his right wing (he had to dip it to look down), someone walked along the beach. *Two* someones, side by side. Surf rolled in white dashed lines toward the shore. The sun reflected brilliantly from holiday blue water.

"Arm up the guns, Opal," Lead called.

It was a long, shallow run-in to the north-west, right up the beach. Lead had plenty of time to let the gunsight settle. Far, far away two tiny figures walked south along the sand toward him. They were close together, close enough to hold hands. One of them might have been a woman, the other a man in black pajamas. They were holding hands. The man, the black-pajamaed one, actually waved at him—the bastard *waved!*

Lead hesitated, tightened his finger against the red plastic trigger on the grip, and exhaled.

*B-R-R-R-R-R-R-R-R-P*

The 20 millimeter explosive cannon shells flew far, far out in a red, almost solid line, and kissed the sand. The sand exploded with entropic frenzy as the shells kissed farther and farther along, walking toward the walking couple.

Toward where the walking couple had been! They weren't there anymore. At the last moment, they had run and dived to the left. Lead released the trigger, delayed the pullout for a moment, then hauled in gs so close to the ground that a rooster tail of sand kicked up in his wake.

The GIB monitored the run-in, his hand lightly guarding the stick. As the plane made its lowest approach, he was looking left out of the canopy. Otherwise he wouldn't have seen it. His eyes were tracking at precisely the right spot at precisely the right rate, or he never would have seen the sight that would haunt his dreams for the rest of his life.

A woman! In a red bikini! Sprawled in the sand, looking directly up at him. And kneeling protectively over her, one hand down on her back, a man in black pajamas shot indignant anger directly into the GIB's eyes, right hand up in a universal salute, middle finger extended.

They got away. They escaped, disappearing into the sand dunes before Two, following, could catch them.

Steve wondered when he heard the story. *Avery?*

He didn't really believe, but he wanted to believe. And perhaps he *did*, a little, just a bit—perhaps he consciously forced himself. It was a psychological salve, self-anointed—it eased the hurt, it soothed, it ...

Steve wondered, but he would never know if Avery was the man.

Never *could* know if that was the man who had been driven by a tenth-of-a-second image that had burned through his eyes, through his brain, and into his heart.

# 44

Frank Bender's hundredth counter came up. Steve still had two to go. They flew a combat proof. At one o'clock in the morning, they rolled onto runway one-seven right and plugged in the burners. Steve punched the clock.

They made a steep, climbing right turn after takeoff, rolling out headed directly for the middle of the DMZ a hundred miles northeast. Frank kept the afterburners on all the way up. They picked up the ground controller in the climb, and he turned them left 5 degrees and slowed them to five hundred and seventy-five knots ground speed after they leveled at twenty thousand.

The controller drove them over a target five miles beyond the DMZ. Frank pickled a load of five-hundred-pound bombs—ten of them—and jerked the freshly cleaned plane into a three-g right turn as he plugged in the burners again. They were supersonic as they rolled out in a descent directly toward Danang. They switched back to Danang tower frequency early—way early—and got permission for a VFR straight-in. They dragged a sonic boom over the peacefully sleeping countryside for most of the trip back, startling no fewer than 273 people into jumping beneath their beds, until Frank came out of burner fifteen miles north of the field, idled the engines, and dumped the speed brakes. They intercepted the glide slope at three miles, four hundred knots, and by one mile had slowed to the maximum safe gear and flap speed. *Clunk* went the gear handle, and Steve saw the leading edge flaps start down. Frank plunked the Phantom smack in the middle of the stripes, smack at the nominal airspeed, while Steve punched the clock.

"Hot *damn*, Frank! We did it, we *did* it! Twenty-seven minutes. A new world record!"

They threw a going away party for Frank the next evening in the BOQ. The evening after that, he was gone.

•     •     •

They had been drinking beer in the DOOM Club bar for about an hour, feeling no pain, when Colonel Sanger walked out of a warm drizzle into the club in high spirits, maybe a little tipsy himself. A clutch of first lieutenants and a few captains, all of them GIBs, loitered at the dart board. It was Steve's turn, and he put the first two darts right on target.

"Whoa, hot shit!" the colonel exclaimed, looking at Steve in admiration. He swayed over to the dart board and put his palm over the center, hairy stubby fingers splayed out. "Wanna try again? Com'on, put it right there between the fingers."

Steve felt an almost overwhelming déjà vu, as if he had experienced this exact same scene on some ill-defined occasion in his past, perhaps in another life. His co-GIBs urged him on, laughing, teetering on their feet. "Do it, do it!" they chanted.

The colonel taunted. "Come on, lad. Front-seaters can nail it between the fingers every time."

A hubbub of drunk laughter and conversation swirled in Steve's head. He did not hesitate. Without aiming, he let fly. Hard.

The steel-tipped missile fired through the air and buried itself into the back of Colonel Sanger's hand, in the flesh between the bones of the middle and ring fingers. Steve thought that if he had thrown it just a little harder, it might have gone all the way through and pinned Sanger's hand to the dart board.

The bar was suddenly quiet. The colonel stood there calmly. He did not wince or jerk or seem perturbed in the least. The dart stood straight out from his hand. In a friendly, expressive voice he announced, "You *missed*, lad."

"No sir, I didn't."

The bar became even more silent.

The colonel nonchalantly brought his hand from the board and slowly pulled out the dart, blood running between his fingers. Someone offered him a handkerchief. Sanger waved him away disdainfully. He turned to the board and pushed the reddened tip of the dart into the bull's eye. He fixed Steve with his eyes and smiled. It was a terrible sight.

"I'd say that's a counter, lad. I'm going to buy you a drink."

# 45

Sam slipped out the door as Airman McNish came in balancing one large carton of cornflakes atop another.

"Where ya goin', Sam?"

"Woof." Sam trotted, hobbling, across the squadron crabgrass lawn into the evening.

It had rained, and Sam sniffed in and sucked down fresh washed air tinged with a faint odor of decay. He ran onto the road where a whiff of asphalt and gasoline yanked his nostrils, and followed it out onto the tarmac past a hangar. A mechanic sat there in darkness, his back propped against the building, the glow of a cigarette faintly illuminating his face. A buddy sat beside him.

"Hi there, Sam." The fatigue-clad mechanic waved and chortled. "Looking for Charley?"

Sam didn't answer but angled southwest across a concrete universe of sleeping metal birds until the pavement narrowed down into a taxiway flanked with blue lights. He limped down the centerline of the taxiway until he was confronted by a rolling explosion of light and a roar from an A-6 coming the other way. He stopped, and it stopped, and they looked at each other for a minute, but Sam couldn't see much because he was nearly blinded by the light. He walked to the side of the taxiway, and the plane rolled on.

He went out into tall, wet grass and weeds. There was skunk out there somewhere. He smelled it. Burrs collected in his damp fur. McNish would curse as he worked them out tomorrow.

Sam pushed through the grass until he came to a small, sandy mound—bulldozer scrapings of yesteryear—fifty feet from the runway named one-seven left for one takeoff direction, and three-five right for the other. He trotted up onto the mound, shook his fur out, turned around twice, and lay down. He curled up, resting his chin across his rear legs.

A flare floated in the sky a few miles away across the runway, trailing a ribbon of smoke. It sputtered and went out. Here and there, the clouds cleared and stars spangled through. To the east, near the horizon, a strange orange light struggled to push through the clouds and make itself seen.

Far away, two Phantoms rolled onto the head of runway one-seven and jerked to a stop in echelon. Taxi lights winked off—one, two—and they sat momentarily bathed in the flicker and glow of their own navigation lights. After a while, Sam heard the engines growl and pricked his ears. One of the planes moved, and Sam saw bright orange flames leap out, filled with blue diamonds and fury. The sound came louder then, swept up in volume, *ka-shoom-m-m*, and Sam's ears filled with the white noise of snarling afterburners. Then the other plane jumped and added its snarl to the cacophony. They came right at Sam, full of sound and fury, signifying something. Sam wasn't sure what. He stood as the first plane came abeam, nose rising into the air, wheels wobbling from the ground, engines screaming through quiet, moist air.

The second came by, jumped into the air, chased its brother, and Sam watched as the orange-blue flames diminished and then tucked themselves away into the bellies of the planes, leaving only the glow of the navigation lights on the tips of the wings, the tails, and the undersides, closing up on themselves in the darkness.

The roar subsided as the lights turned slowly to the left, sliding across the sky, and Sam turned slowly, following them across patches of black, patches of stars, patches of black, until they crossed the strange orange light in the clouds.

The moon. It peeked around a billow of silver-lined darkness. Sam saw the shadowed edge, and watched the waning orb, just past full, slowly work the rest of its gibbous form loose from blackness to finally stand silently alone on a small stage filled by its own light, surrounded by curtains of cloud.

Sam howled. It was not a conscious decision to strain his neck out, open his throat, draw back his lips from fangs, and throw soul into the sky. It was done. He did not care why, whether from loneliness, sex, challenge, hatred, pride, fear, joy, passion, rage, fire, lust, frenzy, ecstasy, or all of these in one. Ancient canine memories came mid-scream, a warm teat buried in damp fur, a mother's nuzzle at rear end, a roll across dusty ground with a brother and sister, and more ancient than that, a crackling fire, a threat from the dark outside, a challenge, a taunt, an invitation, a boiling of blood. "Come fight with me, brother, come play, come dance, come sing."

"O-o-o-o-w-w-w-w."

And across the damp grass from far away came an answer. Slip the surly bonds of reason, it said. Abandon fear, all ye who enter, abandon plans and thought, abandon why and whereof, cause and effect, abandon deliberation, consideration, rationalization, consultation, calculation, speculation....

"O-o-o-o-w-w-w-w."

Act. Do. Abandon. Obey.

Sam shivered, crept down from the hillock, and drove through the grass.

The base was quiet for the slipping of an hour. A KC-135 landed, a massive rolling island of light slowing to a stop along the runway. Low clouds scudded across the lights on Monkey Mountain looming above the inlet north of the runway, making it a ship plowing through fog. Lightning flashed silently far beyond the ship, in an enormous distant thunderstorm that towered over the far horizon. Flares lit and smoked and dropped south of the runway, and blinking lights from one, two, three planes buzzed above them, and there was a deep but distant *pom* of vibration in the air, and another *pom* a minute later, and quietness again except for the barking of dogs far away and the sprinkle of lights on the ground to the east and west and the silence of dreams. Moonlight came and went and came again.

After a while, Sam crept onto the mound again, shook his fur, turned around, and lay down. He licked his right haunch, loosening and dissolving the blood that matted his fur, the taste of salt on his tongue. He panted, tongue lolling, long, collie mouth open in a long, collie grin. There was a nick on his snout, dirt on his coat, and joy in his soul.

Two Phantoms, side by side, came through the air toward Sam. They wailed their phantom wails, louder and louder, until they were directly overhead. Sam howled in response, and then they pitched out to the downwind leg, one after the other, gliding just below the base of clouds.

As the first one started the turn to final approach, Sam slipped off the sandy mound again, pushed fifty feet through the grass to the runway, and climbed the low shoulder to the hard surface. His toes clicked on asphalt. A nearby runway light glared like a naked bulb, pushing shadows past Sam's fuzzy silvered profile.

He pranced in circles. Gone was the hobble. Gone was the limp. The light illuminated quick gushes of fog from his breath, so laden with water was the air, even though the night was no more than cool.

The first plane touched far down the end of a quiet country road touched by soft moonlight. Sam trotted toward it, along the white, broad stripes of the centerline. The plane grew slowly, a widening hulk of metal behind a blinding landing light, then it grew faster and faster as Sam broke into a run toward it.

It became a monster, with uptilted dragon's wingtips, downtilted tail, spurts of light, soft red dragon's eyes atop a body of fearsome metal scales and angles. Sam did not need to know the concept of dragon; he sensed the animal directly. He did a hairpin turn as it came abeam him, not more than twenty feet away, and chased after it, barking happily, for he had seen the little men, two of them, that sit bathed in soft red light at the center of the pupils of the dragon's eyes.

He didn't notice the second plane coming fast behind him, so intent was he on the first.

He didn't notice it, but it noticed him. Late!

Almost too late. It swerved slightly, ponderously at the last instant, the left brake grinding suddenly much harder than the right, and Sam passed to the right of the nose wheel and the left of the right wheel, two feet away from rolling rubber death, as the white underbelly passed over his head, vacuum cleaner intakes sucking, enormous asshole exhausts blowing. He tumbled quickly, rolling into a fur ball from the hot force of dragon's wind. A smell of scalded metal and dirty-burned JP-4 flooded his nostrils as he returned to his legs almost mid-lope and chased behind the planes. Joyfully!

# 46

Ninety-nine down, only one to go.

The last combat sortie Steve would ever fly was another nighttime combat proof, but it did not go as well as the last one with Frank.

He and a new pilot, a major from Wing Staff—a Wing Weenie—flew the second position in a two-ship formation. There were SAM warnings out. The controller put them at eighteen thousand feet and drove them toward the DMZ.

"Why don't you fly," Wing Weenie said, "while I set up the bombs?"

Steve moved into fingertip formation, only a few feet of wing clearance between the F-4s, while the controller flew them across the DMZ into a bank of clouds and then right into the heart of a god-awful thunderstorm. They were engulfed by rain, turbulence, and total darkness. The planes pitched and bucked, and Steve moved in closer to keep sight of the bobbing wingtip light, for all he could see of the other plane was that light and a few outer feet of the wing. As he began to fight the controls in earnest, Mad Dog called a SAM warning on Guard.

*Great, now they can get two birds with one missile*, he thought. Sweat bloomed on his forehead and trickled to his eyebrows.

There was a lurch, and the blinking wingtip was suddenly six feet below them. Steve nearly lost it right there, but he bounced down without panicking and glued himself to the light again while heavy curtains of rain screamed through the space between the planes at four hundred knots. At least there was no hail. Yet. At four hundred knots, hail can kill.

*Wing Weenie isn't flying this*, Steve realized, *because he can't. He'd lose it and we'd either be sharing cockpits with Lead or breaking off to go home with our tails between our legs.*

There was a bright flash. Steve tightened involuntarily, viscerally learning the meaning of the word "pucker" as he imagined a SAM penetrating the belly of the plane beneath his seat. But it was only lightning—so close that he thought he could hear a faint slam of thunder through the cocoon cacophony of wind, engines, canopy, helmet, earphones, and quick rasping intercom breath. A drop of sweat rolled around the edge of his eyebrow and down into his left eye. The salt stung like the lash of a miniature whip, and his only recourse was to blink rapidly to clear it because he didn't dare move his hands from the stick and throttles.

"Good, good," Weenie intoned approvingly. There was the tiniest hint of apprehension in his voice.

"Right. Could you turn up the air conditioning?"

Lead was turning into them—Steve swore—into a bank that racked up steeper and steeper even though the controller droned, "Steady now, steady on that heading, ten thousand yards." Steve continually overanticipated the roll and moved away a few feet, then jerked back in. That wingtip jutting out of deep gloom was his whole world, his only reference, his attitude control. It gave not only instantaneous position, but also trends. And when it began to drift back, his throttles walked back rapidly a quarter-inch to kill the trend. When it tilted ever so slightly toward him, the stick went right a sixteenth of an inch, and when it drifted upward ...

*Wham.* Another stroke of lightning, and for an instant, Steve glimpsed the big picture—a complete plane out to his left as a reference until it was gobbled whole by the blackness.

They were in a screaming right turn, Lead was rolling into him, and they were inverting while the controller calmly intoned, "Five thousand yards, turn right one degree." Once inverted, Steve hung in his straps, until finally he couldn't stand it any more. He *had* to do it. His eyes flicked for the merest fraction of a second from the other plane to the ball of the attitude indicator in the middle of his instrument panel.

The ball was straight up and down, miniature airplane wings glued along the miniature horizon reference of the ball, indicating that they were, indeed, rightside up, and Steve's rational mind breathed relief, but a pack of demons, bats of the mind, screamed, *It lies! It lies! The indicator indicates falsely because we are hanging upside down!*

He *was* upside down in all his sensations and emotions and intuitions, so he flew formation on that isolated wingtip as if it were upside down, as if they were in the middle of a screaming inverted dive that would momentarily end in the silence of intimate contact with the ground even while a single corner of his mind, a single island of rationality surrounded and threatened by an ape pack of ancient human demons jostling on his shoulders, told him, *There, there, don't listen to those ninnies. Pay no attention to that insane crowd about to lynch you. We're really straight and level.*

Sweat rolled into the other eye as Mad Dog announced another SAM warning, the controller called "Pickle," and Weenie announced, "Bombs away." Five seconds later, they flew out of the storm into cool, clear air glowing with stars and peace.

It was a "Winken, Blinken, and Nod" of a night with a wide happy moon dozing peacefully, floating among the stars in a quiet, calm sea of black mystery. Two wooden shoes flew, outlined against a vast, sublime, silver-lined-by-the-moon thundercloud which was illuminated from within by flashes of wonder from childhood dreams and from below by blossoming bombs.

# 47

*Clayton Daily Star*

## Clayton's Lt. Mylder completes tour

By Lt. Steven W. Mylder

When you're a kid, it takes forever for Christmas to arrive. When you're a pilot at Danang, it takes forever to get 100 counters. Today I feel like a kid at Christmas. After nine months that seemed like nine years, after 150 combat missions that seemed like 1,000, I flew the last one this morning, the only one that counted—number 100 over North Vietnam.

We taxied into the chocks and shut down the engines just as the yet unrisen sun began to pinken the cloud tops. A fire truck and a contingent of well-wishers, including Sam, our collie mascot, greeted us. And there was a bottle of champagne. How does it feel to wash your face in champagne? Tingly. Cold. Damn fine.

We partied at the DOOM club until mid-morning. I came back to get a few hours of sleep, then got up to begin planning the rest of my life.

My days at Danang are numbered, but before departing I feel an urge to recount some of the tribulations and—yes—blessings experienced over the past nine months.

High on the list of tribulations and unnecessary items is mustaches. Mine is gone now. Clipped and shaved away. Indeed, many never even knew that I had it, blond and sparse as it was. I was the typical fuzz-faced lieutenant and the brunt of bad jokes because of that line of hair on my upper lip. But was I jealous of those bushy, prolifically mustachioed contemporaries who paraded around as if they owned the world? Not at all.

Why? Because my mustache was my superstition. It pulled me through all the tight missions I ever had. My awkward, blond, nearly invisible mustache warded off rockets and flak, kept my name off bullets, and saved my life time and time again.

It's the same for all the pilots and all the soldiers in every combat situation. Everyone has his mustache or mannerism or small quirk adopted to pull him through the roughest situation. The slightest variation means certain death.

My friend Virgil's superstition was his gloves—the ones issued when he first came here, an ordinary pair of thin, leather, standard-issue flying gloves with a serial number, not important to anyone but Virgil. They saved him as surely as my mustache saved me. After 94 counters, they'd turned stiff and smelly from sweat; there was a hole in the thumb of the right one, worn through by the trim switch on the stick grip. To summarize, they were foul, and he'd be better off without them.

Didn't matter. To trade them in for a new pair would have sealed his doom.

Then, after the 94th counter, he lost the right one. He was extremely upset. It was unthinkable to get a new pair. After intense consideration, he settled on the simplest and the only acceptable solution: rather than change a divine course of events, Virgil flew his last six missions with a naked right hand, wearing only one glove—little more than a sweaty, beat-up, worn-out leather rag—on the throttle hand. When he finished his last counter, he tossed it unceremoniously into an ash can. Superstition has utility, but only up to a point.

One of the recent blessings at Danang is that there are no more mosquitoes. A few months ago, a vigorous spraying campaign began on base. Every evening at dusk as the stars came out, a large tank truck filled with DDT made rounds of the compound, chug-chugging dense billowing clouds of choking chemical, killing almost as many airmen as mosquitoes. There is no substitute for victory.

Cool weather has arrived along with an unseasonable preview of the winter monsoons. But, in typically irrational human behavior, rather than praise the demise of hot weather, everyone gripes about the rain. Would you have the world?

Dusty sidewalks along dusty roads have been concretized, and the roads have been paved. Layers of asphalt replace mud and weeds in new parking lots. The BX has a new roof as a consequence of the last rocket attack. Our squadron has a new dart board.

It's fine to think of improvements now. Everything is rosy to one who is leaving. But there are those who are staying, who will fly more missions, and who may not come back, so I won't belittle the thousands of small things that are still uncomfortable on a tour over here. They are an endless source of pleasurable griping, of fine entertainment. I have participated myself.

Now it's time for farewells. May all the friends I leave behind fly well and come home safely. Good-bye, everyone. Good-bye Sub-Lieutenant Sam, faithful collie companion. Good-bye Major Karl; may the labors of Sisyphus not weigh too heavily on your back. Good-bye, Avery, wherever you are.

And now, it's nice to be alive.

And a little moving.

And damn fine.

●          ●          ●

Lt. Col. R. W. Gannis
666 TFW Public Information Office

Dear Col. Gannis:

This is my last missive. Good-bye and good luck. You were full of shit mostly, but it gave me the opportunity to sharpen my thinking, so thanks for that.

Have a nice rest-of-the-war, and don't forget to turn out the lights when you leave.

Sincerely,
Lt. S. W. Mylder

# 48

"What's this shit I hear about you resigning?" Colonel Sanger was not a happy man. It perversely gratified Steve that the colonel cared enough to give his very worst.

"I don't think I'm suited to the military, sir." Steve sat primly, stiffly on the first six inches of his government-issued chair.

The colonel's fingers drummed languidly against his desktop. The thick bandage that had wound around his hand, covering a festering wound from Steve's dart, had finally been replaced by a small square of gauze held in place by tape on the back of the hand.

"You said that already." Sanger held up the terse, one-page memo Steve had typed and rattled it in Steve's face. "That's no reason." His fist clenched and unclenched over the desk. "You tell me *why* you want out." Uncle Sam's finger pointed at Steve, foreshortened, menacing. *I want you!* "You've already accepted your next assignment. The training commits you for three more years, and it's too late to do anything about it, so why don't you just sit on this resignation a couple of years? It's stupid to burn your bridges in advance. You might change your mind."

"No sir, I don't think so." Burning bridges was just what Steve felt like doing.

"Goddamn it, lad, tell me why!"

There was more than one reason, most of them complex and not well thought out, but one stood out. Maybe it was the only one that counted. A tiny idea had put down a tenuous root in a conversation in the DOOM club bar weeks, months, years, eons ago. The seed had been a long time germinating, but its sudden growth had triggered from the praise of Mike Ross, and the roots had branched and multiplied to the extent that pulling out the young sapling that grew in his mind now would be tantamount to pulling out a sizable chunk of gray matter with it.

Writing.

What would he write? When? Where? Who would he write about? Why? He had no idea. It would come. Maybe. Maybe he could shape the tree as it grew over the next few years, make it a thing of beauty sprouting leaves of truth. But kill it he would not.

Steve had come to realize that he was not really a liberal, contrary to Avery's half-humorous accusations. Nor was he a conservative. He had no love for ideologies either left or right, no tolerance for "-isms" of any sort: communism, capitalism, theism, atheism, determinism, relativism, conservatism, liberalism … all of those doctrinal things that rigidly stricture and structure the human mind and ultimately come to enslave it. Those were for followers and joiners and people who could not think for themselves. To hell with all of them!

Yet he thought that if his life were to have any meaning at all, he would have to serve *something*; he would have to commit his soul to something different from what he had been doing so far. Until now he had blindly served the military and the doctrine of Us vs. Them.

It seemed to Steve that there were two broad areas of human endeavor, two interlocking yet adversarial pursuits: the quests for control and knowledge. Power versus truth. Until now, he had been a minion of power. Henceforth, he would devote his life to serving the truth the only way he knew how—he would write.

And damned if he'd tell the colonel.

"Sir, I just … I'm not a military man. I like the flying, I like … but that's all, I …

"Is it the assignment? You don't want to be an instructor pilot? I could get it changed."

The war had changed Steve, not in an explosion of revelations, but in smaller rendings of fault lines in minor mindquakes as tectonic plates of ideas and experiences ground slowly into each other, pushing up mountains of belief here, dropping the terrain into swampy quagmires of doubt there.

The war had accelerated his growth, had put together the pieces that the Academy had taken apart, and set him on the course toward normalcy, competency, and military professionalism. Until the war, his life had been a series of leaps into larger and larger ponds, from high school to Academy to Air Force, while self-esteem shrank in relative proportion, and now …

In this largest of uncaring fishponds, the war had given him the camaraderie of others, uniting them against a common danger. This brought comfort and a measure of goodness, but there was also a black side, a price. He had become part of the pack, had hunted and run with the pack, had joined its rituals, and had fought as a unit, a cell of a larger body. He had become a member of the first-string team. He was in the game.

He didn't want to play the game. He didn't want to be a team member. He didn't want to run with the pack.

The demons perching on his shoulders, the ancient unthinking human demons, the dark blind bats of human nature—he had embraced them. Even now they moved from his shoulders to burrow through the brain casing and take up residence in his mind.

They were not all bad. They were rooted in human survival and evolution, but he must look forward, not back. He must not let them control him. He must not abandon thought and rationality. Steve didn't want a conservative, primitive life. He would not remain a hyena baring his fangs, mooning other hyena packs with his own gross behind. The war had given to him with one hand, but had nearly taken a quest for the sublime from him with the other.

He had finally decided. He had finally abandoned the Hamlet persona as Avery had urged. He knew now that he would soar and achieve beauty. Or fail. But it did not matter; the quest was the important thing. Without the quest, his soul would be lost.

"I've watched you," the colonel said. "You don't know it, but from the first, I watched and saw you grow and become a soldier."

*A savage, a tribesman*, Steve thought.

"And now you're going to throw it away."

*Throw away doom. Walk into light.*

The colonel lectured about the new permissiveness, about how he hoped Steve was not starting down the track of degradation, of liberalism, of weakness and self-gratification. The colonel tore Steve's memo into two pieces and dropped them into the wastebasket.

Steve was not deterred. *I'll write it again and again if necessary.*

The colonel droned.

Steve thought.

This is what, in essence, the colonel said: "There are too few men with hair on their asses."

This is what, in essence, Steve thought: *Thank God, there's hair on mine. I confess, however, that I have almost none on my chest or face. This probably excludes me from the deeper ranges of masculinity which our soft, permissive society seems unable to cultivate in these degenerate times. Colonel Sanger is a member of a dying breed, a race of rugged individuals hailing back to the Old West when men were strong and hated flowers. He is of the aging restive men who deplore the end of Olympian days, who see in the puny weakling youths, now bred and raised in a culture of loose morals and aesthetic leanings, the beginning of the end of the human race. You may be right, Colonel Sanger, but I don't think so. God rest your soul, wherever it is. RIP.*

And as the colonel rambled further, Steve soared over the Sonoran Desert of Arizona, a hawk-dove sailing through grand canyons of saguaro cactus jutting proudly into a carefree blue sky. A white rabbit hopped across an arroyo and up a hill.

The war had given, and the war had taken away. One thing the war had given Steve without exacting a price was a new sense of self-confidence.

*But what if I'm wrong?* he wondered and worried.

And laughed.

# Epilogue

A long time ago men walked on the moon and boys flew naked through the skies of Vietnam.

A long time ago the war came to an end.

After three years of instructing fledgling pilots (who came as close to killing him as Vietnamese gunners had), Steve Mylder resigned from the Air Force, came back to the Sonoran desert, and began writing from the junior offices of the *Clayton Daily Star*. In the beginning, he covered obituaries, weddings, and weather. Eventually he graduated to business, sports, and crime, and he incorporated local and world events. Finally his domain expanded to encompass the stratospheric heights of books, theater, and editorials.

One day a senator named Mike Ross passed through Arizona. He stopped in Clayton and visited Steve.

"Why don't you write a book, Steve? Tell the story of you and me and Avery and everything that happened."

Steve was much too modest to commit to such a project. Senator Ross laughed and shook his head. "You haven't changed much, Steve. You're still an inferiority-driven overachiever. I know damn well you could write a great story." He winked. "Just use lots of metaphors, avoid passive construction, and don't put in too many commas."

They shook hands—the senator's arm, broken so badly in that long-ago ejection, had mended completely—and parted.

Many of Steve's friends didn't survive the war. Pat Truhaft didn't, Don Casper didn't, nor did a boy named Steven Mylder. Steve had gone to war and discovered in himself a little bravery mixed with the fear, some daring to go along with caution, and a little action stirred in with thought. By the end of the war, a fuzz-lipped Lieutenant Steven Mylder had perished in a Phantom somewhere over the skies of Vietnam, actually fading slowly like a phantom, but not before fathering a full-grown child who combined those traits in a more harmonious blend, who could see a bit more of himself.

There is a name for the process. That name makes the process sound trivial. It's not. It's called growing up, and when someone grows up, it's traumatic and sad because a child has to die.

But there is also reason for celebration because someone else is born of new hopes, fears, and vitality, and that is the story of our lives—of the continual death and rebirth of who we are.

When the papers came out with the names of returning POWs, Steve searched the list. Ron Catarsis was on it, as was Lewis Luxington, Harvey Camero, Art Hoppovich, Jake Phelps, Phil Stanton, …

And more. But Will Styles was not—Will Styles never did walk across the surface of Mars. He never will.

Nor was the name of Avery Aughton on the list.

Steve never easily accepted Avery's fate, and even years later he entertained the possibility that Avery lived somewhere over there with an impregnable wife and their children. The children would have been boys, feisty like their father, but grown of course, as old as he was when …

Listen. The story the pilot told that day of the man in black pajamas on the beach—he was blond. Tell us that isn't hope, that somewhere an indomitable spirit doesn't walk the earth!

Yet one day Steve put his fingertips to polished stone to trace Avery's name across the dark reflections of the Vietnam war memorial, and tears streamed down his face.

There were other victims, of course, many of them killed by the Gunfighters of the 666th Tactical Fighter Wing. They are gone, mourned by their families, but they never existed for Steve and his friends. The young pilots were self-contained, encased in dark masses of gelatin, moving slowly through night skies, watching flares throw pools of light on country roads. Their bombs dropped silently through cold night air, and people on the ground never existed.

The warriors were neither ogres nor heroes. There were reasons at the time—they thought—for fighting, but ultimately there are no reasons. Finally there is acceptance, there are apologies, and even celebrations and cerebrations of violence, but back then they knew nothing of that. They were boys barely out of adolescence, warmones coursing their veins.

Enough philosophy. Enough of this stupid war with its mosquitoes, rocket attacks, bombs, death, destruction. Leave it behind. Supplant it with more pleasant dreams and memories. Somewhere, Sub-Lieutenant Sam the Collie slips the surly bonds of mortality and chases phantom planes down an ancient runway, sailing joyously into the air behind them.

And somewhere, the Red Baron slips between clouds—now visible, now not—and taunts the young fledgling pilots who look his way from the ground. Come up and play, come dance, come fight.

And what do we do about you, Baron? The fatal attraction of combat, the scarf flying in the wind, the hunt, the kill, the glory ...

What do we do about you?

978-0-595-46427-2
0-595-46427-0

Printed in the United States
134100LV00006B/130-141/P